MURDER ON THE MOORS

A gripping murder mystery

PRISCILLA MASTERS

Detective Joanna Piercy Mysteries Book 6

Originally published as *Embroidering Shrouds*

Revised edition 2022
Joffe Books, London
www.joffebooks.com

First published by Macmillan in Great Britain
in 1999 as *Embroidering Shrouds*

This paperback edition was first published
in Great Britain in 2022

Cover art by Nebojša Zorić

ISBN: 978-1-80405-509-0

NOTE TO THE READER

Please note this book is set in the 1990s in England, a time before smartphones, and when social attitudes were very different.

1

Sunday 25 October, 6 p.m.

She mumbled while she worked, hands lumpy with arthritis selecting the right shade of thread. Pink for the child's skin. She measured a length, snipped it, made it rigid with saliva and concentrated on threading it through the eye of the needle. *Harder for a rich man.* She made her stitches fine, a difficult manoeuvre with such stiff hands, but she would manage it. She was determined.

It was an intricate design, the most complicated she had ever attempted. The baby in the centre, lying on its back. Its mother in the background, hands over her face, unable either to witness or to stop the event. The soldier with his sword raised, his next move easy to anticipate. Nan had stitched the title beneath, the sentiment originating from Tintoretto, though it was not a copy. His painting had been far too detailed. But she had liked the title, thought it apt, and had adapted it. *Massacre of the Innocent.* The border was her particular pride, complicated and wide, bearing emblems — a cross, Remembrance Day poppies, a chalice, supplicating hands.

Nan's eyes drooped slightly. Tapestry work was tiring, hard on the eyes, and she wasn't so young now. She smiled, half dozing. She had captured all that she had wanted — and more: that implication of piety. She closed her eyes again and dreamed.

Lydia sat back, listened to the wind screaming like a banshee and sighed. It would be wreaking havoc on the hen-house roof. She'd spend most of the next day nailing the corrugated tin back to the rafters. She too felt tired. It was time to stop; she'd done enough for one day, completed her quota. She could take the evening off and listen to the radio. She folded the exercise book and stared out through the blackening window at the silhouettes of trees forced to dance in submission to the storm, only now realising that from outside she was illuminated. If anyone was out there she could be picked out as though she sat in the centre of a lit stage. The thought made her suddenly apprehensive. She should have closed the curtains earlier.

* * *

Two miles away, the same thought was flitting through her sister's mind. Nan's eyes had drifted from the work toward her reflection in the darkening glass. She saw herself clearly, unkindly. Marion Elland, the home help, did her work well. The light picked out details on the glass that she would have asked it to spare. Knobbly joints, a stooped back, sparse white hair, her face creased with more than seventy years of living. Worst was the reflection of her expression, her native aggression watered down by fear. The fear of an old lady living alone, the fear of the vulnerable, the fear that someone was outside, watching her. She should have closed the curtains earlier.

Her eyes were caught by a movement outside. Too big for a cat or a dog. Taller, less graceful, white-faced. She tried to stand up — too quickly — and fell back in the chair with a gasp of pain.

She should have been slower, taken her time as Dr Edmonds was always telling her. 'Take your time, Nan.

What's there to hurry for?' He didn't know that taking time was the luxury of the young. For her, time was running out as fast as the sand in an egg timer. Faster than she knew. Faster even than nature intended. Nature would have allowed her the slow slide toward death. He would not.

She reached for her walking stick; varnished blackthorn, stout and strong. It provided her with some small measure of confidence, a delusion of security. She thought that with it she would be able to defend herself.

It was some use; with it she *could* stand, take the vital couple of steps and reach the window. Sharply she snapped the brocade curtains *almost* together. She did the same at the other two windows, then with a feeling of relief she dropped back in her chair, exhausted by the effort.

Robbed of his view, Christian Patterson padded away from the window and crossed the garden toward his front door.

Nan always mumbled while she worked, the habit of a woman who had lived alone for years. Sometimes she uttered bits of well-known poetry, a few bars of songs, acerbic comments to herself about other people or acid rejoinders to the radio commentators. Tonight it was the turn of 'The Lady of Shalott', an old favourite.

And so she weaveth steadily
And little other care hath she

She liked the image it threw out, the picture she longed to portray, of a young, graceful woman, bent over her needlework. Suddenly she looked up, her eyes threatening to flood. More than fifty years too late. And Sir Lancelot? Would he come riding by? She shivered. God forbid. But he would come one day. He would come. And as with the Lady of Shalott, it would prove her downfall; the mirror would crack.

She bent back over the canvas, stretched across a wooden frame to keep the pattern taut, the stitches neat and even. It was for the church, meant to replace the top of one of the threadbare footstools. People didn't bother about the church nowadays. Folk would interpret the work as they wished. Nan Lawrence's face twisted in angular spite. They would look at it and see one thing, when she knew it represented something quite different. And when she rested her knees on it while she prayed, it would be a fitting symbol of her dominance.

What she could not know was that this design, colourful as it was, would soon become even more colourful. Drops of scarlet would rain randomly to alter the picture, but while she would be the one to apply the colour, it would not be of her design. And in time the piece of canvas would be studied, but it never would reach the church.

She leaned back to appraise it. It was almost finished. He would be — no — he would not be pleased. But he would be surprised — yes — surprised.

It was an understatement. She felt desperately tired. Her chin dropped. Her mutterings changed to snores.

* * *

Joanna Piercy had no such problems. She was wide awake. Replete and mellow with thought, wine and food, she sat back on the sofa listening to some soft pop classics. *The Very Best of Love*. She stretched her arms above her head. 'Well,' she challenged Matthew with a sideways grin, 'am I a good cook or not?'

He was still sat at the table, a half-empty wine glass in his hand. He returned her grin, put his glass down and answered with mock gravity. 'No, not good, Jo,' he said.

She stood up in one swift, graceful movement and moved behind him to fold his head against her. 'Not good, Matt? Careful,' she warned.

He tilted his head right back to kiss her full on the mouth. 'It wasn't good,' he said. 'It was wonderful. I'd almost forgotten how well you can cook — when you try.'

'Sarcasm', she said, combing her fingers through the thick, honey-coloured hair, 'will cost you dearly. You can load the dishwasher, Matthew Levin, for tucking that spiteful little comment behind a compliment.'

'Later', he said, 'I will throw the plates in the dishwasher. Not now.'

But she wasn't going to let him off the hook yet. 'Promise?'

'I promise,' he said. 'But for now I should really give the chef her just desserts.'

She giggled and pulled him away from the table back toward the sofa. The CD changed tracks.

Matthew glanced up toward the window. 'Hang on a minute, Jo,' he said, letting go of her hand abruptly. 'Don't want the neighbours peeping, do we?'

Joanna giggled again. Relaxing evenings spent with a bottle of good French wine were infrequent and heady. She felt almost drunk with happiness. 'We haven't got any neighbours', she mocked, 'except Hubert and his sheep. And they won't tell — whatever we get up to. And anyway,' she said recklessly, 'who cares?'

He drew the curtains. 'I care,' he said. Then he sank down next to her on the sofa.

She lay with her head in his lap, looking up at him; it was minutes before either of them spoke.

'I am', Matthew sighed, 'a lucky and contented man. A very contented man.'

Joanna studied him slowly. During the year since they had moved into the cottage in the moorlands village of Waterfall, Matthew had undoubtedly been happy — for most of the time. The final break-up of his marriage had seemed the right step for both of them. It was a new phase, this contentment, after the angst and guilt and doubt had evaporated, and they were still savouring it. Throughout the summer he had played cricket with renewed vigour every weekend while she had joined her fellow members of the cycling club. They would meet at the end of the day exhausted but happy and hungry. Through the winter they walked together in the Peak District, discovering country pubs and unknown villages

— unknown to them as a couple, a whole new Garden of Eden. Through the week they both worked hard; their leisure time together was precious and valued.

She closed her eyes to shut out a rogue thought. 'You don't think saying you're a contented man is tempting the fates?' She was asking the question lightly, dreamily, but they both knew her fear, that contentment was an illusory state. And as though to confirm this, the phone rang before Matthew could answer. The destruction of the atmosphere was swift and complete.

Matthew moved first. 'Leave it.' Joanna tugged at his arm.

'Jo,' Matthew was impatient, 'I can't. It might be—'

She knew who it *might* be. Who else would disturb an idyllic Sunday night when they were both relaxed. 'Leave it,' she said again, sharply. 'Let the answerphone—' But he shook her from him and picked up the phone.

Straightaway she knew her instinct had been right by the way the lines on his face deepened, by the way his hand pushed his hair from his forehead, exposing deep furrows that had not been there seconds earlier. Dammit. The little witch must have an instinct for the precise moment of happiness to destroy it so utterly. Joanna put her shoes back on. *She* might as well load the dishwasher.

* * *

Nan Lawrence's rest had been short-lived; a loud thud had disturbed her from her dream. She had been digging, digging into damp soil, preparing the ground for . . . *Dig, dig, dig for victory. Dig, dig, dig for . . .*

She sat up, startled. She knew what she had been digging for. There was a second thud, followed by an ominous grating sound. And now she knew what it was that had disturbed her.

It was the long-case clock in the corner. Christian had explained to her why it made that noise; there was a fault in the movement. He had even made a joke about it. He had said it was old, stiff, misshapen and arthritic, like her.

Thinking of the clock reminded her of Christian, and the lines in Nan Lawrence's face melted with a streak of sentimentality. A vivid picture presented itself of his tanned forearms disappearing into the trunk of the clock while his grin challenged her. Emotions fought for their place: pride, bitterness, fear. Pride that the boy had inherited some of her powerful character. Bitterness because however hard Nan wished he was her true grandson, he was not. Fear that the male sex was so much stronger, more aggressive, more cruel than the female, and his youth made him raw and reckless. A rare pang of conscience hit her; maybe, maybe she had influenced the boy too much. Certainly his mother had thought so.

She tried again to concentrate on her sewing, but it was impossible now; her eyes were too tired. And now she had a new worry: she couldn't remember if she had turned the key in the front door or pulled the bolt across. Foolish the way she forgot things these days — important things. But it wasn't safe to leave the door open; she must check.

She stood up and stumbled across the room, using her stick for support, as the physiotherapist had showed her. But even with the aid, her progress was slow, and someone was knocking at her door.

* * *

Lydia normally felt safe behind drawn curtains and closed doors and didn't bother with locks and bolts. But that night something was making her restless; maybe it was the wind, howling outside. And it wasn't just her; the soft clucking in the corner was louder than usual. She crossed the room to stand over the basket. 'Quiet, you two. Nothing's happening. It's just a storm.' But the hens failed to respond to the soothing tone in her voice and clawed at the straw in their basket.

Lydia Patterson picked up the larger of the two hens, a fat, black-and-white pencilled bird. 'What is it?' she asked. 'Is there a fox outside?'

The hen gave a noisy cluck.

Lydia placed the hen back in the basket and returned to the window, pulling back the curtain to stare outside. The wind was gaining strength, noisily tearing through the night. There *was* something restless in the air; she wasn't imagining it. She pulled the front door open and stood at the top of the steps, peering around the yard. *Was* something slinking along the hedge, or was it her imagination?

She took the gun from its cabinet and slotted two cartridges into the barrel.

* * *

Joanna wasn't clattering the plates on purpose, they just *seemed* to be making a louder noise than usual. Matthew glared at her, frowning.

She wasn't *trying* to listen either, but she couldn't help it. Matthew's voice was very clear. And when he spoke to either Jane or Eloise he had a habit of speaking even more slowly, more deliberately and more clearly than usual. Added to that was the fact that Eloise's voice was high-pitched and shrill, particularly when she was trying to coax something out of her father.

Even in the kitchen, scrubbing the green Le Creuset saucepans that she had learned not to ruin in the dishwasher, she could hear Matthew's replies to Eloise. But she could not make out Eloise's words, only the tone. She's laying down the law, Joanna decided. What was it now, a half-term treat? A weekend somewhere? Money? She picked up the wine glasses, wondering whether or not to risk putting them in with the dishes. There was still half a bottle of wine left. They wouldn't be drinking it now. Correction, she thought sourly, they would drink it, they just wouldn't enjoy it. In a sudden fury she slammed the dishwasher door shut, ignoring the protesting clatter from the crockery, and switched it on, her mind working overtime. How many evenings did she and Matthew have together? With his work and her irregular hours, few. Too few. So how did his daughter sense when it was their turn for an evening at home when he wasn't on call? How did she *know*?

Sunday, of course, the traditional *family* day.

Sulkily Joanna listened to Matthew's apologies to the ex-wife now. 'I'm sorry, Jane. I do realise.' A pause before a patient, 'Yes, I do understand. It's fine. No, no, I'll be glad to see her.' Another long stop while Jane Levin continued the tirade. 'Joanna will love to have her, I promise.' Said more firmly. Joanna froze in the doorway. Matthew shot her a swift, anxious, apologetic grin, meant to be reassuring, a *we can manage it together* sort of grin, at the same time as he was speaking into the telephone. 'I'm sorry, Jane, but I shall have to go now.' And, surprisingly, without waiting for her lengthy sentences to end, he put the phone down, stood motionless for a moment, then finally turned toward Joanna. He held out an arm in pacification and typically didn't wait to drop his bombshell. Matthew always broke bad news quickly.

'I've promised to have Eloise for half-term. Okay?'

Monday 26 October, 7 a.m.

Lydia was out of bed and already writing.

Dora nestled over the brown egg, feeling the comforting shape of it beneath her feathered rump. She eyed the other hens with a certain air of smugness. None of them could have produced such perfection.

Lydia stopped writing and stared through the window, her thoughts years away. How different all their lives could have been if . . .

She tutted to herself; no use dwelling in the land of *if.* She must accept what was, and be practical. So instead of searching through dreams she forced herself to see what *was* through the window: a yard, muddy and strewn with branches and twigs blasted from the trees by the storm; a corrugated tin roof lurching at a drunken angle over the hen house. Damage had been done and now there was work to do.

* * *

Joanna's contentment temporarily returned as she wheeled her bike round to the front of the house and took a long glance back at their home. Waterfall Cottage never failed to delight her. Built in the earlier part of the 19th Century, it had originally been a farm worker's cottage in the attractively but misleadingly-named village: there was no waterfall; there were stocks and a pinfold, an ancient parish church, and a school that had been closed for twenty years but still served as a village hall. Waterfall Cottage stood opposite the triangular village green. It was a small, pretty stone cottage that backed on to the churchyard. She and Matthew had gutted the entire house, preserving what they could and at the same time improving it with a damp course, central heating and a kitchen that masqueraded as traditional yet held every available modern labour-saving device: a microwave, a dishwasher, a fridge-freezer. They had decorated throughout in modern, bright colours, chosen every stick of furniture together: an antique pine dining table and eight chairs, a feather-stuffed sofa, a cabinet that she had filled with her only inherited heirlooms, a collection of Victorian Staffordshire figures, bequeathed by an aunt.

She negotiated the blue brick path, mounting her bike at the front gate and carefully manoeuvring around Matthew's maroon BMW, which still stood outside. He would leave in half an hour.

It was a perfect day for cycling, blustery and cool, fresh and damp, the moors bathed in a sunshine too golden for any season but a fine English autumn. The only hazard left by the previous night's rain were slippery leaves that lay rotting on the lanes and a few branches strewn across the road like objects in an obstacle course. Joanna wheeled around them carefully; she didn't want another broken wrist.

She sped down the hill, quickly crossing the flat patch of moorland that lay between her and Leek. But as the town came into distant view, she felt a sudden reluctance to abandon the countryside with its fields bordered by dry-stone walls, the grass speckled with grey stone cottages and isolated farms. As she flicked her feet around the pedals she scolded herself; Leek was really a peaceful town, and she was usually glad to see it slide into view. It was as she changed gear to climb the hill that she finally acknowledged the reason for her alien emotion: a spate of burglaries that had begun early in the spring had escalated to robbery with violence. What had started as petty pilfering from empty houses had progressed to a spree, where the burglars didn't care whether the owners were in or out. Twice the crimes had been committed while the owners had been obliviously watching television. And then a few months back, through a wet summer, the crimes had altered again. In July the burglars had pushed past an old lady, causing her to fall down some stairs and break her hip. In August another of Leek's elderly widows had reported that masked men had broken into her home and robbed her of £300 that she had kept with her tea bags ready to pay the gas bill.

While the town was still nervous from those pointless acts, the crimes had taken on an even more threatening turn. Two weeks after the last robbery, the thieves had seemed to *wait* for an elderly widow to be in at the time of their attack. Cecily Marlowe had been out shopping all afternoon, presenting ample opportunity for burglars to break, enter, steal and get away. But they had made themselves a cup of tea, turned the television on and awaited her return, then slashed her across the face with a Stanley knife and stolen a few trifles, including her pension book. And the police still hadn't caught the gang.

Finding her rhythm now, Joanna pedalled along the Ashbourne Road, the Peak District National Park rising to her right, the small farming valley to the left. A few sheep were dotted around on pale grass, a tractor climbed toward the ridge, its engine spluttering noisily. The town loomed ahead, its landmarks already discernible: the spire of St Mary's, the green dome of the Nicholson Institute, tall square mills. She returned to her thoughts. Fear of the crimes had spread throughout the small town, the flames fanned by the front page of the local paper that had been devoted to the pathetic picture of Cecily Marlowe, aged 75, scarred by a Stanley knife. The paper had spared none of the details;

its description had been graphic enough even without the picture that took up half of page one. The picture had been clear enough to pick out every one of the twenty-five sutures that had criss-crossed the old lady's right cheek. Worse still, when she had tried to save herself, putting her hands up to protect her face, one of her fingers had been slashed to the bone and almost severed. The headlines had reported nothing but facts, and they had been enough to spread panic through the elderly population of the quiet moorlands town.

The article had had its inevitable spin-offs. Police investigations had been hampered by a disproportionate increase in reported incidents where there had been no crime, just another elderly citizen who *thought* they had seen or heard something suspicious. The call-out rate had more than quadrupled. Fear had crept, like a draught, under every door where people felt vulnerable. And as the police constantly admitted, they could offer no solution, only repeated advice not to let strangers through doors.

A bare ten days after the Stanley knife assault — and before the newspaper had finished commenting on the crime — another old lady had been threatened and the panic had spread further. Locksmiths and burglar alarm suppliers had had a field day fitting out homes like fortresses. But however many precautions they took, the elderly folk of Leek no longer felt safe in their own homes.

For the police it had been a nightmare. Each reported incident had to be followed up by an investigating team, lest one of the elderly victims who cried wolf should be a real target. But every moment Joanna and Mike spent chasing up 'incidents' was time lost from the real investigation. Frustratingly, they were getting nowhere. Neighbouring police forces had been of little help either, having few reported incidents of attacks on elderly women in their own homes that had not been solved. And this had led them to deduce that this gang had struck only in Leek.

Joanna had almost reached the town. As she approached the outskirts she breathed a silent prayer that peace would reign again, both in the town she thought of so affectionately and in her own home. Miss Eloise Levin she shoved roughly to the back of her mind.

She turned right into the station car park, locked her bike against the railings and stood for a moment, her mind still wrestling with the problem. Gangs who robbed old people had a standard *modus operandi*; they didn't *wait* for old ladies to return, but took advantage of an empty house. They stole videos, cash, jewellery: small, valuable objects. Not a pair of brass candlesticks of no great value and a pension book that was too risky to use. Joanna tramped toward the glass doors, feeling a prickling of apprehension. The violence was roller-coasting; they would attack one frail old lady too many.

Soon there would be a death.

* * *

Bill Tylman liked to think of himself as a traditional milkman, friendly, whistling, jolly and helpful; the man in the adverts; a sort of community service to solitary households, the lonely, the elderly, the vulnerable. And there were plenty of those. He knew all his deliveries from one end of the town to the other, knew who supplemented their milk order with orange juice, cream, eggs or pop — because he didn't just sell milk. He turned into the tufted lane that led to the two houses; the decaying, grand mansion and the concrete box that stood in front. Nan Lawrence restricted her order to one pint of milk a day, two on Saturdays because he didn't deliver on Sundays. Her order never varied — no eggs, no cream, no pop — just the one pint of milk a day. As he drove toward the ugly concrete house Bill had a vision of her emptying the last drop of the pint into her early morning cup of tea before rinsing the bottle and setting it outside the front door for him, just so she could stick to her rigid, regular routine. This never varied either: two empties on Mondays, one to pick up every other day of the week.

Most mornings Bill would rattle the milk cage and whistle extra loud, then see Nan eyeing him balefully from the

14

window, as though if she didn't watch him he would leave sour milk on the doorstep. He would smile and wave, still playing the part of the milkman of the year, which he had been declared only a month earlier. It was his ambition to win the title again the next year. Tylman grimaced. If he did, it would not be through Nan's nomination; she certainly didn't appreciate him, never even waved back, and she didn't smile either. Instead she would stare right through him, her eyes fixed on the milk bottles. Gave him a nasty feeling, that, but he'd chuck her a cheery grin anyway. At least she always paid her bills — in cash. No *I'll give you double next week, Bill.* Just handed the money over on Fridays with her frosty stare. But he didn't mind; he'd got used to her now.

He glanced at the window, his smile in his pocket ready to stick on his face, but the curtains were drawn. Strange. She always sat in this room, bent over her sewing, and she wasn't one to leave her curtains drawn either. When he put the bottle down on the front doorstep another puzzle was waiting; only one rinsed bottle was there. Tylman eyed it superstitiously. It was Monday, wasn't it? Yeah, of course it was. Tylman scratched his head. This was most unusual, no doubt about it. He picked up the solitary empty, his eyes fixed on the closed curtains, half expecting them to be flung back and for Nan Lawrence's sharp features to appear. But the curtains stayed firmly shut.

Still pondering the problem, Tylman slipped the empty bottle into his basket, put the new pint on the doorstep and backed away, his whistling for once silenced.

He was still chewing things over as he returned to his milk float to pick up Arnold's pint and two bottles of pop and placed them at the front doorstep of the shabby but still grand old hall where Nan's brother lived. Maybe he should ask Arnold? He put the thought straight out of his mind; no point asking him. He stood at the front door and stared up at the old house, thinking the same thought he always did. It was all such a shame. His whistling started again, slowly, softly, speeding up as he picked up the empties. He returned to the milk float, backing the few yards into the drive until he was able to turn around and return to civilisation. At the bottom he glanced back, but he saw nothing unusual and accelerated along the Macclesfield road toward Leek town. By the time he reached the outskirts he had forgotten all about the minor anomaly.

* * *

Joanna greeted the desk sergeant and went straight to her office, shooting the bolt across the door while she changed out of her cycling shorts into a scarlet sweater and black skirt that skimmed a few inches above her knees. She slipped her feet into some thick-heeled black leather shoes, pushing the sleeves of her sweater up toward her elbows. As she settled behind her desk she began reading through all the reports relating to crimes against old ladies. It was peaceful and quiet, an ideal time to think, until Korpanski walked in with a face like a thundercloud.

'Morning, Mike.'

He grunted a return greeting.

'You want a coffee?'

Even that failed to raise a smile.

Detective Sergeant Mike Korpanski was a man who never bothered to conceal his emotions. And that morning anger was transparent in the square face. The son of a Pole who had fought for Britain in the war and a local girl, he had black hair, a quick temper and a bulky, muscular frame nurtured by hours spent at the local gym, pumping iron. Mike was, rightly so, very proud of his body beautiful. In the early days following her promotion, Joanna had felt the full force of his resentment; resentment directed not at her personally but at a system he believed had favoured a woman *because* she was a woman. Now they understood each other better and he gave her his fierce and energetic loyalty. She knew she could count on him absolutely, and they had worked closely through a number of difficult cases. Whatever affected him would, directly or indirectly, affect her too.

She fed the coffee machine with change and returned moments later, putting the polystyrene cups on her desk and observing him.

'Well,' she said eventually, 'are you going to be like this all day?'

'Probably.'

It was a deep bad mood then. She let it lie for a few minutes before probing further, putting a friendly hand on his arm. 'What's up, Mike?'

The hand that put his cup back on the desk was shaking. A splash of coffee landed on one of the papers. She ignored it.

'Fran and I have got a visitor.'

'Which you're obviously enjoying.'

As always, he missed her sarcasm, remaining silent.

'They don't stay for ever, Mike.'

'It feels like it.'

Then she noticed how tired he looked. There was an angry, defeated expression on his face, tiny worn lines under his eyes. 'And who is the honoured guest?'

'Fran's mum.'

Joanna stifled a laugh. So it was the old music-hall joke, the mother-in-law. 'How long's she staying?'

'Her doctor says she needs a rest.' There was burning animosity in his voice. 'Fran works, we've a couple of kids, I'm out all hours, and the doctor says the old bag needs a rest. She's sat there all weekend with a disapproving look on her face — doesn't like the kids watching so much telly.' Mike was bursting with indignation. 'She switched the bloody film off last night halfway through — said the language was disgusting. Fran and I are adults, we can make up our own minds what we want to watch in our own home. It's none of her business. And then she said she didn't like the kids having to go to someone else's house after school until Fran finishes her shift. Bloody hell, Joanna, we have our lives worked out. It's nothing to do with her. She's upset us all.'

Joanna was silent. She had no comfort to offer except to repeat, 'She won't be with you forever.'

'It only feels like it,' Mike said, scowling, and was soon back in full throttle. 'She's talking about moving up here. She's even been to look at a bungalow in the next street; says the kids can go to her after school; says she'll give them wholesome food — no chocolate bars — and she'll help them with their homework. They're just kids; they want chocolate biscuits and telly when they get in, not some old boot interfering.' His dark eyes met hers with a tinge of desperation. 'We aren't a perfect family, Jo, but we've got our own way of doing things. If she doesn't stop her meddling I don't know where we'll end up.'

Joanna leaned back in her chair and felt inadequate. 'Oh dear,' she said lamely.

Mike was pacing the room now with heavy, thumping footsteps. 'I don't know how her husband stands her. I bet he's glad to get rid of her. He's happy if he can get his fishing in once a week. He's a nice sort of chap; puts up with anything. I wish', he said savagely, 'that when you married someone you didn't have to take on their whole bloody family.'

'I quite agree,' Joanna said heartily.

For the first time that morning Mike's attention was diverted away from his own problems. 'Eloise?'

'Half-term.'

'Oh.' He gave her a flicker of a smile. 'I'm sorry.'

'So am I.' She was tempted to pat his shoulder but realised it might be interpreted as a gesture of more than friendship, and she had learned to tread carefully with Korpanski. He was a sensitive man. She gave him a chummy grin instead. 'Let's get on with some work, shall we? And check through the statements made by the residents of Hope Street.' She handed him a sheaf of papers and they settled down silently to read.

Hope Street was a long row of terraced houses behind the High Street. Cecily Marlowe had lived about halfway along, in number 14. About a quarter of the houses were inhabited by elderly, retired people, the remainder by an assortment: young professionals, couples and four families.

Plenty of people had been in their homes on the day that Cecily had been attacked. All doing something. Housewives ironing, a night-worker sleeping, mothers tending children, some elderly folk watching daytime television. No one had seen or heard a thing. No stranger walking along the street, no one knocking. And no one had heard the old woman's screams when she had been attacked. If she had screamed. The Cecily Marlowe Joanna had met in hospital two hours after the assault had been too terrified even to speak. Joanna leafed through the papers. 'The usual,' she said resignedly. 'Deaf, dumb and blind. The three monkeys. Nobody saw or heard a thing.'

Mike was studying the police photographs that showed the injuries in black-and-white detail. 'You'd think a local attack like this would scare my old bat of a mother-in-law away from Leek.'

She looked up. 'You'd like that?'

'I want her to go.' Mike was off again. 'What right has she got to spread so much misery?'

'You're exaggerating.'

'I am not.'

By now she had realised that as Mike could not be reasonable about his wife's mother it was a subject best ignored.

Without talking, they read through every statement for the nth time, hoping to find something hidden, implied even, between the lines. But the morning was wasted. There was nothing.

'So let's look at the others and leave out the early burglaries. There are no clues there — all entry through back door or downstairs window, the usual stuff taken. Which brings us to July the fifteenth, a Wednesday, seven o'clock in the evening, and Emily Whittaker. Upstairs, putting sheets in the airing cupboard, hears voices, sees someone in another bedroom, screams. He pushes past her. She *thinks* someone else is downstairs but can't be sure. Description?'

Mike shrugged. 'A man. She said young, in his twenties. But when pressed, he could have been thirty or more. Can't be sure about height. She *thinks* he was wearing a balaclava. No other description.'

'Okay,' she said slowly. 'So what did the SOCOs find?'

Again Mike read from the report. 'Drawers tipped on the floor, jewellery taken: a couple of rings, an old pendant, a gold watch. Downstairs television unplugged, also the radio. Evidence the burglars wore black woollen gloves.'

Joanna knew these details off by heart. She'd been mulling them over in her mind for three months. 'That was a fairly typical robbery,' she said decisively. 'Now what about Florence Price?'

'There's even less there, Jo. She was watching the evening news in the front room, heard a noise in the kitchen, found a masked gang rifling through the cupboards. They stole three hundred pounds she'd saved for her winter gas bill.' Mike looked up. 'If the money wasn't missing, I'd think she'd fallen asleep and left the telly on, the story was so melodramatic.'

Joanna was cupping her chin in her hands and staring dreamily into space. 'How big is her kitchen?'

'Small,' Mike said. 'Very small.'

Their eyes met.

'I know, I know.' Mike finally dropped into the chair opposite her. 'It's the word "gang". How does a gang fit into a tiny kitchen? None of us could picture it somehow, but she insisted.'

Joanna sighed and pushed her heavy hair away from her face. 'I hate cases like this when you know the real villains are out there, laughing their socks off and deciding when to go hunting again. It's so difficult.' She glanced down at the desk, strewn with piles of papers. 'And just look at all this paperwork. All the man-hours wasted so far. And half the time the felons are hauled in by chance; by some other force for a motoring offence and they find the Stanley knife or something. Police work can be so frustrating.'

Now it was Korpanski's turn to grin. 'Patience, Jo.'

She sighed. 'Not my strongest point, Mike.'

'I know.'

They clocked off at one, retiring to a local pub for lunch of an oatcake filled with Buxton Blue cheese and sun-dried tomatoes. The cheese was more of a local dish than the tomatoes, which needed a rare commodity to ripen them. It had been the wettest summer in the moorlands since Joanna had taken up post there more than eight years earlier. The sun had stayed, sulkily, behind clouds for all the months without an 'r' in them. And the rain had not let up during the autumn. Nearby Endon had been cursed by flooding. Farmers had been reluctant to let their cattle roam the fields and turn the grass into a soggy mulch. Everyone, it seemed, was fed up with the rain. It was just starting up again as she and Mike left the pub, giving the town a generally depressing atmosphere. They walked quickly, heads down, threading their way through umbrellas and people in mackintoshes.

By two they were back at the station, dealing with a call that had come in during their lunch break, reporting someone loitering around a garden shed. The uniformed officers had sped round, lights flashing, in the hope of showing up the CID boys. *They* would be the ones to catch the villains terrorising the old ladies. They'd found nothing and had driven back slowly, blue lights extinguished, their tails between their legs.

Joanna and Mike exchanged resigned glances. 'We may as well go and talk to her,' said Jo.

They spent a fruitless half hour taking a statement from a querulous septuagenarian.

'*Someone* was there. I know it.'

'Did you see him?'

'Not clearly.' Rose Turnbull wrinkled her forehead. 'I *heard* him though,' she insisted. It was as though she knew her words would be doubted. 'I *did* hear him.'

'Where?'

'Near the garden shed.'

For form's sake the pair of detectives trooped out into the garden: a tiny lawn smothered with fallen leaves; a gravel path; stringy, dying plants, plenty of deadheads. At the bottom stood a wooden garden shed. The door was swinging open.

Mrs Turnbull was distraught. 'I *know* I locked it. It has a padlock. It's quite secure. How else would it have come open?'

'Is there anything . . . ?'

'One lawnmower. It was new in the spring.'

Patiently they took security numbers, details, filled out forms, took the vaguest of descriptions that would have fitted every male in the town between the ages of 14 and 60.

But as they drove back to the station Joanna voiced the thought that had occupied both their minds. 'It isn't our boys. These are simple shed-breakers, kids or drug addicts, not our villains.'

Mike agreed. 'Her lawnmower'll turn up in the car boot fair next week.'

Joanna nodded. 'And in the meantime we wait.'

3

Just to prove how capricious the weather could be, the morning was once again bright with autumn sunshine as Joanna biked into Leek. White clouds drifted in a Wedgwood blue sky, inviting optimism that spilled over into her work. Maybe the gang would be caught and the elderly of Leek would once again feel safe. Joanna squinted up at the sun and wished she could believe that, but behind the warmth there was a nip in the air. A few more weeks and she would have to stop cycling. The weather would become cold, the journey hazardous in the dark. Cyclists were never as visible as cars, and the moorland roads were remote and unlit. She loved yet hated this time of year, the dying time, when Christmas beckoned with scarlet and tinsel fingers. This year the festive season would be a particularly tricky time for her, a time when she would wrestle against Matthew's sense of duty toward his daughter. It would be their first Christmas under the same roof since they had bought the cottage in Waterfall and already she was dreading it. What would happen about Eloise? Would Matthew go to York, leaving Joanna alone? Or would Eloise expect to stay at Waterfall? Joanna's face changed as she pictured the sullen, blonde 14-year-old with little of her father in her features. Joanna bent low over her handlebars, turning her aggression against Matthew's first wife into speed, and she tried to imagine a different Christmas. Maybe she could invite Caro and Tom up, cook a turkey for them? 'Roll on next spring,' she muttered, and pedalled furiously until she reached the station.

The exertion served its purpose, absorbing all her concentration. Eloise was forgotten — for the moment.

* * *

Bill Tylman stared for a long time at the previous day's pint of milk still stood on the step. No empties. Something was wrong. In all the years Bill had known Nan Lawrence she had *never* broken her rigid habits: she had *never, ever* left her pint of milk out for the day or forgotten to replant the empties. This was out of character.

And Bill Tylman wasn't exactly sure what to do about it. He stood for a moment, glancing nervously around him, scratching his head and pondering. That was when he realised the curtains were still closed.

* * *

Joanna used the locker room to change out of her cycling gear into some black trousers and a loose, white silk shirt. Mike was in her office when she walked in. She greeted him warily. 'How are things?'

He made a face. 'Fran had this almighty row with her last night. The old boot's been feeling sorry for herself, quiet since then, acting the martyr.'

Joanna flopped down in the chair behind her desk and made a token effort of leafing through the pile of papers. 'No mention of her going, I don't suppose?'

'Not yet.' He grinned, looking a little more like the Mike of old. 'We all live in hope.'

* * *

The milk float lumbered along the main road, Tylman trying to push the vehicle over its top speed of 25 miles an hour. Cars raced past him. Tylman's face was white. He had looked in through the tiny crack in the curtain. Now he wished he hadn't, because he knew he would *never* forget. It would stick in his mind. Every time he closed his eyes he would see it. Her. He gulped back a deep, nauseated breath. Once he had seen her he had raced back to his milk float with one blind thought. The police. He had to get to the police. Panicked, he drove past telephones and houses, people and parked cars, ignoring the chance of summoning the police to him.

He had to reach the police station.

* * *

Joanna was drinking her second coffee of the day when the call came through from the desk officer, a stolid local lad named PC Robert Cumberbatch, who had spent the last five minutes trying to make sense of the agitated story.

'Got a milkman here, ma'am.'

She suppressed any instinct to order one pint or two. 'Mmm?'

'Called at an old lady's house this morning. Her milk was still on the step from yesterday.' Cumberbatch's tone was flat.

'Social services, Cumberbatch,' she suggested gently.

'Says he looked in through the window.' Cumberbatch looked again at the shaken milkman. 'Curtains was drawn but they didn't quite meet. He could make her out; says she's lying near the window. And he says there's a lot of blood around, he thinks . . .'

Joanna stood up, still holding the phone, trying to still the sudden snatch of fear that the thing she had dreaded had now happened. 'Have you dispatched a car round?'

A pause. 'Yes.'

'And an ambulance?'

'Yes.'

'Where does this old lady live?' Joanna asked sharply.

'Macclesfield Road.'

'The number?'

There was a brief, embarrassed silence.

'The number, Cumberbatch? Macclesfield Road goes all the way from Leek—'

'To Macclesfield. I know that, ma'am. Well, it doesn't really have a number. It's Nan Lawrence's place. It's in the grounds of . . . The locals call it Spite Hall.'

'Spite Hall?'

'On account of—'

Joanna interrupted; she had no time for local legend. 'How far out of Leek is it?'

'Two or three miles, on the right-hand side, just beyond the trout farm and the turning for Rudyard.'

'Okay, Cumberbatch,' she said sharply. 'Get a statement from the milkman and let him finish his round. Alert Sergeant Barraclough and the rest of the SOCO team; just tell them they might be needed.' Already she was sliding her jacket from the back of the chair.

Later she might reflect that while PC Cumberbatch had had no difficulty telling her about the finding of a woman's body, he had found it hard to repeat a vernacular house name.

Mike said nothing as they walked across the station car park, but as she glanced at his square profile, she could see his jaw had tightened. She could read his mind. They had expected this, anticipated it, yet they had been unable to prevent it.

They used a squad car, left the blue light off. The town was quiet and traffic-free compared with Wednesday's market day. Three minutes and they were on the northern outskirts, speeding past the Courtaulds factory on the right and Rock House on the left. Another couple of minutes and they were at the trout farm.

Mike pointed out a narrow track on the right, almost concealed by an elderly oak, its trunk disfigured with cancerous-looking burrs. The track itself seemed little used, with turf sprouting up its centre. She turned the car in. The lane bent around to the left, and two houses came simultaneously into view: a grey concrete, single-storey building, flat-roofed with 1940s metal window frames; and behind it, its ground floor completely hidden by the other, a beautiful 18th century symmetrical bow-windowed Georgian manor house, red brick and elegant. The best of the 18th century, and rammed up against it the very worst of the 1940s — little more than a troop hut. Long and thin, the smaller building spanned the entire length of the Georgian facade. It was criminal.

Mike made a face. 'Now you know why it's called Spite Hall.'

Her eyes returned to the red brick. 'And the other building? What do they call that?'

'Brushton Grange. Nice, isn't it?'

There was no answer. It was more than nice. It was beautiful. And that made the contrast between the two buildings even more tragic. Only real beauty can be so completely marred.

'How can they have allowed this to happen?'

Mike shrugged. 'Post-war.'

'But to leave it standing.'

'The owners are brother and sister,' he said, as though that explained everything.

She climbed out of the car. Signs were already waiting to be read: the milk bottle still stood on the doorstep; ridges in the gravelled drive where someone, presumably the milkman, had struggled to escape the scene; another squad car, its blue light still flashing.

Mike hammered on the door and met six and a half feet of PC Will Farthing walking back around the side. 'There's no answer, Mike,' he said, 'and there's someone in there. I was just going to break in.'

They stood outside the front door, solid wood, closed and undamaged, set in the narrow width of the building with two small windows either side. 'I've tried it, ma'am,' Farthing said. 'It's locked. I looked through, though.' He led them around the right-hand side of the building to a large metal window.

It didn't take them long to see what the milkman had seen: through a frustratingly narrow gap in the curtains, they spied what looked like a heap of bloodstained rags lying on the floor near the window. In the darkened room they could just make out white hair, caked in a dark, dried pool of blood. Joanna peered through silently for a moment before speaking to Will Farthing. 'Did you notice any sign of forced entry?'

He shook his head.

'Then we'd better break a door down.'

Will Farthing led them round to the back. The door was partly glazed with panels of reeded glass, and coated in dull green peeling paint. Joanna wrapped a tissue around her hand and tried the handle. It was locked. 'Let's get in there,' she said.

Mike gave the glass a sharp blow with his elbow, slipped his hand through the hole, turned the key and shot back the bolts. 'No one got in this way', he commented, 'or out.'

They put on overshoes and stepped into an old-fashioned kitchen, small, dark and narrow, running the rear width of the house. It contained a tall green and cream cabinet, an ancient grey gas cooker, a red Formica table and two chairs neatly pushed back. They moved through to a long, dark hall and headed for the room on their left.

Seconds later Joanna was bending over the crumpled body of an old woman. 'You can cancel the ambulance,' she said.

4

Joanna stood in the doorway and looked around her, inhaling the fusty atmosphere. This was not the first body she had seen, but it still had the capacity to make her retch. She forced herself not to think but to observe.

It was a narrow, dingy room, the same basic shape as the house. To her right was a small window that overlooked the front door, its curtain tightly shut. She slipped a glove on and pulled it open. Now a little light was let in she could see the room and its contents more clearly. The old woman in a dark skirt and black cardigan lay sprawled with her head toward the window, an upholstered armchair tipped over behind her. At her side a small occasional table had also fallen to the floor together with an electric table lamp, its bulb smashed into tiny shards. Already Joanna was starting to anticipate the minds of the scene-of-crime officers. Such sharp fragments easily worked their way into soft-soled shoes.

Joanna moved her head slightly. From the position of Nan Lawrence's body it seemed she had been sat facing the window when she had been struck from behind. Her feet, in brown woollen slippers, were still almost touching the stretcher rail. Joanna's eyes avoided the bloodied pulp that had been her head; instead she continued her silent study of the room. It was shabbily-furnished, an oblong of faded green carpet covered the centre, while the border was of dark wooden parquet. An upright piano stood at the end farthest from the door; a cheap, old-fashioned instrument of dark wood with brass candlesticks on its front. An elderly, brown leather-covered sofa curved around a green-tiled fireplace, a crude print above of a vase of cornflowers the only picture in the room. In the corner, next to the piano, stood the sole piece of quality, an antique long-case clock with a brass face. Everything else was mass produced and tasteless, dating from the 1940s.

Korpanski touched her arm and motioned toward something on the hearthrug: a walking stick, varnished blackthorn, splintered and stained along its length.

She nodded. 'It could be the murder weapon,' she said, still scrutinising the room. 'We'll have to see what Matthew says. What's that?' Careful to avoid the glass splinters, she crossed the room toward the armchair.

The reason the old woman had sat in the window, by a lamp, instead of nearer the fire, was a tapestry frame, also knocked over but unbroken. Nan Lawrence must have used the daylight to see, and in the evening she had worked beneath the lamp. Joanna bent down to peer at the work, neatly done, evenly stitched in bright silk, and now spattered with blood. She read out the title: '*Massacre of the Innocent*'.

Behind her, Korpanski shifted uncomfortably. 'You could call it that.'

'Bit ironic,' Farthing commented, and Joanna was forced to agree. She took a good look at the tapestry. Prettily bordered with scarlet poppies and a bright blue chalice, the content matched its title, a bloodthirsty, classical religious subject. She'd seen paintings like it in art museums the world over — a baby, its mother, soldiers — the depiction of Herod's attempt to slay Christ. A common enough choice for an artist funded by the church, but a very strange selection for an old woman to choose to sew late into the nights, even an old woman who lived in a house commonly known as Spite Hall.

Mike's gaze was on the spots of red. 'I suppose it's her blood.'

She simply nodded.

Their attention was diverted by Sergeant Barraclough arriving noisily with his team of SOCOs. He took a swift look around and gave a long whistle. 'Nasty,' he said. 'Very nasty. No time to waste.' He unpacked his scene-of-crime bag and started work straightaway, unfazed that he had arrived before the pathologist. 'Plenty for me to be getting on with here', he said cheerfully, 'before Dr Levin starts his poking and prodding.'

He began by directing the police photographer to record the entire scene. Barra was experienced enough at dealing with crimes to start already to tie his evidence to a sequence of events. His observant eyes picked out a box of embroidery silks scattered near the window — pinks, blues, browns. Some of them were blood-spattered too.

Joanna waited as the SOCO team erected lights before speaking to Barraclough. 'What happened, do you think?'

Barra gave her a straight look. 'Well, we'll know a bit more when your boyfriend gets here,' he said, 'but it looks to me like the old lady left the door unlocked. She was sat here.' He indicated the chair. 'I guess she was deaf, didn't hear someone come creeping up behind her. He grabs the walking stick and *crash*. Over she goes.'

She knew the hint of flippancy hid a revulsion for the crime as deep as her own. 'So our killer simply walks in through the front door?'

'Well, the back door was bolted and there's no damage to the front door. It wasn't forced. It's an old-fashioned mortise and tenon lock, rather than a Yale, which he could have forced easily. Look, she would have had to turn the key to be safe.'

He led her from the murder scene along the dingy corridor, brown-painted walls, more parquet flooring. 'There isn't a single bloodstain along this entire corridor,' he said. 'I've already had a quick look. She was attacked in her own sitting room as she sat with her back to the door. As far as I can tell — so far — that's the theory the evidence supports.'

'She'd left the door unlocked?' Joanna said incredulously. 'A woman who is careful enough to *bolt* her back door? After all the panic there's been in this town amongst the elderly population? After what happened to Cecily Marlowe? I find it hard to credit.' Behind her, Mike nodded in agreement. They moved back into the sitting room and Joanna continued. 'I suppose the only other way it could have happened is that she let her assailant in and returned to her sewing, which is even less likely.'

'Well, it's one or the other, Jo,' the SOCO pointed out reasonably. 'I haven't had a good look at *her*, but there really is no blood anywhere except in the area surrounding the chair that's tipped over. There's a lot of blood on the top rail of the chair.' He fingered some dark staining on the upholstery. 'So, from the way she's lying, it's 90 percent certain she was in it when she was initially struck.' He bent over and touched the tapestry with a gloved finger. 'And then there's this. It tells its own tale. I think we have enough evidence to reconstruct the massacre of this particular innocent.'

His grey eyes looked distressed. 'Judging by the spilt embroidery silks, I think she was actually bending over her sewing when the first blow was struck, and she never looked up again. The back of her head's a bloody pulp, but I can't see any injuries on the side of her face, and I don't want to touch her until . . .'

Joanna's frown deepened and Barra continued to expand on his theory.

'She was an old woman. It's perfectly possible she was a bit deaf.'

Joanna's gaze took in the small stitches that made up the picture. 'Deaf maybe, but not blind. I can't even see any glasses.' She made a mental note to speak to the dead woman's doctor.

Footsteps along the corridor announced Matthew's arrival. He grinned at her from the doorway. 'Seems only a couple of hours ago that I saw you, Jo.'

She made a wry face. 'And I thought I was safe until tea time.'

Matthew eyed the body. 'Well, this little lady wasn't, was she?'

She waited while he slipped on a pair of examination gloves, his green eyes busily scanning the room, absorbing the upturned table, the lamp, the splashes of blood, the tapestry frame, lastly the state of Nan Lawrence's body. 'I think we can say with certainty it's a homicide.'

He'd finished a cursory examination of the body within a couple of minutes. 'I don't think there's a lot of point my making a meal of this, Jo,' he said. 'I can tell you she's been dead for more than 36 hours. Rigor mortis has practically worn off. She died of multiple wounds, blows square on to the back of the head with our old friend the blunt instrument.'

Barra indicated the walking stick. 'Anything like this?'

Matthew's green eyes gleamed. 'Could well have been. Bring it along to the PM, will you? I'll see if it matches the injuries. And I'll want some X-rays doing before I start.'

Joanna raised her eyebrows.

'I have my suspicions she has a good number of broken bones,' he explained. 'She's old. She took a hell of a beating. Her bones will have been brittle.' He looked up. 'Primary cause of death almost certainly head injuries. Could be shock, but . . .' He lifted the skirt of the dress, revealing thick lisle stockings heavily stained with blood, a leg twisted to an unbelievable angle. Joanna winced. He pushed the thick sleeve of the cardigan aside. 'Red wheal s on the forearms. Look at this.' He lifted Nan Lawrence's right hand, and even Joanna could tell the wrist had been snapped. The fingers too were discoloured and swollen.

'Arthritis and trauma. Whoever did it was either in a hell of a temper, drunk, or a complete psychopath,' Matthew said, disgust making his voice husky. 'I think it's what the newspapers may well call a frenzied attack. I wouldn't disagree with them.' Joanna watched him speak, noted the set of his chin, the tightening of his mouth. No one could say pathologists do not feel for their patients. She knew that Matthew was moved. He stared silently for a time at Nan Lawrence's face. 'How old was she? Eighty?'

'Something like that, I don't know exactly.' Joanna's mind was already grappling with the problem she had started the day with. Was this the work of the same gang of burglars who had preyed on the other old ladies of the town?

Never quite at ease in Matthew's presence, Mike had watched silently from the doorway. Now he spoke, and from the comment he made, Joanna knew his mind had been tracking along the same highway. 'So it's happened,' he said. 'They've struck again. Only this time they have killed someone.'

Matthew turned to face him.

'We've had a couple of attacks on old women,' Mike explained. 'The last one had her face slashed with a Stanley knife.'

Matthew was still regarding Korpanski. 'Yeah, I knew about that,' he said. 'But do villains usually change their weapons? I thought once a slasher, always a slasher. I mean, this is a different sort of attack; the walking stick just happened to be here. It isn't the sort of weapon villains take on their sprees.'

'Violence is violence,' Korpanski countered. 'They were all old ladies attacked in their own homes — defenceless and weak. I don't suppose a bunch of psychos care what they use, just so long as they hurt someone. The stick was here so they used it. Violence always escalates, Dr Levin. We thought something like this would happen in the end. She probably just annoyed them, so they bashed her about.'

Joanna looked up. 'How could she have annoyed them? She was sat in her own home doing some sewing.'

Mike shrugged.

Matthew was continuing his examination of the room. 'I take it she lived alone?'

'Yes,' said Barraclough, sellotaping bloodstains from the walls. 'Her brother lives in the big house next door. Matthew.'

He called the pathologist's attention to the state of the chair. 'Do you agree this is where she was sat when the first blow was struck?'

They all peered at the chair, then at the tapestry. A long spray of blood decorated the canvas, and they didn't need Barra to tell them that the first blow often gave this pattern of spattering before the injuries became severe and the blood loss less vigorous. Even so, Matthew took his time before answering. 'Could be, Barra. I can see what you mean. Blood sprayed. No oozing. It could be.' He was clearly unwilling to draw too many conclusions. 'I can't be sure yet. I'll need to study the injuries.'

Joanna was busy with her part in the investigation, directing the team. 'Let's get the body moved to the morgue, and we'd better call on the brother. I'll see you later, Matthew.'

She left Matthew continuing his discussion with Sergeant Barraclough, and she and Korpanski walked out of the house.

They had time for a brief exchange as they rounded the side of the concrete block and approached the front of Brushton Grange.

'So it's happened,' she said. 'They've killed someone. Though why, I can't imagine.'

'They don't need a reason, Jo. There isn't any point to any of it. It's the same as all the other muck we get shovelled on top of us — pointless, mindless, stupid crime. There isn't a motive within fifty miles of this bunch. They just go out and *do*, they don't think.' Korpanski's attitudes were all too familiar to her.

'Well, try this for size. We have four old women, one has been accidentally hurt by being pushed down the stairs, two have been badly frightened and robbed, one has been deliberately set upon, and now we have this.' The mortuary van was pulling up outside the front door of Spite Hall.

They negotiated the path between the two buildings. It was a dark space no more than six feet wide where the sun failed to penetrate, blocked out by the newer house. The result was that the area was damp and overgrown with ferns, the stone slabs slippery with moss. 'The trouble is, Jo,' Mike said slowly, 'the whole picture is confused. It's almost like each crime is separate, even though we can be sure it's always the same gang.'

She smiled at him. 'Like one of those Cubist paintings where you know it's a face but the eyes and nose seem in the wrong place and of the wrong proportion. I know, Mike, it is confusing, but there must be a rational explanation somewhere.'

Mike climbed the steps ahead of her, throwing his comment back. 'Look, Jo, like I said in there,' he jerked his thumb backwards, 'violence escalates. We could have expected this. We should have had more men on the job from the start. Tell Colclough this time we need a proper team. Not the couple of extras he let us have after the Marlowe attack.'

Joanna nodded. They would have all the officers they wanted now. Murder escalated an inquiry, opened the purse strings, gave them access to unlimited funds. *Too late for one victim.*

Above them the October sky threatened another downpour. Joanna turned to look at Spite Hall. 'Her brother must have cursed this place every time he stepped outside his front door. Why on earth did they build so near the house? Was it built as a troop hut?'

'No. Rumour is she had it built just after the war, to live in after her father died.'

'Right in front of the family home? Did she dislike her brother so much?' At the back of her mind the question was already forming. Did her brother dislike her enough to want to kill her? It opened up the possibility of a different motive for the old woman's murder. Was this possibly not the work of a gang but a sudden eruption of sibling rivalry after years of hatred?

Mike was looking uncomfortable. 'They're just old stories.'

'Then perhaps Spite Hall was well named.'

He glanced up at the decayed Georgian facade. 'Perhaps he didn't mind. It doesn't look as though he cared too much about the place.'

Mike was right. Brushton Grange looked neglected: the paint was peeling, the woodwork rotten, the windows dusty, with faded curtains carelessly draped across. Even the bricks were crumbling, the mortar between them deeply scored. The paint on the front door had once been red, now it wore a pale bloom like the paintwork of a very old car.

There was no visible door knocker or bell. Joanna lifted her fist and banged.

5

There was no response from inside the house. It remained completely silent. The only sounds were the gathering police officers, working inside and outside Spite Hall. Joanna stared up at the neglected facade. Maybe no one did live there. Her mind began racing. Perhaps the brother had so hated Spite Hall that he had moved away, and that was why Brushton Grange wore such an empty, uncared-for air. He had abandoned it. Joanna looked questioningly at Mike, who simply shrugged. Without expecting an answer, Joanna banged again. They were about to descend the steps and look around the building when the door creaked open, just a crack, and a face peered out. That was when she realised she did not know his name.

'Mr . . . ?'

He supplied it. 'Patterson. Arnold Patterson. Who are you?'

'Detective Inspector Joanna Piercy, Leek Police. And this is Detective Sergeant Mike Korpanski.'

The door opened wider. Through it they could make out a dark expanse of hall. Dull, tiled, Victorian. 'So what do you want?' His voice was neither hostile nor curious, but strangely flat, as though all inquisitiveness had abandoned him years ago.

'Are you the brother of . . . ?' Involuntarily her gaze jerked backwards.

Patterson gave a ghost of a smile. 'I am.' He opened the door a little wider.

He was an old man of eighty years or so, bent almost double, condemned by arthritis to peer always at the floor unless he made a superhuman effort to look up, which he did now. And Joanna could read the pain twisting his face. Yet her first instinct on meeting Nan Lawrence's brother was one of relief. This man could not conceivably have killed his sister, however much he had hated her; there was not enough strength to batter a mouse to death in those weak arms.

He lifted his face to peer up at her. 'So what have you come about?'

She was alert to the fact that this was a frail old man and she had some shocking news to break to him. 'Are you alone?'

There was a flash of wariness in the pale eyes. 'I often am, but as it happens my grandson is with me — upstairs. He lives here.'

'Would you like to call him down?'

'Not particularly.'

Whatever frailty Arnold Patterson possessed in body, he made up for it in spirit. Joanna wondered if it was a family characteristic. Hard to judge when all she had seen of the sister had been a huddled heap of old clothes containing a battered, lifeless body.

Mike tried to help. 'We've got some rather bad news for you, I'm afraid, Mr Patterson. It's about your sister.'

Patterson didn't bat an eyelid, but he struggled to straighten just an inch. There was something curiously dignified about the movement, almost military. 'Then you'd better tell me what it is.' A wisp of wry humour softened his features. 'I can tek it. I've a weak body but my heart is sound — so the doctor tells me.'

* * *

Lydia's pen was scratching across the surface of the exercise book. At last the story was absorbing her to the exclusion of everything else. Everything.

* * *

Patterson was still keeping them on the doorstep. 'May we come in?' Joanna asked.

'If you must.' He invited them in with obvious reluctance.

The old man moved with difficulty through the wide, tiled hall, pain evident in every slow step, forcing his back lower until it was nearly at a ninety-degree angle to his body. At the end of the hall he turned left, pushing a door open.

It was another dull, neglected room, furnished with 1940s utility furniture. A cupboard, a couple of huge, hide armchairs, an oblong table with two chairs pushed back, a carpet square in the centre that had lost its colour long ago. It was reminiscent of the room they had found his sister's body in. Once it must have been the servants' kitchen; a row of bells hung motionless on the wall. Now they played host to ancient spiders' webs and layers of dust. The atmosphere was made doubly dingy by threadbare red curtains half-nailed across a sash window. The only source of light was a forty-watt bulb, minus a shade, swinging from the centre of the ceiling. Patterson eased into one of the armchairs and held his bony hands out toward the fire — one electric bar barely glowing red. Joanna sat opposite him. Mike took up his customary stance in the doorway, legs apart. His face was wooden and he said nothing, preferring to leave sensitive issues to Joanna.

She opened with a deliberately neutral phrase. 'We've come about your sister, Mr Patterson.'

He wasn't going to help her. 'I know. You've already said. Which one? I've two, you know.'

'The one who lives . . .' The name stuck in her throat.

Not in his. 'Aye. Spite Hall. Well named, isn't it?'

She tried again. 'Have you noticed lots of cars coming and going this morning?'

'Can't say that I have. I've had no milk delivered, that I do know.'

'I suppose Mr Tylman is your milkman too.'

Patterson made as though to stand up. 'If you've come for domestic detail, I've no time to waste.'

'No. No, Mr Patterson. The milkman, Mr Tylman, he found Monday's milk still on your sister's doorstep.' She was trying to ease this frail old man into gradual realisation, but he seemed determined to force her hand.

'They've not got the police in over that — un-drunk milk.'

'No, Mr Patterson.'

'Then spit it out, young lady. What *have* you come about?' There was a touch of impatience now, only slightly tempered by the gentle humour.

'He found your sister. I'm sorry, Mr Patterson. She's dead.'

A spark of malice hardened Patterson's face. 'So,' he said, 'I've outlived her. She's dead.'

'Not through natural causes.' Joanna leaned forward. 'Your sister', she said, 'was battered to death. I'm sorry.'

Patterson looked visibly shocked. 'What? Nan? You're trying to tell me someone's killed *Nan*? I don't believe you.'

'I'm so sorry,' Joanna said again.

Nan's brother seemed to have shrunk in seconds; the chair suddenly dwarfed the wizened form.

'Tell me about your sister Nan, Mr Patterson.'

For a minute she wondered if the old man had heard her. He gave no sign but sat and stared into space. As Joanna was about to repeat the question he uttered just one word. 'Nan.' Then, after a pause of a few seconds, he asked, 'When did it happen?'

'Sunday night — Monday morning — early. You didn't hear anything?' Joanna tried again. 'When did you last see her?'

Patterson still seemed burrowed in his own thoughts. 'Last see Nan?' he mused. 'I can't say.'

'Over the weekend?'

'No.'

'Last week?'

Patterson gave a wry smile. 'Last week?' he said. 'Last year, more like.' His gaze slid away, toward the door, in the direction of Spite Hall. 'Our paths didn't cross.'

Joanna had a sudden vision of two old people, brother and sister, hobbling about their business, their front doors almost opening into each other's homes, deliberately avoiding one another.

Patterson stood up with difficulty. 'Come with me,' he said. 'Just come and look. You'll understand then.'

Slowly he led the way back through the hall to open one of the other doors, leading to a room at the front of the house. The moment he pushed the door open, Joanna was aware of stale, musty air, a room that had not been opened for months, years even. The curtains were drawn tight shut; not a chink of light peeped through. When the door was closed the room was in total darkness. Patterson moved toward the window and drew back the curtains using a long pull cord. 'Look,' he ordered. 'Just look.'

The window was one of the semi-circular bays that looked so authentic from the outside. But from here the entire vista seemed filled with grey concrete. Though Spite Hall had been built at a lower level, the window overlooked part wall, part flat roof; now pooled with rain. It was as bleak and depressing a view as Joanna had ever seen. The ruination was absolute. No wonder the room was never used.

'This is the south of the house,' Patterson muttered. 'Any sun would get lost on its way passing that.' His face changed as he gazed through the window. It twisted, seeming to gain an energetic malevolence of its own. 'I used to think you could adjust to anything,' he said. 'I was wrong; quite wrong. I tried. For years I tried, but I just couldn't. She won — in the end. She beat me.' Without another word he drew the curtains back, and the room was again in total darkness. But Spite Hall still managed to intrude.

As he closed the door behind them he again muttered, 'So Nancy's dead, is she?' And all three of them must surely have been thinking the same thing: that with Nancy dead, Spite Hall could be pulled down.

So the Georgian house could be restored to its dignity, its isolation, and its view. But looking at the bent, tired old man, Joanna felt his release had come too late; he lacked the energy, the strength, the health to do anything but sit and wait for his own death in this crumbling mansion.

And although Joanna believed it could have no bearing on his sister's murder, she was compelled to ask it. 'How did all this happen?'

'My father,' Patterson said simply. 'He had a wicked sense of humour. Left me the house, Nan the land.'

'But surely . . . ?'

'You'd have to understand my dad. He had a streak of . . .' Patterson fumbled for the word, failed to find it. 'Well, put it like this, Inspector, he liked to put the cat among the pigeons and watch the feathers fly. Only this time, of course, he couldn't, because he was dead. But I reckon while he was dying he must have been chuckling, having a good belly laugh. He knew how Nan felt about this place.' Involuntarily Joanna glanced around her, at the high-ceilinged hall, at the dirt, the decay. The neglect.

Patterson was watching her. 'It weren't always like this,' he said. 'Fifty year ago it were grand, just grand. As a child, Nan would go strutting around these very rooms playing the part of the great lady. Much good it did her; much good. She wanted to live here more than anything in the world, and all I ever cared about was the land to farm. So what does the old devil do? He leaves me the house and her the land, with the condition I was not to sell the place in my lifetime or it reverted to her, and she couldn't sell the land either; she had to take up residence on some portion of it or else I got it.' He looked up at the ceiling. Joanna could see cobwebs. She had the feeling he could see something quite different: the old man laughing down at him.

Patterson's eyes returned to them both. 'He knew I was condemned to stay here. That I couldn't move.'

And so the seeds had been sown, the stage set carefully by old Mr Patterson. To give his children contention for their entire lives, Spite Hall had been built close to the house Nan Lawrence felt she'd been cheated out of. She must have inherited some of her father's malicious characteristics to have built it so intrusively near.

'Couldn't you have come to some agreement? Let her live here, with you, and allow you to manage the land?'

'You didn't know Nan,' Patterson said. 'There was not a bone in her body that weren't contentious. Her and my wife,' Patterson's face cracked into a smile, 'like crossed swords they were.'

'And Nan? She was married?'

'David. He was a local farmer. Broke by the war. Died soon after. A wreck of a man before he was thirty.'

'Children?'

'Me or her?'

'Both of you.'

'I got the one son,' Patterson said grudgingly. 'Nan never had any. She was married in the war, and when David came home, well, let's just say he weren't up to it.'

'And your grandson? The one who lives here. How old is he?'

'Nineteen.'

Both Mike and Joanna were thinking the same thoughts; the attacks against the widows, the robbery, the violence, the escalation bore the marks of youthful, possibly drug-related crime. They would find it interesting to meet Arnold Patterson's grandson.

Patterson turned to stare at Joanna and she felt embarrassed. He had read her thoughts, all of them. 'My grandson's name is Christian. He has the top floor.'

'Permanently?'

'Aye. His mother turned him out, so he moved in here. He'll be upset when he hears about Nan. Fond of the old girl he were. Too fond, if you ask me.' Patterson swivelled round. 'It don't do to swim in vats of poison,' he said.

The statement was so sudden, so unexpected that Joanna was taken aback. She wanted to ask, had Nan Lawrence been such a malignant influence?

'We'll need to talk to your grandson.'

'You'll have to come back later if you want to speak to him.' Behind the weariness there was still some fight. 'Lydia,' he said.

Korpanski eyed him. 'Who's Lydia?'

'My sister. My younger sister.' Patterson's face screwed into a smile. 'She'll have a laugh about this.'

Joanna looked at Mike. What a strange, perverted family. *Have a laugh?*

'We'll inform her for you, Mr Patterson. Where does she live?'

'Quills,' he croaked. 'A stupid name for a stupid house. It's a wooden place, a hut, no more than a shack, near Rudyard Lake, along a track. You tell her, and you watch how she takes it. She'll laugh, I can tell you.' With difficulty he straightened his bent back. 'Now when can we hold the funeral?'

And this was the bit Joanna hated. First of all you inform a family their relative is dead, then you tell them they can't even have the body for the funeral until the coroner releases it, when the police and the pathologist and the rest of the legal team are convinced every conceivable piece of evidence has been extracted from it. It could take weeks, months, even on rare occasions years, however sympathetic the coroner might be to the family's needs. As gently as she could, she explained to Arnold Patterson that there might be some delay. To her surprise, Patterson seemed to grasp the situation quite easily.

He nodded. 'Will you be wanting me to identify her?'

It crossed Joanna's mind that contact between brother and sister had been slight, but Patterson was frail and his sister had been badly beaten. Maybe someone else should do the job, someone physically stronger? 'We usually want a relative, someone who knew her well.'

Arnold Patterson chuckled. 'Then you'd better have Christian,' he said. 'He's the only one who knew Nan what you might call well.'

Joanna and Mike moved toward the front door. 'We'll come back.' It was time to leave this old man alone with his emotions, although Joanna was not at all sure what they were.

They had almost reached the front door when music began, thumping out overhead. An unmistakable jungle beat.

'I thought you said your grandson was out?' she said sharply.

'I didn't say that. I told you earlier he were in. I simply said you'd have to come back if you wanted to talk to him.' Arnold Patterson was sharper than he looked. 'He just doesn't get out of bed until late, keeps different hours from us working folk. He's a student.' To Patterson it seemed an answer to everything.

Joanna's curiosity about young Christian Patterson compounded. Nan Lawrence would have opened the door to her great-nephew, welcomed him in, unsuspecting, returned to her tapestry. She moved away from the door, read Mike's dark eyes and knew he was tracking along the same lines as herself.

'I think we'll just pop upstairs and say hello to him.'

Patterson would have liked to have stopped her, they could both see that. He lifted his arms up, then dropped them again, in the end turning his back on them. 'I won't come up,' he said grumpily. 'Arthritis.'

They were guided by the music thumping throughout the house. Two flights of stairs to what must once have been servants' attic rooms. A blue-painted door ahead was closed. Joanna gave it a few hard knocks and the music abruptly stopped, although the pounding beat still seemed to reverberate around the walls.

The door opened and a freckled face peered out, tousled red-gold hair tied back with a bootlace, pleasant brown eyes and an engaging grin. Considering Christian Patterson lived here alone with his grandfather, who was almost certainly confined to the first two floors, and that he probably hadn't heard their approach up the stairs, he didn't seem in the least bit surprised to see them. 'Hello there. I thought I heard voices. I was going to come down and investigate, but I had an essay to finish.'

Joanna's eyes roved past him to the desk littered with papers, scrunched balls spotting the floor. The bed was unmade, yet the room looked clean and there was a pleasant tang of a spicy men's deodorant. So far her impressions were good. When she looked back at Christian Patterson he was appraising her just as critically. They smiled at one another.

She decided then that Christian Patterson was clever, personable and by the same token someone to be wary of. But she could see quite plainly why the old woman had formed an attachment to him. He must have seemed like the very essence of youth to the lonely, childless old woman.

'So?' Christian Patterson was watching them both enquiringly.

'I'm Detective Inspector Piercy, Leek Police. This is Detective Sergeant Korpanski.'

'Oh?'

There was something about the classic innocent reaction. Too classic. Too innocent. Eye contact straight, true and prolonged, wide open. It made the back of her neck prickle, as though she had touched something electrically live, and she was curious.

'You didn't notice the police cars outside this morning?'

'Nope. As I just said, I thought I heard voices for the last half hour or so. That's all.'

Considering the music, it was perfectly possible. But the attic window clearly overlooked the entire front of the house, including the drive, and it was open a few inches. *She* could see the police cars, so why hadn't he? Had he been *so* absorbed in his essay? Or asleep?

Belatedly Christian showed curiosity. 'What are the police doing here anyway?' He frowned. 'Why *are* you here?'

'Your great aunt,' Joanna began.

Christian interrupted. 'Not fallen and cracked her hip, has she? I'm always telling her to be more careful.'

'She hasn't fallen.'

'What then?'

'She's been found dead.'

'In suspicious circumstances.' Mike spoke from behind her shoulder.

The innocent eyes widened even further. 'Aunt Nan?' There was a slight tremor in the youth's voice. 'What's happened?'

Either he was a good actor or he had been genuinely fond of the old woman.

'She's been murdered.'

Christian looked shocked. His face turned white. 'How? How did it happen? I was always telling her.' His eyes narrowed intelligently. 'How did they get in? She bolted that door every night. She never let *anybody* in.' He tried to make a joke of it. 'Even I practically had to show an identity card to cross the threshold. She's been ever so careful, ever since . . .' He looked from one to the other. 'Well, she'd heard about the attacks and burglaries against old ladies in Leek.'

'Did she know any of them?'

The brown eyes regarded her thoughtfully. 'Inspector Piercy,' he said with the ghost of a smile, 'Leek is a small town, *all* the old ladies know each other, or did once. The newspaper headlines made Aunt Nan extremely cautious. So how did they get in?'

'She must have left the door unlocked.'

Christian shook his head slowly. 'No,' he said firmly. 'No way.'

'Well, there's no sign of forced entry; the back door was locked and bolted and the windows were all fastened.'

Mike threw his suggestion in. 'Perhaps she forgot to lock . . . ?'

'Look, just because she was old,' Christian defended his great aunt vigorously, 'she wasn't stupid or demented. Not Aunt Nan, she's pretty amazing.'

'Was she deaf, Christian?'

The brown eyes held surprise. 'Deaf? Aunt Nan? Absolutely not. She could hear a pin drop in the next room. She had brilliant hearing and brilliant eyesight. She wasn't like other old women.'

There was something strange about the way Christian Patterson spoke about his great aunt. As though she were no ordinary mortal but something else, something special, someone revered.

What had her brother said about the relationship between the grandson and his great aunt, about swimming in a vat of poison? So had Christian swum in the venom too often? Had he then become tainted? Looking at the youth in front of her, Joanna could see no evidence of this.

'How was she killed?' he asked.

'We don't know. The post-mortem will tell us. It's probably tomorrow. But it looks as though . . .' Joanna searched for a nice way to say it. There wasn't one. 'She might have been battered with her own walking stick.'

Christian stared at the floor, still pale; when he looked up, Joanna was surprised to read the shock in his face. 'You know the awful thing? She kept that walking stick to defend herself.'

'Perhaps you'd take a look at the stick?' Mike suggested. 'It would help if we knew for certain it was hers.'

Joanna looked at him sharply. He wanted to see Christian at the scene of the crime.

And it did seem to rattle him; he licked his lips. 'You mean you want me to come round to . . . ?'

Joanna wondered if he would call it Spite Hall. He didn't. He used no name. Instead: 'When did you say she died?'

'We didn't.' Mike seemed to produce the sentence like a trump card.

Joanna hesitated. Usually she could read Korpanski like a book, but she didn't know what he was up to. She let him take the lead.

'The signs are that she died sometime on Sunday. When the milkman called on Monday morning the empty bottles had not been put out.'

'Then she died on Sunday.'

'How do you know?'

'Aunt Nan was a real stickler for habits. If the empties weren't on the step for Monday morning, she died on Sunday night.'

'You can be as certain as that?'

Christian nodded.

'When did you last see her?'

'Sunday evening,' he said, after some thought. 'She was sat in her window, sewing. I was thinking of knocking on the glass and telling her to shut her curtains. *Anyone* could have been watching her.'

Joanna wondered then whether it had been Nan who had drawn the curtains or someone else who didn't want to be seen.

As she Mike walked back toward Spite Hall, having decided to spare Christian the ordeal of going down to the murder scene straightaway, Joanna ran through her list of things to do: there was the formal identification of the body to come, then there was the setting up of an incident room, the gathering of a team. They would all be working long hours, in close proximity, discussing the case from all angles. Past experience had taught her that time spent together, pooling knowledge and discussing possibilities and prob-abilities, testing theories amongst themselves, could prove as productive as the other long hours spent interviewing neighbours, friends and suspects. But the first thing she had to deal with was making a full report to her senior officer, Superintendent Arthur Colclough. He of the bulldog jowls, the dubious wit, the almost paternalistic attitude toward her. A senior officer whom she had grown to respect. And only to herself would she admit that the respect was tempered by affection. He was, in a way, the father she had never had. Her own father had been a Peter Pan of a man, who in his middle fifties had found himself a much younger wife and had paid for his passion with a fatal heart attack. Joanna had never quite forgiven him; neither had her mother, nor her sister.

She rang Colclough on her mobile phone. As always he listened without comment, saying nothing until she had finished. His mind followed her reasoning. 'So you think the same gang is behind first the robberies, then the assaults on the old ladies, and now this?'

'I think so, sir,' she said cautiously.

'Piercy,' he said, 'you're a senior police officer. I don't need to tell you how to work at this.' He did anyway. 'Look at the MO of these gangs. How did they get in?'

'Front door entry, sir.'

'And in the Marlowe case?'

'Almost the same method, sir.'

Colclough picked on the word like a vulture finding carrion. '*Almost?*'

'It was a downstairs window, sir, smashed in. Cecily Marlowe had had window locks fitted after news of the robberies broke.'

'Right.' A brief pause. 'And forensic evidence?'

'There was very little, sir, except in the Jane Vernon case. I mean, these gangs, they know what they're up to.'

'Mmm.'

It was a dissatisfied sound followed by a long pause. Colclough was thinking. And as frequently happened, his decision followed closely what Joanna had already decided to do for herself.

'It might be an idea, Piercy, for you to talk to all these old women again. *If* you're right and the crimes have been committed by the same gang, these old biddies have met Nan Lawrence's killer.'

'The thought had crossed my mind, sir. But they were all very traumatised by the incident. We never did get good statements from any of them.'

'Well, they've had time to get over it,' he snapped. A touch of humour shone through as suddenly as the sun appears from behind the blackest of clouds. 'Use those famous kid gloves of yours, Piercy. Now when's the PM?'

'We don't know yet. I'm waiting for Matthew to let us know.' She paused. 'He wanted some X-rays doing.'

'Mmm?' Surprise this time in the expression.

'He thinks quite a few bones were broken in the assault.'

'I see.'

They discussed routine points next: available officers, extra phone lines, the incident room — a huge caravan to be parked in the drive of Spite Hall — methods of alerting the local public without firing the entire town with panic.

The call ended with Colclough's usual parting shot: 'Keep me informed, Piercy.'

And her habitual rejoinder: 'Yes, sir.'

She found Mike stood outside the front door of Spite Hall, talking to PC Will Farthing. He crunched across the gravel toward her. 'Post-mortem's fixed for tomorrow morning,' he said. 'Just had the coroner's office on the phone; coroner wants to speak to you. And the desk sergeant's been sending messages too; Tylman's come back to make his statement.'

'The milkman? Then that's where we should be.' She handed him the squad car keys. 'You drive, Mike. I want to think.'

As he turned the car around, she couldn't resist turning back in her seat to study the two contrasting houses that had brought so much pain.

* * *

Tylman was sat nervously in the anteroom. He was a ruddy-faced, plump man wearing a royal blue overall splashed with the name of the dairy, Addison's. Joanna introduced herself and Mike, and they made themselves comfortable in one of the interview rooms. Tylman looked anxious. 'I'm not a suspect, am I?'

Joanna bit back the Clouseau reply, that she suspected everyone and she suspected no one, instead reassuring him heartily and adding her thanks to him for acting so promptly both by alerting the police and by attending for interview.

Tylman's face visibly relaxed.

'Let's take you back to Saturday,' she began.

'I just left two pints.' And Tylman explained Nan Lawrence's regular habits. 'She *always* had two pints on a Saturday.'

'Did you notice anything unusual?'

The milkman shook his head.

'Did you see her?'

Tylman thought for a moment. 'Not on Saturday,' he said finally.

'And Sunday?'

'I don't deliver on a Sunday.'

'What do you do?'

Tylman's face broke into a grin. 'What half the population do,' he said. 'Catch up on some sleep.'

'And?'

Again Tylman looked uneasy. 'I went to the DIY store,' he said. 'My wife's got this thing about having a dishwasher. It wanted plumbing in. I did that most of the afternoon, then I watched a rugby match. In the evening I watched a film.'

'And that takes us to Monday,' Joanna prompted. 'What can you tell us about Monday?'

'There was only the one empty on the doorstep,' Tylman said. 'Washed. She always washed them. I picked it up. I thought it was a bit funny. I mean, there was always *two* empties on a Monday. I'd never known her leave only the one.'

Joanna cast her mind back to the tiny, old-fashioned kitchen. A fridge had stood in the corner, to the left of the door. She made a mental note to ask Barra what it had contained. Would they be able to pinpoint the time of death by how much milk was left in the bottle rather than rely on scientific means? Probably. Already she could see that science and social science would together provide answers; if both agreed, it would be fixed.

She spoke again to Tylman. 'And so to Tuesday.'

Tylman swallowed. 'It was still there,' he said, 'Monday's pint, stood on the doorstep. I knew then that something was very wrong. I was worried,' he said. 'I turned the engine off and walked right round the house. The curtains were drawn but there was a narrow crack. Then I saw.' He looked up. 'You *know* what I saw.'

'Okay. Okay.' Joanna stood up. It all seemed logical enough. 'Thank you very much, Mr Tylman. Is there anything else you want to add?'

The milkman shook his head.

Mike interrupted. 'Nothing *else* that you noticed?' Again the milkman shook his head, more emphatically this time.

Joanna put the statement in front of him and handed him a pen, and he signed it.

Afterwards, watching the milkman leave, Joanna had a nagging feeling that there *was* something else she should have tackled him on. It would be later that afternoon before she knew what it was.

Lunch breaks — even late ones — were already a thing of the past. She and Mike wolfed down sandwiches while preparing for the first briefing, washing the bread down with coffee. Neither spoke.

The assembled officers were waiting for them as they walked in.

Joanna crossed straight to the whiteboard and penned in the facts of the case. First she wrote the details of the eighteen burglaries that had taken place between January and July. All preying on elderly women, widows, stealing easily disposable goods, money, televisions, videos, pension books, the odd piece of porcelain. No sightings of the perpetrators. Then in July Emily Whittaker had stood at the top of the stairs to find two or more youths ransacking her house, one of whom on leaving a bedroom had pushed past her. She had fallen and broken her hip, and that had been the start of a change in the crimes. She had described her attackers as young, although later she had applied the same description to the consultant who had operated on her — a man of around fifty. When pressed by a gentle DS Hannah Beardmore, she had said that the burglars were boys of about twenty. Further descriptions had been elusive; she couldn't remember what they wore, what they looked like, anything, even how many there were.

Joanna moved on.

If Emily Whittaker seemed to recall nothing, what Florence Price remembered was equally unhelpful. She had been robbed by a 'masked gang'. But the money taken had been real enough. Cash. Three hundred pounds saved out of her pension. Money meant to pay for her winter gas bill. A local businessman had donated the money instead. Florence Price may have been badly frightened, but ultimately she had not been out of pocket.

Joanna stood back from the board and frowned. What sort of a 'gang' broke in, robbed and threatened and left no trace of evidence? Beneath Florence Price's name, she wrote 'Cecily Marlowe' in large black capitals. She hardly needed to remind the assembled officers of the details of that crime; the slashing of an old lady was memorable enough.

Barely a week after the assault on Cecily Marlowe had been the puzzling robbery of Jane Vernon. Thankfully no violence that time. Her purse had been emptied of 27 pounds, and this time the forensics boys had hit lucky. They had found a long, blonde hair. A natural blonde, the report had said. For the first time they had wondered if a female had been involved. None of the other victims had mentioned a woman's presence; their assailants had been unequivocally male.

And finally Joanna wrote the last name on the board. That of Nan Lawrence. Murdered. Battered with what was almost certainly her own walking stick. Joanna recalled the murder scene, *Massacre of the Innocent*, and they didn't know yet if anything had been taken.

There were plenty of lines of enquiry open to them, but the questions she penned onto the boards were, 'Did Nan Lawrence know her killer?' and 'Was the door left unlocked or did she unlock it herself?'

Joanna stepped back from the board. Christian had told them a few things, facts that did not exactly deflect suspicion from him. His great aunt had not been deaf. No one therefore could have crept up on her unawares. Barra's theory of a deaf and slightly scatty old lady had been blown right into the sky. And from the statement given by Nan's own brother, her great-nephew had been the person who had known Nan Lawrence best.

6

Still puzzling, Joanna wound up the briefing, but as she was leaving the room, Will Farthing caught up with her. 'There's something you should know.'

He and Joanna walked along the corridor together. 'I'm sure it's nothing to do with the case,' he said earnestly, 'but you should know.'

'Know what?'

'The milkman.'

'Bill Tylman?' A more innocent bystander Joanna had never met.

'He was the one. He found that other old lady.' Then it clicked. Joanna knew what it was about Tylman that had given her the feeling of déjà vu.

'You mean Cecily Marlowe?'

'Yes.' Farthing looked uncomfortable. 'He found her the morning after the attack. I'm sure there's absolutely no connection. I mean he's probably one of the few people who calls round regularly on these old ladies, but he did have a big fuss made of him at the time. They gave him the milkman of the year award last month on the strength of it.'

'That's right. The papers have been running stories about his bravery, haven't they? Made him quite a local celebrity. Thanks, Will. As you say, I'm sure it has nothing to do with the case, but . . .'

Farthing grinned at her. 'Just thought I ought to remind you.'

As soon as she was back in her office, Joanna asked Mike to get her the Marlowe file.

'There's only one thing that bothers me about Tylman's involvement in another major incident,' she said. 'Why didn't he mention it? It would have been the most natural thing in the world. He was first on the scene both times. He was honoured for it the first time. He wasn't exactly evading the spotlight before. So why, all of a sudden, does he hide his light under a bushel?'

Mike had located the file. He handed it across the desk. 'Yeah, a bit suspicious, don't you think?'

Joanna laughed up at him. 'You think everything's suspicious, Mike.'

Korpanski grinned back. 'Surely you can't imagine that Tylman gets a gang to assault old ladies purely for a moment of glory?'

Their good humour didn't last long. Cecily Marlowe's file made grim reading. The photographs were bad enough. Sad eyes peered out from a mournful face criss-crossed with suture lines. The mask of someone who had seen too much, lived too long. And the shock was evident in a fixed stare directed at a cruel world.

Then there was the doctor's report. Contusions. Numerous slash wounds across the face, some superficial, some not. Joanna bent over the file and continued reading, sickened to the stomach. A general anaesthetic had had to be given, in spite of the victim's poor physical state. There was underlying damage to deeper tissue: muscles, blood vessels, nerves. A finger had been almost severed. Joanna stopped reading, too queasy at the thought of the cruelty behind the hand that had slashed, without pity, at a defenceless, scared old woman. For no reason. She stared sightlessly at the wall. There was no mention of the irreparable damage that had been done to the woman's mind, the fright, the loss of confidence. Joanna knew that Cecily Marlowe suffered from permanent terrors since the attacks; her dreams were filled with pain, with knives slashing.

She leafed through the statements. Yes. The milkman had heard whimpering from inside the house. He had gone to her rescue. He had found her hiding underneath her kitchen table, too terrified to come out, screaming hysterically as *he* approached her; someone she had known for years, had seen day in, day out. She had been too frightened to be rational. He had coaxed her from under the table as though she were a small child. He had rung the emergency services, waited with her until they had arrived. He hadn't done much, but he had been there. The milkman had been commended, singled out as one of Leek's true heroes. A local charity for the elderly had adopted him as their patron. Leek's business population had proved generous. He had been voted the Millennium Milkman by a local newspaper. Joanna stopped reading. Tylman peered out from the newspaper cuttings, justifiably proud of himself, fitting the caption of 'Hero Milkman' perfectly. So why hadn't he said that Nan Lawrence was not the first battered old lady he had discovered?

Joanna moved on to Nan Lawrence's murder and asked herself the same question that had troubled her before. Why? There were plenty of motives for murder; and plenty of murders that had no apparent motive: blind lashings out, unplanned frenzied attacks, usually committed under the influence of alcohol. In fact, Nan Lawrence's murder bore some of the hallmarks of such a crime. The weapon had been opportunistic, not one taken to the scene to kill. The injuries had been far beyond those that would have been necessary to kill her. The killer had carried on beating and beating, almost certainly after she had died.

Was Christian Patterson telling the truth when he insisted she had *always* locked and bolted her doors and had perfectly good hearing? But why would he lie? If anything, it heaped suspicion back on him.

Mike was watching her. 'Penny for them, Jo.'

'I'm trying to work out the sequence of events, Mike, and I'm not doing too well,' she said frankly. 'I can't think how our killer gained access, and I can't think why. If it wasn't for the numerous recent attacks on old women, and if it wasn't physically impossible for him to have done it, I might start turning my suspicions on the brother. Heaven knows he had motive enough. Every time he walked down those steps to be confronted with that place, he must have loathed his sister. I sensed real hatred there.' She met his dark eyes. 'That is why it's called Spite Hall, isn't it? The entire edifice is a mausoleum to spite, hatred, malice. I mean, it's an ugly old place, but the emotion that created it and stuck it right in front of her own brother's front door is even uglier.'

'I don't know, Jo,' Korpanski said uncomfortably. 'It's just folklore.'

'And how many times does folklore have its origins in the truth, Mike? They hated each other, this brother and sister. Encouraged by their father. They lived as close as it is possible to live, without actually sharing a roof, and virtually ignored each other's existence. How did that ugly building come to be built there in the first place? I thought there was such a thing as planning permission.'

'I don't know. Maybe just after the war they relaxed it — if it was in place at all. And besides, it won't have any bearing on our little gang of granny-bashers.'

'We should keep an open mind, Korpanski. Anything we learn — at all — about Nan Lawrence might help in finding out about her death.'

Korpanski planted himself right in front of her desk, centre vision. 'It's a waste of time, Jo,' he argued. 'We should be talking to Stockport Police, Manchester; look at parts of the Potteries where they've had a problem with break-ins, the Meir for a start.'

'I know that, Mike.'

He was smiling at her. 'You're just being nosey.'

'Yeah, well,' Joanna admitted, 'I concede that. You know me, always want to sniff out the scandal in people's lives. That's where crimes are born, Mike, and don't you forget it. For now, I'd like to talk to the third member of the family. The other sister. Besides,' she fixed him with a stare 'if you're so certain this is a random attack, perhaps you'll tell me why you're keen to lure Christian Patterson down to his great aunt's place.'

Korpanski made a face. 'You're usually the one going on about feelings, Jo,' he said. 'I've got a bit of a feeling about Christian.'

'What sort of feeling?'

'That he's not quite what he pretends to be,' Korpanski said. 'I can picture him being quite vicious.'

'You're joking.'

'Never more serious,' Korpanski answered. 'There's something about him. Half the villains we come across, they go stamping on people's heads, baseball-batting victims till they need a life-support machine, but then put them in court, hair slicked down, in a suit, and they look respectable. He just reminds me of hooligans like that. And judge and jury get fooled every time.'

'But not you, Mike.'

'No,' he said. 'Not me. I know the type too well.'

The exchange was interrupted by the ring tone of Joanna's mobile phone.

'I'd better do breakfast in the morning,' Matthew told her cheerfully when she answered the call. 'PM's fixed for 8.30.'

'Thanks,' she said sweetly. 'No fry-ups then, Matt, just a light one'll do. Or none at all?'

'Fine by me. Listen.' A pause. 'I've cleaned her face up. There's quite a bit of damage, enough to turn anyone's stomach. I think it would be kinder to the relatives if we relied on dental records for formal identification.'

'Good idea. I'll be late home tonight. Bound to be, really, with everything that's happened.'

'Then I'll see you when I see you. Hope you're around to tuck me up.'

Joanna smiled. 'Count on it.'

'Bye then, darling.'

She stood up. 'PM's at 8.30 in the morning,' she told Mike. 'Not that it'll tell us much we don't already know. In the meantime, let's go and visit Nan Lawrence's sister.'

* * *

Rudyard was a straggling village a couple of miles to the north-west of Leek. Its centre was a huge reservoir housing a small sailing club. In the summer this would be full of day-trippers in search of any large expanse of water, ice creams and the chance of a short ride on the tiny railway. The Victorians had loved the place, and a certain Mr and Mrs Kipling had been so impressed that they had named their son after it. That day, however, not a sail was to be seen. The lake looked grey and unwelcoming as the rain bounced on its surface.

Quills was not easy to find in the fading light, up a mud-died track and through a wide farm gate; nothing pointed the way to a home at all. It seemed that Lydia Patterson did not encourage casual callers. If one of the WPCs had not been familiar with Rudyard and given them directions, they might have missed it altogether. As it was, they had precise instructions, along with the description Nan Lawrence's brother had provided, so they were already prepared for a home somewhat different from the traditional cottage. To be expected, considering her brother's and sister's residences.

It was still a surprise. A 1920s square wooden shack, single-storey, small and neglected in the centre of a field. Once emulsion, the paint was now peeling. It hadn't been touched for years. The garden was non-existent. Hens, sheep, even a pig wallowed in the mud outside. Ducks paddled in a huge puddle. Had it not been for a lamp burning in one of the windows, a passer-by would have thought the place was derelict. No one was to be seen.

Mike pulled the car up at the gate. 'You want me to open it?'

It was only fair that she should do it; Korpanski was driving. But the rain had started up again in a vicious, blustery drizzle, and one step out of the car would have put Joanna straight into the mire. *Bugger all this feminism*, she thought. *Give me chivalry any time.*

She grinned at Korpanski. 'Do me a favour.'

Manfully he stepped out, dirtying the bottoms of his trousers straightaway. Joanna watched him through the windscreen; big, burly, a contrast to Matthew's slight figure. Korpanski caught her watching him, grinned ruefully, opened the door and sank back into his seat. 'It's a mud bath out there.'

He stopped the car right in front of the two steps that led to Quills' front door. The scent of the farmyard was strong as Joanna closed the gate, this time accepting that her shoes would be soiled. She didn't want to antagonise Nan Lawrence's sister by allowing her animals to escape. Some movement caught her eye. She glanced up at the house; she was being watched. A face had appeared at the window. She had a swift impression of doughy features and pale skin. The next instant the door was flung open and a robust woman was silhouetted in the doorway.

'Who the hell are you?' she snapped.

It was hard to be dignified when you were up to your ankles in foul-smelling mud. 'Detective Inspector Joanna Piercy and DS Korpanski, Leek Police,' Joanna shouted, holding her hands over her eyes to keep the rain out.

'Why have you come?'

A sudden gust of wind forced Joanna to shout even louder. 'I've got some bad news. It's about your sister.'

The woman put her hands on her hips and stared. 'What bad news?'

'I'm afraid . . .' Joanna took a couple of steps toward the front door of the cottage.

'Don't be afraid.' Lydia Patterson had stopped shouting and her voice was soft and surprisingly gentle. Closer to,

63

Joanna realised she was more of a plump, elderly hippie, in a floor-length tartan skirt and a frilled cream blouse with ribbons at the throat and puffed sleeves — an incongruous outfit for such a rural environment. And the puffed sleeves on such meaty arms added to the strange effect, making her look almost like a man in drag. Joanna watched her, fascinated.

'Sod off.'

The words, said gently, almost affectionately, startled her. She glanced back at Mike. But Lydia Patterson was not speaking to either of them, she was addressing one of the brown sheep, which had climbed the two steps toward the front door.

'Go on, Mint Sauce. Sod off.' The sheep bleated a response and scuttled back down the steps again. 'Sly, stupid animals,' Ms Patterson said calmly. 'Think they'll sneak in while I'm occupied with you.' She scrutinised them both before turning around and heading back indoors. 'Well, the pair of you, you'd better come in before you get soaked, and tell me what this "bad news" is about my dear sister. I'm all agog.'

They followed her into a small, cosy room that smelt the same as the yard outside. A couple of hens flapped from the sofa.

'And you can bugger off too,' Lydia Patterson said. 'If you can't provide me with a few more eggs, I shall wring your bloody necks and put you in the broiler. Now off with you.' She picked up one hen under each arm and threw them both into a wicker basket in the corner. 'Bloody things,' she said without rancour. 'Take advantage of your good nature. Maybe I should expel them to the hen house.' She sank onto the sofa, glancing from one to the other as though trying to read the news for herself from their faces. 'We-ell,' she prompted, 'I suppose Nan's finally released the world of her odious presence and popped her clogs?'

Joanna opened her mouth, but it was Korpanski who filled the silence. 'She's been murdered,' he said bluntly.

Lydia stared at him for a few moments without a twitch of reaction. 'This isn't a joke?'

Joanna shook her head.

Then Lydia Patterson fulfilled her brother's prediction by laughing. 'Someone really has bumped the old cow off?' She moved quickly to the door of the chalet and threw it wide open. To the dark, to the blustery rain, to the animals in the yard, to the world in general she shouted, 'The old cow's dead.' And again: 'The old bag is finally with us no longer. We can all breathe again.' She stood for a moment on the threshold, filling her lungs, it seemed, with the Nan-free air. Then she closed the door, stared first at Korpanski and then at Joanna. 'And what does my big brother have to say about this?' Lydia Patterson's eyes gleamed. 'Let me guess,' she said, looking from one to the other. 'He's delighted?'

'He doesn't appear', Joanna ventured cautiously, 'to be too upset.'

Lydia Patterson opened her mouth and gave yet another quivering belly laugh. 'I'll bloody bet he isn't,' she said. 'So, who did the foul deed?'

'We don't know yet.'

'Well, let's go for how then.'

'She was battered to death.'

Lydia Patterson's intelligence was impressive. 'So you have someone who hated her.'

'There have been numerous attacks committed against old women in the Leek area,' Joanna began.

Lydia turned a pair of small, amber eyes full on her. 'You can't class my sister with just any old woman from Leek,' she said. 'She was a one-off, a spiteful old cow. She devoted her life to causing trouble, and now her chickens have come home to roost.' She leaned right back on the sofa and smiled. 'You know,' she said, 'I rather like this theme of chickens coming home to roost. It might almost convince me there is justice in this chaotic world of ours.' She beamed from one to the other, looking pleased with herself. 'So, why have you two abandoned your investigations purely to come and see me? I mean, any old junior officer could have broken this particular piece of news. Let's see.' She pinched a lardy double chin between her thumb and forefinger. 'It wouldn't be curiosity, would it?'

Joanna flushed. 'We need to know where you were between Sunday lunchtime and Monday morning.'

'Where I always am — here.'

'You have an alibi?'

'Well, not a human one. But if you're wondering who might have wanted to murder my sister, the list is long. You believe this to be the work of a gang, don't you?' Her small, strange eyes flicked from Joanna to Mike and back to Joanna again as though waiting for confirmation. 'Well, there you have it.' She stood up. 'Do come back if you'd like to talk to me again.'

* * *

'What an astonishing person,' Joanna gasped when they'd finally escaped from Quills.

'Uncomfortable,' Mike agreed.

But she caught the humour in his voice. 'You liked her.'

'In a way — yes.' He turned to look at her. 'Well, at least she didn't pretend.'

'No.' There was no pretence about Lydia Patterson, not of grief or sorrow or affection for her sister — even if the circumstances surrounding her extinction had been tragic. Already Joanna sensed that Nan Lawrence's family held secrets. And they were sceptical that their sister's murder had been the work of a gang.

As Mike drove the car back toward the Macclesfield road and Leek, she turned to him. 'I don't know what you're looking so cheerful about; we've got a long night ahead of us.'

'Yeah — well. That's exactly what was making me so cheerful. I was thinking. With all this overtime I won't be home much, will I?'

She tut-tutted. 'So you'll leave poor old Fran to deal with her mum alone?

'She's *her* mum. Not mine.'

So we disassociate ourselves from unwelcome relatives. Mike from his mother-in-law, Joanna from Eloise, Arnold and Lydia Patterson from their sister.

7

Peering through the window, Lydia watched the car reverse out of the drive and head back toward Leek. The insouciance she had displayed while the two police officers were present had been part affectation. Underneath she was agitated. She paced the small room, muttering to herself. 'I must be wrong,' she repeated over and over again. 'It can't have been him. He *couldn't* have done it, not him. It would have been impossible.' But a small voice inside her was arguing, 'Talk to the policewoman. You don't have to point the finger. She'll be reasonable. Listen. They think it was the work of a gang. So, let them think.'

After all these years there was still enough turbulence to disturb her mind. There was only one way to silence it. One escape. She bent over her exercise book and wrote.

> *It was Fredo who attempted to put some sense back into Dora. 'You don't know it was Cassandra who took the egg.'*

Lydia Patterson stared, unblinking, at the rain cascading down the window, and snapped the curtains shut.

* * *

Joanna had not been lying when she had warned Mike it would be a late night. Using a large sheet on the flipchart, she again wrote Nan Lawrence's name in block capitals. Underneath she scrawled the questions they wanted answering.

'First, Mike, who killed her? Why? Is anything missing?' She looked across at him. 'We'll get Christian to take a look in the morning as soon as the post-mortem's out of the way.' She stood back. 'Have I left anything out?'

'How did they get in? How was it that she was still sewing when she was hit?'

She scribbled again on the board and Mike continued. 'Is there any connection with previous assaults and burglaries? And if there is, can we learn anything from them that will help us find Nan Lawrence's killer?'

Both were silent for a few minutes before Joanna shook her head. 'I can't think of anything, can you?'

'No.'

'Motive? What are they after, Mike?'

He shrugged. 'Kicks. Money. Dominance. Cruelty.'

She winced. 'Nicely put, Korpanski. Cruelty. So, how many do you think are in the gang?'

'Two. Three. No more than four.'

'And we think it is a gang because of?'

'Victim evidence and . . .'

Joanna finished it for him. 'Because this is just the sort of crime a group of youths would commit.'

'Yeah.'

'Right. I agree with you so far. But was it our gang? If so, were they working up to murder?'

'Jo, you're the one who's always been worried about that.'

She nodded. 'But as a group, or one malevolent person within the group? The leader?'

'One, probably.'

'Yes. I agree with that.'

'So, did they go to Spite Hall to kill?'

'You mean rather than to rob?'

Again she nodded.

Korpanski met her eyes. 'It's a rough thought.'

'Very rough.'

'We know there was no sign of a break-in. Would a suspicious old widow let in a gang of strangers?'

She leafed through some documents — Bill Tylman's statement and the SOCOs' report. 'Remember what Christian Patterson said, that he practically had to display an identity card to gain access? Nan Lawrence wasn't just suspicious, she was very careful in practice. It doesn't seem at all likely that she let anyone in. Add to that the fact that it was a stormy night. She wouldn't have left the door open. Then think back to the geography of Spite Hall. There are two windows looking out on to the front door. If she was at all security conscious, she would have peeped through. Which further underlines the fact that she would not have opened her door to strangers. Let's go one step further, Mike, and say she didn't let strangers in. Therefore, whoever she opened her door to was not a stranger.'

Mike opened his mouth to speak, but she held her finger up. 'No, just wait a minute. Let's turn this entire case on its head. Just try this. According to Barra, the evidence at the scene points to Nan Lawrence having let someone in and then returned to her embroidery.'

'That doesn't fit.'

'I know, I know. It doesn't fit the story, Mike, but we can't change evidence to suit our theory. Barra's finds will have to form the framework of our case. The blood splashes over the tapestry indicate Nan Lawrence was bending over it when she was struck — from behind. All the blood is centred around that and the top rail of the chair. She was seated when struck, fell, and didn't move again while her killer hit her over and over again.' Joanna hated even speaking the words. 'You'd have to know someone terribly well to let them in sometime on a Sunday evening, then calmly continue with your sewing.'

Mike drew in a deep, sharp breath. 'What are you saying, Jo?'

'You know exactly what I'm saying.' She stood up. 'Right. Tomorrow we're going to set the team on Nan's last movements all day Sunday. But you and I, Mike, are going to get to know Christian Patterson a little better. Your idea of taking him to visit—' she paused — 'or *revisit* the crime scene seems like an excellent idea to me.'

She gave a sharp yawn and stretched her arms above her head. 'I'm too tired to cycle home. It's too late anyway.' She grinned at Korpanski. 'And I can't drag poor old Matthew out at this time of night.'

'So you want a lift?'

'Would you mind?'

Quite suddenly Korpanski's face clouded over. 'Well, anything that'll delay the evil moment of going home.'

Again Joanna was tempted to put a friendly arm around her colleague's shoulders. But the action would have been open to misinterpretation. Instead she gave a chuckle as she put her jacket on. 'Damn and blast it, Mike.' She grinned impishly at him. 'Why don't I ever get a straightforward murder case? Just a simple stabbing where the husband confesses and hands me the knife?'

* * *

Matthew had fallen asleep over his *Journal of Forensic Medicine*. Joanna kicked her shoes off, tiptoed into the kitchen and poured herself a glass of wine. Then she sat on the sofa opposite him. He looked different asleep; open-necked shirt, tie flung across the arm of the sofa, long legs outstretched, honey-coloured hair tousled.

It had been almost eight years since she had first met him, on a case very like this one, an old woman battered to death. Fresh out of university, already a detective sergeant, she had been dreading her first post-mortem, and had felt queasy at the first cut. Matthew had halted the post-mortem to find her a chair. She had read warmth in the green-brown eyes. And he must have seen something answering in hers.

After the PM had been completed, while her colleagues were still finishing their notes, he had engaged her in conversation.

Joanna smiled, went to pour herself a second glass of wine, and returned to the sofa. He had asked questions mainly, she recalled. A grilling about why she had done a psychology degree, why she had then joined the police force, how the degree helped her — if at all. And she had found herself drawn into the sticky web of an affair with a man she had always known was married. It had helter-skeltered out of control, her actions increasingly careless, her mind, her soul, her thoughts no longer her own; by the time they had started sleeping together, she had completely lost all sense, all reason.

And then one day she had woken on a chill November morning, alone, knowing that Matthew would be sleeping beside his wife, and had acknowledged that, for her sanity, it must stop. She had written him a cold note, begged him not to contact her. He had respected her wishes — for more than a year. Eighteen months had passed. Eighteen months when she had tried — hard — to have other relationships. No one had measured up to him.

And then the nurse had been murdered. She had seen him again, listened to his voice, loved him more deeply even than before, because it was no longer a crazy passion but an intense knowledge that Matthew was the only man she would ever love. However doomed it was, there never would be another. The realisation had brought misery, the terrible knowledge echoing around her head. *He is married.*

Suddenly she wanted him to wake up, put his arms around her, tell her he felt as she did.

He gave a little snore, a jerk, and his journal fell to the floor. He woke up, yawned, stretched, rubbed his forehead, smiled sleepily and sat up.

'Hi, Jo. Why didn't you wake me?'

'Mr Sleepy,' she said affectionately. 'So tired?' Her eyes drifted toward the journal. 'Or was the article so boring?'

He laughed. 'It had better not be,' he said. 'I wrote it.'

'Why didn't you tell me you were a budding author?'

'I didn't know they were going to publish.'

'What's it on?'

'Contusions after death. Now are you going to share the rest of that bottle of wine, or hog it all to yourself?'

She moved across to his chair. 'Share it.'

It was half an hour later that he referred to her case. 'Hand on collar yet?'

'Nowhere near. I can't see us making an early arrest.'

Matthew's face changed. 'So lots of burnt dinners, microwave meals, takeaways and pizzas.'

''Fraid so, my darling.'

8

Wednesday 28 October, 8.30 a.m.

Matthew drove Joanna to the mortuary for 8.30 in the morning.

'I should have the results of the X-rays waiting for me,' he said. 'And I have a feeling they won't make pretty reading.'

She was familiar now with conditions at the mortuary, with the bright white lights, the banter of the two morticians, the apprehensive faces of two young police officers and the business-like approach of Sergeant Barraclough. All these people helped to preserve an air of normality during the macabre procedure. And central to the operation was Matthew himself, only half familiar in his theatre clothes; dark green cotton top and trousers and a long, heavy rubber apron.

He began by leafing through the X-ray reports pinned to the board. 'As I thought, numerous skull fractures, a couple of them depressed enough to cause unconsciousness followed by death; both radii and ulnae; four ribs; scapula; and a nasty displaced fracture of the right femur. Extensive injuries consistent with prolonged battering.' His eyes met Joanna's as he clipped a scalpel blade to the handle. 'Now let's test my theories about contusions sustained after death.'

They all stood back as the mortician drilled though the skull. Then Matthew moved in to examine the brain. Joanna watched him. He worked in silence, holding his thoughts back until he had completed his work. It was a measure of the concentration he was giving this job; usually he spoke into a small Dictaphone.

He had finished when he turned to the waiting police officers. 'Seven or eight blows to the head,' he said. 'The first hit the back of the head; that was enough to render the victim unconscious. Many of the blows were delivered after death. It was a hell of an assault, Jo.' Softly he added, 'Catch him, Jo.' Then, 'What people you are forced to deal with.' And she knew that hidden behind his revulsion and curiosity was a fear — that she might soon be in contact with the psycho who had broken these bones so viciously.

She gave him a watery smile. 'Thanks, Matthew, for the PM. And now, I suppose, we'd better get out there and do some work.'

He caught up with her as she was leaving. 'Be careful, Jo, please. If you must do anything even remotely risky, keep Korpanski by your side.'

'You think I need a bodyguard?'

'I'm not saying that.' He searched her face. 'I'm simply asking you to be careful, for my sake.' He brushed her cheek with his mouth. 'I don't want anything to happen to you.'

'Point taken, Dr Levin,' she said lightly.

* * *

Barra took her round to Spite Hall, where she met Mike.

The drive was full of police cars. Mike pulled the door open. 'What if the grandson's not in?'

'We'll talk to the old man again.'

They found Patterson stood on the top step, leaning on his walking stick and staring at Spite Hall, the front door gaping behind him. He glanced only briefly at them, and again

Joanna found herself curious as to the relationship between brother and sister.

'Would it be convenient for you to come and look inside your sister's house?' she suggested. 'Maybe you could tell us if anything's missing.'

This time the old man didn't take his eyes off the concrete block. 'Wouldn't be any use me doing that,' he said. 'I haven't never been inside the place. She had a home help. She'd know better than me if anything's been took.'

'The home help's name?'

'Marion. Marion Elland. She lives on the Tittesworth estate.'

Joanna made a note. 'Have you thought any more about when you last saw your sister, Mr Patterson?'

For the first time, the old man seemed to have something he wanted to hide. His gaze slid away from his sister's house and toward Joanna. 'I . . . We . . .' He cleared his throat noisily. 'Our paths didn't cross.'

Again Joanna was reminded of the proximity of the two houses. Six feet apart? Their paths could not fail to cross. She waited.

'A week ago? A month ago?' Mike prompted.

Patterson swivelled his bent back toward Korpanski. 'I think the end of August, Sergeant. I don't get out much.' It was a reminder that Patterson was old, he was infirm, but he was in possession of all his faculties.

'Can you be more specific?' Joanna prompted gently.

'Somewhere round the end of August, the bank holiday. I think the Monday. We didn't speak.'

She could understand the obvious animosity between brother and sister, but she still had to ask. 'Was it just the house?'

'Aye, well, you can get used to anything. Almost anything.' Patterson was silent for a moment. Then, 'Well, so now, Nan's dead. Well.'

And Joanna was curious. 'Your father must have been an unusual man.'

Patterson didn't even pretend not to understand. 'He was.' He clenched his walking stick. 'I've already told you how it was. He loved to set us up against one another. It was his main hobby. He knew how me and Nan would fight.'

'And Lydia?'

'She's unusual too. You've met her?'

Rheumy old eyes pierced hers and Joanna nodded slightly. Yes, Lydia Patterson was a strange woman.

'That old bugger.' Arnold Patterson turned back toward his decayed home. 'He knew how I loved the land. I would have farmed it, made it productive, and Nan would have kept this house beautiful. For years I've had to watch the fields go to waste. The only way I could punish her was to let this place fall apart. And what does she do? Builds the ugliest place imaginable, as close to me as is humanly possible, right up against me own front door, and condemned me to that place.' He could not bear to turn around, but he held his hand up. And neither Mike nor Joanna could have any doubt what it was that he was referring to. 'Nan never set foot in this place after me dad died, and I never ever went inside hers.'

'What did her husband say? Surely he could have farmed the land, opposed the building of Nan's home?'

'David? He was nothing after the war. Farmer's sons don't make good soldiers, Inspector Piercy.'

Joanna's knowledge of the war was hazy. 'But surely as a worker on the land he was exempt from call-up?'

'Not David. Patriotic. Stupid. Just the type to let his conscience drive him to the very place he didn't want to go, the front line, the worst place for him. Messed up a lot of people's lives that war did.' He was a master of understatement.

Joanna found it difficult even to feign interest in this slice of history. Surely it could have no bearing on his sister's murder? At her side she guessed Korpanski was anxious to interrogate the grandson, not this rambling old man awash in his past.

At last Patterson showed curiosity about his sister's death. 'And who do *you* think did it?'

'There have been other attacks on old women in the town.'

Patterson nodded. 'I do read *The Leek Post*.'

'At the moment we're connecting them. We aren't sure, but it seems likely.'

Once again Patterson displayed his native calm acceptance. 'Aye, well. We'll see.'

'Do you know the terms of your sister's will?'

Patterson smiled slowly, he had good teeth for such an aged specimen. 'On her death it all goes to Christian.'

By her side she felt Mike jerk. It seemed the perfect cue to speak to him.

The thumping jungle beat seemed to fill the entire house with a threat. Something flashed through Joanna's mind. Her father had taken her once to the pictures, a rare occurrence. It had been an Indiana Jones movie. They had watched some white men being kidnapped by cannibals in the jungle. Her father had leaned across and whispered, 'When those jungle drums stop, they're going to eat them!' As a child she had been terrified. And the music still seemed to hold a threat.

As she and Mike climbed the stairs toward the attic, she felt her tension mount. When they reached the second floor, the music stopped abruptly.

Christian Patterson's freckled face peered out. 'I thought I heard footsteps.' An engaging grin appeared. 'Not always easy to hear when I've got the decks going. Hello again. Come for me?'

'Yeah.'

'I'm still working on that damned essay. You want to come in?'

Christian Patterson had made himself perfectly at home there. The walls were painted in bright colours; lime green, citrus yellow. The floorboards had been sanded and polished. Rugs were scattered around. There was a long foam sofa covered in a multicoloured throw. Through the open door Joanna glimpsed a second bedroom, again tidily organised.

On the landing there was a small kitchenette and a door to what she presumed must be a bathroom.

He was watching her.

Joanna was puzzled. She had thought she had connected with this young man, but now that she really studied his face, she realised she had been wrong, quite wrong. He didn't look concerned now but detached.

'I've been thinking,' Christian said airily. 'How did they get to her?'

She felt he should have displayed concern, not curiosity. The police should be the ones to ask these matter-of-fact questions. He had known her, for goodness sake.

Christian Patterson turned the full gaze of those melting, toffee eyes on her. Maybe she had been wrong about the lack of emotion; something was there, not quite grief, something else. 'None of the windows were broken?'

'No.'

'Well then, curiouser and curiouser.

'I've just had a thought, Inspector. I bet I was the last person to see her alive.'

'On Sunday night,' Mike said steadily.

'Exactly,' Christian replied calmly. 'And earlier that day: I saw her walking to church on Sunday morning. Offered her a lift, which she refused, stubborn old cow,' he said with some affection 'She had real trouble walking, with her arthritis. But she forced herself to go every Sunday. Look,' he said eagerly, 'let me come down to the house. I bet I can work out how they got in.'

Inwardly Joanna groaned. *Oh God, not an amateur detective.*

'All right,' she said. Behind her she felt Mike exhale deeply.

Arnold Patterson watched them troop out through the hall. Christian was quick to reassure him.

'It's okay, Grandad. Just popping over to Aunt Nan's to see if anything's missing. Shan't be long.'

The old man nodded and shuffled back to his living room.

There were still police cars filling the drive. But now they had been joined by a huge incident van, white with a bright orange stripe. They skirted past it. The front door of Spite Hall stood wide open, inside was chill. Gently Joanna reminded Christian of the reason they had brought him there. 'Just take a superficial look around, see if anything's missing. And please, don't touch anything, it might obliterate prints.' She handed him a pair of overshoes. 'And you'd better put these on.'

He gave a self-conscious smile and walked along the narrow passage to the sitting room. They saw him visibly wince as he entered. Barra had ringed each individual bloodstain with chalk, numbered them too. The shape of the body was obvious, chalked in. Furniture had been left where it had been tipped, ready for removal to the science laboratory. Christian's face was pale as his eyes found the first of the stains. 'Is this *her* blood?'

Joanna nodded.

'I don't think I've ever been in this room when she wasn't over there—' he pointed — 'sat by the window, sewing.'

He picked his way through the marks, stopping when he reached the stained tapestry. He reached out to touch it, then must have recalled Joanna's instruction and withdrew his hand again. 'She was always doing this,' he said. 'Spent ages choosing the right colour silks so carefully. It all seemed so important.' He smiled. 'She used to mutter to herself like a maniac, bits of poems, old songs, little comments to herself.' His eyes were warm as they returned to Joanna's face. 'Sometimes', he said, 'she'd sing. She had a bloody awful voice.'

Afterwards Joanna would ask herself if the brightness in his eyes had been tears.

9

Lydia stopped writing and her hand, as though it had a will of its own, slid to the edge of the desk and touched an antimony box that sat on a small table. She opened the lid and fumbled through the contents. Her fingers found the picture. She held it up in front of her face. It was an old photograph, sepia tinted, of three solemn-faced children, a boy and two girls. The girls both had long hair and serious dark eyes. They were wearing white cotton pinafores. The boy was older, taller, seemed protective.

Lydia stared at it for a few minutes, then she bent her head on her arms and gave a long, shuddering sigh. 'Heaven help us,' she said. 'Heaven help us all.'

* * *

Christian had halted in front of the long-case clock. 'Stupid thing,' he said affectionately. 'I spent no end of time trying to fix it. She never could understand why it wouldn't work properly. I used to try to explain, but in the end I just gave up, told her it was old and arthritic — like her.' His eyes swept over the sofa, the rug, the burnt-out fire. Then he moved back toward the window and stared out at the older house. 'She was quite a character, you know. Powerful.'

'So we believe.'

'Not what you think.' He was swift to defend her. 'Just because she built this place, people thought—' He stopped. 'You know what they call it? The name grew up around it, but it was unfair. She had her reasons, you know.'

'Which were?'

Christian looked away. 'It wasn't right. *Him* getting the house.'

'It wasn't your grandfather's wish,' Joanna pointed out to him, 'but the terms of *his* father's will. Besides, you should be grateful. Brushton Grange has provided a roof over your head.'

'It would have been a better roof with *her* under it. Look at it,' Patterson said, scornfully gazing upwards through the window. 'It's been there since the 18th Century, and he's let it go. I mean, neglected doesn't quite sum it up, does it? It's a ruin. If *she* had lived there . . . Well,' he shrugged, 'it wouldn't have been like that.'

Joanna suddenly had an insight into the times Christian Patterson had sat right there, looking through the window, with his great aunt stitching by his side, feeding him poison. And she instinctively knew that Christian's grandfather had been right. Nan Lawrence had been an adverse influence on the youth.

His eyes swept around the room. 'And she had to live here. Awful, isn't it?'

She felt bound to counter his criticism. 'There was no need to build Spite Hall quite so near or so ugly. There must have been plenty of other sites on the land. She could have designed a bungalow or a cottage. It didn't need to be so functional, such an eyesore.'

'It was a joke,' Christian said, almost disdainfully. 'Just a joke.'

Mike and Joanna exchanged glances and wondered if anyone had ever laughed at Nan's joke. They doubted it.

* * *

Lydia sighed and closed the exercise book. It was no good. The stories always had a mind of their own. *They* dictated the text, not her. She put her pen down and stood up. That was enough for one day. She must work outside, with the animals; hammer back the hen-house roof. Anything to escape the memories.

The photograph lay on the desk, bleaching in a sudden burst of sunshine.

* * *

'Is there anything missing?'

Christian looked carefully around the sitting room before shaking his head. 'Not that I can see. But then there isn't much in it, is there?'

'No.' He was right. What would burglars have stolen? There *was* no television, no video. 'Did your aunt keep cash in the house?'

'Hardly any. She was probably one of the few of her generation to actually bank her pension.'

'So the only item of value was the clock,' Joanna mused. 'Was that a family heirloom?'

'Not from *her* family. She had *nothing* from Brushton Grange. Not so much as a pair of curtains. The clock came from her husband's family, the Lawrences. She used to say it was the only decent thing to come from them.'

The implication was, then, that Nan Lawrence's marriage had not been a happy one. It was not a surprise. Arnold Patterson had already hinted as much, and Spite Hall hardly matched up as a post-war love nest.

Before they left the room, something else was intriguing Joanna. 'Why did your great aunt choose such a gory subject for her tapestry?'

He shrugged. 'I don't know. All I do know is that it meant a great deal to her. She'd been stitching away at it for a couple of years.' He glanced down. 'I never really looked at it properly.' There was the hint of a smile playing around his lips. 'I can't say I'm very interested in needlework, Inspector.'

'What actually is it?' Korpanski asked.

'Something for the church, I think. I don't know what. She never told me. I'd guess it's an altar cloth or a prayer-stool cover.' He smiled. Joanna was again struck by the intelligence behind those melting brown eyes. 'And then someone clobbers her while she's bending over it.' He hesitated. 'And the marks on it *are* blood. Her blood.' He gave a dry laugh. 'So it never will get to the church, will it? All that work and it'll be police evidence in a murder trial — if you nail anyone, that is. You've failed so far, haven't you, Inspector Piercy?'

After his careful politeness, the barbed comment was unexpected. It put Joanna into defensive mode. 'We've had very little evidence to go on so far.'

'And you're hoping my aunt's murder will provide you with a solution?'

'We didn't *wish* this on her purely to—'

'I wasn't suggesting you did,' Christian said smoothly. 'But it must be fortuitous.' His gaze lingered on the chalked figure.

'Murder is never fortuitous,' Joanna said sharply. 'Even if through the crime we find out who the gang are, we would wish your great aunt still alive.'

A half-smile played around the youth's lips. 'Then you must be about the only one who does wish that.'

'Except for you, Christian?' The gloves were off.

His eyes gleamed at the challenge. 'Naturally.' He seemed thoughtful for a few seconds. 'Inspector Piercy,' he said with a touch of humour. 'No wonder you were so keen for me to accompany you back here.'

It was the perfect cue. 'Who do *you* think did it, Christian?'

'Well,' he said slowly, appraising first her, then Korpanski, 'I really can't imagine. But I can't see myself concurring with your theory of a gang bursting in. The evidence surely would point to a gang creeping up on her.'

It sounded silly. He was mocking her, but Joanna felt equal to the challenge. She could use it to her advantage even. 'You're right. It isn't possible they crept up on her, is it? And you've already assured us she wasn't deaf, so she'd have heard them.'

'That's right, Inspector.'

'And she didn't have poor eyesight.'

'Doesn't leave you many suspects, does it?'

He was so brazen, so cocksure, and she could have added more. That all the break-ins so far had been in the town — not three miles out along a long, straight drive, clearly visible from the road. That Nan Lawrence had had nothing of value. That anyone peeping through the window would have *known* there was nothing to steal, not even a television or a video. That a gang bursting in would certainly not have found Nan calmly sewing. That Nan Lawrence's injuries had proved she hadn't even turned her head around to look at her killer but had ignored him. That unlike every other felony they had been investigating for the entire year, there had been no sign of a break-in, not a forced lock or a broken window. And lastly her own gut feeling that the evidence of a frenzied attack she had watched Matthew uncover at the post-mortem was the exact opposite of the cold-blooded carving of Cecily Marlowe's face. Everything in *this* crime was different. But she had no intention of confiding in Christian Patterson. Instead she gave the youth a broad smile and appealed to the amateur detective in him. 'Actually, Christian, you might be able to help us.'

He returned her smile with a relaxed 'Yeah?'

'I daresay you're fond of trotting round the pubs with your mates at night. That's where a lot of the gossip gets picked up. Whoever the gang are, they could be from Leek. If they are local they just might visit the pubs round here. It'd be very helpful if you could keep your ear to the ground.'

Christian nodded dubiously. 'I'll do what I can, but I wouldn't think they're likely to be from Leek. There are plenty of big, rough towns within an hour's drive of here. They're more likely to be from one of those places. I'll ask around if you like; see what I can come up with. But I don't think—'

Joanna gave him another smile. 'Great. Thanks. Now let's take a trip round, shall we? And don't forget, anything you notice as being different or missing is worth a mention.'

It didn't take long; Spite Hall was little more than a troop hut. Two rooms at the front, a bathroom behind the bedroom, and a kitchen that spanned the width at the back. Everything about the proportions of the place was displeasing — the dark corridor that led up the middle, the long, narrow sitting room, the tiny kitchen, shabby and bare except for a glazed cabinet that seemed to hold nothing but cereal packets, a now mouldy loaf of bread, some tea bags and a tiny jar of marmalade. Two teacups, plain white, sat in the sink, a half-eaten packet of Rich Tea biscuits on the draining board. An old-fashioned radio of grey, grubby plastic with a vinyl handle stood on an oak table spread with a faded cotton tablecloth.

It was less than meagre. It was spartan. Christian took some time to scan the kitchen, then he shrugged. 'It looks the same as it always does,' he said.

And Joanna found herself puzzling over his character. A conflict of opposites. Sometimes pleasant, sometimes covertly aggressive, and at other times deliberately on the offensive. Deep within her a question was forming. Had the boy loved his great aunt or not? She couldn't tell. At times she was convinced of his previous affection and current grief, at others he seemed indifferent to the crime — almost amused by it. His grandfather had hinted at a close relationship between the old woman and her great-nephew; more than close, unhealthy. When Christian Patterson had first entered Spite Hall he had seemed upset — disturbed. But now all those emotions appeared to have melted away. He seemed calm, unconcerned, not curious, almost challenging the police. So which was the true Christian? Or had he adjusted so quickly?

Joanna's judgement on the old woman was that she had not been a woman to be weakly liked or disliked but someone who had polarised the emotions. Nan Lawrence would have been either loved or hated. Out of the three people closest to her, two of them had disliked her with fierce intensity, and the third she wasn't sure about.

Sergeant Barraclough joined them in the kitchen. 'My granny had a kitchen just like this,' he said, looking around him. 'Takes me right back to when I was a little boy and she used to bake scones for tea.' His eyes twinkled. 'I tell you what, Jo, nothing in my entire life has ever tasted half as nice as those currant scones with a dollop of butter and jam.' He tapped his corpulent stomach. 'Probably the beginnings of the ruination of my figure. But it was worth it.'

Joanna laughed. 'Now we've had that trip down memory lane', she said, 'perhaps you'll tell me how much milk was left in the bottle?'

'A little less than a fifth of a pint. About enough for two cups of tea.'

'Then she died after supper,' Christian said firmly. 'She always left enough for two morning cups of tea. Then she rinsed the bottle through and put it on the step before the milkman called in the morning.'

'At what time did she have her supper?'

'Half past six.'

'And you saw nothing on Sunday evening? No car draw up?'

Christian hesitated. 'I saw her', he began, 'through the window at about six. She'd left the curtains open. She was sewing.'

'But you didn't call in?'

'No.'

'Really?' Korpanski's voice was heavy with scepticism.

'What time did she get up and have her morning tea?'

'Half past seven.'

Joanna glanced at Mike and knew that if Christian's statement was to be believed, Nan Lawrence must have died sometime between six on Sunday evening and early Monday morning. And if Tylman had been less observant, they wouldn't even have been able to narrow it down to that.

The three of them left Barra in the kitchen with his reminiscences and trooped into the bathroom. It was tiled, with a white 1940s suite, grey-white threadbare towels, mould on the sills, plastic curtains and blue lino on the floor. They were in there for less than a minute; it was obvious nothing had been disturbed. And lastly they went to the bedroom, where Sergeant Barraclough was concentrating his investigation. Articles from the wardrobe were strewn all over the bed: a couple of ancient furs, crimplene dresses, skirts, blouses, a toppling pile of shoeboxes, and with them a fusty, moth-balled air. Again Christian seemed momentarily moved; he held on to the door as though unwilling to cross the threshold. Joanna and Mike almost cannoned into the back of him.

'Is anything wrong?'

'It's the smell,' he explained. 'The mothballs. That awful, pungent stink clung to her, it did.' He grimaced. 'Funny, isn't it. Aunt Nan is reduced to two things: an unfinished tapestry spattered with her blood and the stench of mothballs. So much for immortality, Inspector.'

Joanna scrutinised his features, searching for some clue as to his true feelings, but his face was calm and relaxed despite the comment. However, he still seemed reluctant to enter the room but waved his hand in front of him. 'I wouldn't know what was in her wardrobe or her bedroom,' he said. 'I never came in here, as a matter of fact.'

Joanna could see Mike mentally tallying up this piece of data. If Christian's fingerprints were found on any permanent fixture in this room it would prove this statement a lie. And one proven lie was often the first sign of a crumbling suspect.

Christian still seemed determined to be helpful. 'I can't *see* that anything's missing from here. I don't think there was anything of value here anyway. But, as I said, I never came in here.' The repeated dogmatic statement felt like a challenge to the police to prove it wrong.

'Why don't you ask Marion Elland, Aunt Nan's home help? She was always flicking dusters and brandishing the vacuum cleaner around this place. Knew it better than her own home, I should think. If anything's been taken, she'll know.' His eyes looked thoughtful.

Mike stirred from the hallway. 'And as far as you know, your aunt didn't keep any money around the house?'

'That's right, Sergeant,' Christian said. 'That's what I said.'

Mike persisted. 'Did you ever *see* much money lying around the house?'

'A few pounds,' Christian replied, mirroring Mike's eyes with hostility. 'Enough to pay off the milkman. Nothing worth killing for, Sergeant.'

'That depends, Christian,' Joanna said quietly. 'Although many millions wouldn't stir me to murder, people have been killed for a few pence.'

And that seemed to make Christian Patterson very uncomfortable. 'Do you mind if I get on now?' he asked, glancing at his watch. 'I've got a lecture to get to.'

Joanna waited until he had vanished through the front door before she spoke. 'So, what do you make of that?'

Korpanski was holding his counsel. 'I don't know, Jo,' he said. 'I can't work him out. If he was the one, he's such an obvious suspect, and right on the doorstep too, that he can't have thought he'd get away with it. He's not that stupid. And anyway, why would he have killed her? The question is, do we have enough to get a warrant to search Brushton Grange?'

'I'd like to anyway.' She glanced at her watch. 'But for now I'd like to talk to the home help. You see, Mike, I've just had a thought about this gang business.'

'What sort of thought?'

'What if the crimes weren't committed by the same people? What if we've been deceived and the only common factor is that they were all committed against elderly women? Apart from that—'

'Hold it, Jo.'

'The early burglaries, they were done by the same people. Yes, a gang, maybe from the city, maybe from Stockport or Macclesfield. But starting with the assault on Emily Whittaker, things were different. And the Cecily Marlowe case was different again. I don't know. I can't prove it, not yet. I'll have to spend more time thinking, and we need to talk to *all* the old women.'

Korpanski was patently unhappy. He scratched his head and hesitated before speaking. 'I think it's dangerous, Jo, to start jumping to that conclusion.'

She turned the full force of her gaze on him. 'I'm not jumping to any conclusion,' she said. 'You know me better than that. But I'm keeping it at the back of my mind. Something will crop up either to prove or to disprove my theory. Until then it's on a back burner.'

'Okay,' he said. 'Okay.'

'Glad you agree.'

They were stood outside the ugly building. An icy wind had blown in from somewhere. Dark fingers beckoned from the trees, a last remaining leaf was blasted from a branch, winter was arriving.

Joanna shivered. 'I could almost believe she was a witch.'

Mike stared at her. 'You need a night off.'

'Maybe. Come on.' She clicked back to normality as suddenly as she had left it. 'Where next?'

'I wondered', he suggested, 'if it might be worthwhile talking to someone.'

'Anyone in particular?'

'Yes.'

She put a restraining hand on his arm. 'You're not talking about Melvin Grinstead?'

Mike shrugged.

'That old lag?'

'If anyone knows some dirt about this business,' Mike said, 'he does. There's nothing about petty crime in Leek that he doesn't have a whiff of.' He interpreted her silence correctly. 'I know you disapprove of using moles, Jo, but what else have we got? Hundreds of hours of police time have been and will be spent on this case and the others that went before it.' He paused before firing his last shot, knowing it would sway her. 'If we'd caught the people who carved up Cecily Marlowe, Nan Lawrence might still be alive.'

'Okay, then, you have my permission — but not, Korpanski, my approval.'

Mike grinned. 'I can live with that.'

10

Unseeing, Lydia stared at the words for a moment then pushed the exercise book aside. Beneath was the photograph. She looked at it for a long time before putting down her pen. She would write no more that day.

* * *

Mike and Joanna collected sandwiches from Coffee Beans, the crowded little cake shop at the bottom of the High Street, and munched them as they drove along the Buxton Road. Marion Elland lived a couple of miles out of Leek at the foot of the Roaches on Blackshaw Moor. The Tittesworth estate was little more than two opposing rows of council houses just past the army camp.

The burglaries must have disturbed the home help too. In answer to their knock, she opened the door only as far as a brass chain would allow. Three inches of wary face stared out.

'Mrs Elland?'

The woman fixed her eyes on Mike. 'My husband's inside, you know,' she said defensively. Then, taking a look at Joanna, 'And if you're Jehovah's Witnesses, I'm agnostic.'

'Police,' Joanna answered.

She looked from one to the other. 'Then where's your cards?' But when they showed their cards, she hardly glanced at them before unhooking the chain and opening the door wide, giving them a full view. She was a small, tired-looking woman in her early fifties, with faded salt-and-pepper hair. She was wearing a flowered overall and yellow rubber gloves. 'What is it you want?'

'We understand you were Nan Lawrence's home help.'

'Yes,' she said cautiously, adding quickly, 'I can't tell you anything. I mean, I just cleaned there.'

'What days, Mrs Elland?'

Women always responded well to Korpanski, even tired fifty-year-olds. Marion Elland gave him her first smile. 'Wednesday and Friday mornings,' she said. 'Social Services put me in there.' She made a face. 'She didn't appreciate me though, hardly spoke, ever so unfriendly. When I made her a cup of tea she sometimes didn't even say thank you, so I don't see how I can help. I didn't really know her at all.'

Korpanski grinned at her. 'We just want to ask you a few questions.'

Again Marion Elland responded to him. 'All right, come in, won't you? Cup of tea?'

'Thanks.'

Inside was neat and very clean, decorated in pastel colours; peach and blue. There was a strong scent of Airwick and polish. The three-piece suite looked as though it had just come out of a furniture showroom. The only aspect that made this house different from millions of other homes in England was a huge picture window that overlooked the brutal crags of the Roaches. Instead of sitting down, Joanna crossed the room and stared out of it, remembering a time when a spiral of smoke had drawn some soldiers to its base.

'Lovely view, isn't it?' Marion Elland said.

The two officers agreed.

She had brought in a tray bearing three cups of tea. She placed it on a small occasional table and looked at them brightly. 'Sugar?'

'Just half a one,' said Joanna.

The home help brought it to her and stared with her through the window. 'It's the one thing that would stop me ever moving from this house,' she said, 'that view. It's so special.'

'Unique.'

Reluctantly, Joanna moved away and sat down on the sofa.

'Tell me about Nan Lawrence,' she said.

The home help's answer was frank if not flattering. 'Oh, she was a difficult old thing. Cantankerous. But then lots of old ladies are. She was just worse than most. In one way, anywhere she'd have lived would have been a Spite Hall; she was that sour. A troublemaker. Always accusing me of doing things either too thoroughly and wearing the surface off or not thoroughly enough and leaving dust; saying I'd pinched things when she'd just lost them, or broken them when they'd always been chipped. That sort of thing. I clean for six old ladies. And she was by far the worst. And as for the influence she had over that boy. Well, it wasn't healthy.'

'You mean Christian?' This was the second time it had been hinted at.

'He had a sort of fascination with her, and she encouraged it. I think he almost believed she had supernatural powers — that she was a sort of witch. She'd tell him old stories, silly old tales about people who'd crossed her coming to grief, and he believed her, or maybe he just pretended he did.'

'Why would he do that?'

The home help shrugged. 'I don't know. Maybe to encourage her to tell him more stories, or perhaps he was just stringing her along. You know, letting her think he believed them when really he was just laughing at her. Who knows with that young man?' She hesitated then moved in closer. 'You've heard about the dog?'

Joanna shook her head.

'Mr Patterson had a little dog. Fustin, his name was. A sort of terrier. Used to sit in the front window and bark.

Annoyed Nan something terrible, yapping half the day. He had a habit of sitting on her front doorstep too and doing his business. I saw her watching him one day with a look of venom.' The home help shuddered. 'I feared for that dog.'

'What happened to it?'

'*Someone* must have soaked it in petrol. It was found, just a charred heap it was, at the bottom of the steps to the Grange.'

'Nan?'

'I don't believe for a minute that she was the one to get hold of a gallon of petrol,' Marion said darkly.

'Christian?'

'Nothing was ever proved,' Marion said self-righteously. 'Mr Patterson, he's a lonely old man, all he ever had was that dog. I watched him bury it out the back, shovelling the earth so slowly. Each time he lifted the spade there was a terrible sadness around him.

'The whole family were strange in different ways. Have you met Miss Lydia Patterson yet?'

They both nodded.

'Have you been to her place?'

Joanna smiled, contrasting the mucky carelessness of Quills with the neat order of the Elland household.

Marion Elland moved in closer. 'It's a health hazard. But Nan, she wasn't dirty, just spiteful; loved to cause trouble. It was like a hobby with her, stirring things up, old things. I've seen her talk to couples who'd been married for forty years or more and remind them of some time long ago when the man was caught with his trousers down and his arms around another girl; or spread unfounded gossip about women, about children who bore a resemblance to some local philanderer.' Marion Elland made an expression of disgust. 'She was plain nasty. Most of what she said wasn't true anyway. It wasn't even founded on fact. Not that that stopped her. She didn't care how much hurt she put about. It entertained her. And Christian would listen, his eyes as round as oatcakes, drinking the whole lot up as though it were gospel. From a young lad he was mesmerised by her. I think that's why his mother fell out with him.'

'So he came to live at Brushton Grange?'

'Only so as he could be near her. Aye. She was an old witch.' She fished a pink tissue from her apron pocket and dabbed her eyes. 'And for all that, her death has upset me. Such an awful way to go. I have prayed for her to be at peace, because she never was in this world; leastways, not while I knew her. There was something poisoning her that made her like that. Like an abscess.' She stood up abruptly, almost upsetting the dainty tea table, and crossed to the window to stare out at the rocky crags.

'Do you know what it was that made her like that?'

Marion Elland shook her head. 'No,' she said simply. 'Maybe she always was like that. Maybe it was just the terms of her father's will. I don't know.'

Mike spoke up. 'You're religious, are you, Mrs Elland?'

Marion nodded her head vigorously. 'I am that. Went to the same church as her, the one near Rudyard Lake.' She sighed. 'That's one of the reasons I put up with her difficult ways. We were both children of the Lord.'

It was a sweet, simple belief; one that Joanna almost envied. 'Did you see her in church last Sunday?'

Marion smiled. 'Oh yes, sat very stiff and straight, right at the front where she could watch the vicar from, in an old-fashioned black straw hat. We offered her a lift home but she refused, said the walk would do her good, it wasn't far. We saw her later, stumping along the pavement with her walking stick, toward her home. For all the world looking like a modern-day witch. If she'd been born a hundred and fifty years earlier she'd have risked her fate on the ducking stool, I'm sure. I watched her for a while in the wing mirror, fading into nothing. It was the last time I ever saw her.'

'What time was that?'

'One o'clock. That's when the service finishes.'

'Was she alone when you saw her?'

'Oh yes, almost always was. Sometimes Christian would meet her and walk back with her. It was a struggle for her with her arthritis. But she was a stubborn old thing. You had to admire her in some ways. She had terrific strength of character.'

'Did you talk to her on Sunday?'

'Not for long. Ralph, my husband, was ready for his dinner.'

'Did you see her speak to anyone else?'

Marion Elland shook her head. 'Most people gave her a wide berth.'

'And you've never noticed anyone hanging around Spite Hall? She never mentioned anyone watching her? Unexpected callers?'

Mrs Elland didn't even need to think. 'The image I shall always hold of Nan Lawrence', she said firmly, 'is of a very lonely old woman, friendless and unloved.'

'Except by her great-nephew,' Korpanski put in.

Marion Elland gave him a hard look. 'And that', she said, 'is the greatest puzzle of all. Ralph and I have often wondered about young Christian. He's a very clever boy, that one.'

Joanna stood up. 'Would you mind coming round to Spite Hall to check if anything's missing?'

'Now?'

'The sooner the better,' Joanna said. 'If anything was stolen, tracking it down might help catch her killer.'

Marion Elland put a hand on the detective's arm. 'I'll do anything', she said, 'if it'll help catch him.'

They left then and headed back into Leek, passing straight through to the Macclesfield side and Spite Hall.

It didn't take long for the home help to scan the four rooms. 'Nothing's gone,' she said. 'Nothing at all except—'

Joanna interrupted briskly. 'The tapestry has been taken away for forensic analysis. Nothing else?'

Marion Elland shook her head. It wasn't a surprise; they had never really thought burglary a serious motive for Nan

Lawrence's murder. They thanked her, and one of the squad cars returned her to her home.

Joanna and Mike got back in the car. 'Fasten your seat belt, Korpanski,' she said with a grin. 'It's your afternoon for visiting the sick and elderly, and I want all your impressions.'

* * *

Since breaking her hip, Emily Whittaker had moved to a ground-floor flat on the Buxton Road. It was sheltered accommodation with a warden easily summoned by a pull cord in every room. As Joanna parked the car in the forecourt, she reflected that here lived yet another old woman whose life had failed to return to normality following a crime. It never would now. Before the assault she had been independent, someone who had organised church fêtes, baked cakes for good causes, made jams and pickles, visited the sick. Now she was just another old woman who needed visiting and supervision herself, who sat in a chair, watching TV and getting older.

Joanna pressed the bell with a feeling of deep depression. Another life permanently destroyed as effectively as Nan Lawrence's had been. Emily Whittaker had lost so much more than her health; the attack had taken away her belief in people. They heard slow, uneven footsteps approaching the door, which opened as far as the brass chain would allow it. She looked less than pleased to see them. 'I hoped you wouldn't come again,' she said, 'ever. I want to put it all behind me, forget about it. Every time you come to interview me it reminds me. Why have you come *again*?' Her voice was querulous and weak. 'I've nothing more to tell you.'

'We want to find the people who are doing this,' Joanna said. 'If we had caught them when they first attacked you, other incidents wouldn't have happened.'

'You mean Nan Lawrence's murder,' Emily Whittaker said shrewdly, releasing the brass chain and opening the door fully. 'So you do think it was the same people.'

'It's likely.'

'And you think if I could have given you a better description back in July . . .' She had obviously been pondering the point. 'It's not my fault I couldn't recall things,' she snapped. 'It all happened so fast I didn't get a good look at them. If I'd remembered anything more I'd have got in touch with you.'

'I'm sure you would,' Joanna soothed. 'But with your co-operation I'd like to try a slightly different idea. I think it's possible that if we can get you to make yourself comfortable and fully relaxed, in the comfort of your own home, and with the benefit of a few months' recovery, something might surface that helps us. It might be just a minor detail, but who knows, it could be enough to pinpoint a suspect.'

She didn't want to do it. 'But . . .'

'Please.'

After brief consideration, Emily Whittaker seemed to warm to Joanna. 'All right,' she said, 'I'll do it. But I don't think there's anything stored in my brain that hasn't already come out. How do you know it was the same gang who killed Nan Lawrence anyway?'

'We don't, not for sure. It's just one of the ideas we're following up. But Leek is a small town; it would be a huge coincidence if there were two gangs preying on old ladies.'

It seemed to satisfy her. 'You'd better come inside then.'

They followed her into a small, square room lined with bland flowered wallpaper and a pale, patterned carpet. Two easy chairs sat in the centre, a sofa against the wall and a television in the corner. The television's sound was turned off but the moving picture gave the room brightness and colour. 'It's like company,' Emily explained. 'I never feel I'm quite alone when it's on. Silly, isn't it?'

Joanna smiled. Not silly — natural for an eighty-year-old woman who lived alone and must expect few guests. 'Do you mind switching it off?'

Emily shook her head. 'Do what you think's best.'

They noticed how stiffly she crossed the room, as though there was no flexion in the hip joint, that it had been set in the one position. As she bent to switch the TV off, they saw her wince with pain.

The journey back to the easy chair was equally tortuous. She sank with a sigh and leaned back with her head against the head-rest. 'You really want me to close my eyes?'

'Please.'

She complied.

'Now think back to July the fifteenth.'

To both their surprise, Emily Whittaker smiled. 'It's a hot day,' she said, 'even for July. I've changed the sheets on the bed. They've been out on the line. And now they're dry. I can put them away in the airing cupboard. I can smell newly-mown grass on them.' She closed her eyes even tighter. 'I can hear traffic, flies buzzing in the bathroom window. I must get some spray.'

Korpanski interrupted. 'Can you usually hear traffic from inside the house?'

Emily Whittaker opened her eyes. 'No,' she said, puzzled, 'I can't. Not really. Not as loud as this.'

They both knew. Her front door had opened straight on to the pavement of a busy road, used by motorists as a short-cut from the Buxton Road to the Ashbourne Road, avoiding the sometimes congested town centre. This then had been the moment when the front door had been opened.

'Go on,' Joanna prompted.

She closed her eyes again. 'Some of the towels in the airing cupboard aren't folded properly. I'm taking them out and tidying them up. One of the sheets has a hole in it. Funny, isn't it? I'd forgotten all about that hole. Quite ragged too. I wouldn't be surprised if I'd caught it on something when I took it off the line.'

They let her ramble on. This was how you learned what had happened, by allowing your witnesses to transport themselves back.

'I can hear something in my bedroom.' Her face changed to an expression of alarm. 'Something tinkling. Maybe I've left the window open and a cat or a bird has got in and . .

.' She paused. 'Something's breaking. Glass. I go out to the landing. A man's there. I open my mouth to ask him who he is, what he's doing, why he's in my house. He pushes me. He's a big man, strong, arms like weightlifter's.'

Joanna felt Mike's eyes hot on her. 'A big man? How big?'

'His head is up to the top of the door frame,' Emily Whittaker said softly. 'And he nearly fills it, like a boxer. He moves like an ape, a bit bent.'

'Hair?' Joanna prompted again.

'I can't see his hair. He's wearing a black woollen hat.'

'A bobble cap?'

Emily Whittaker opened her eyes and smiled faintly. 'No bobble,' she said.

'Shoes?' Mike asked this.

'I don't see his shoes. He gives me a shove. A hard shove, right in the middle of my back. And he says something.' She screwed up her face in concentration. 'Something like, *Bye-bye, sister.* That's what he says, *Bye-bye, sister.* And I'm thinking, *I'm not his sister.* I'm falling. Someone else is at the bottom. Perhaps they'll break my fall. They step aside. Now I'm in such pain. He's coming down the stairs two at a time, leaping. He *is* like an ape or a chimpanzee. He's near me. I hold my hand out for him to help me, but he doesn't. He runs straight past me, jumping over my head. He's laughing; he doesn't care. I don't remember anything else', she said, 'except the pain. I'm sorry.'

When they left, tears were still glistening on her cheeks. She put her hand on Joanna's arm in a gesture of surprising strength and desperation. 'Will he come back?'

Joanna shook her head in a promise she had no right to make.

* * *

Jane Vernon was less co-operative. She stood at the door, reluctant to let them in. 'I've told the police all I remember,' she snapped. 'I'm in a hurry now; I have to go out. There's no point you coming back. I haven't got anything more to add.'

And Florence Price seemed almost unaffected by the robbery on her. At sixty-eight she was the youngest victim of the assaults. She answered the door promptly and they took in her heavy make-up: pink lipstick, blue eyeshadow, rouged cheeks, bleached hair in a mass of tight curls. She put her head to one side. 'Ye-es?'

Obviously she didn't recognise them. Joanna reintroduced herself and Korpanski and they were rewarded with a bright smile. 'I don't know what you've come for,' she said. 'I told you all I could remember back in August.'

'Some of the other victims,' Joanna said cautiously, 'are able to remember details they'd previously forgotten or blocked out. Now that a couple of months have passed, we wondered if you'd go over the night once again.'

Florence Price opened her mouth. 'Yes, of course,' she said reluctantly.

She ushered them into a room with a bright blue carpet and terracotta-coloured three-piece suite.

She took up her position in one of the armchairs and gave an alert smile.

'Why don't you close your eyes,' Joanna suggested. 'It might help.'

Florence Price eyed her suspiciously, the smile wiped off her face and replaced by a frown. 'What *is* this?' she asked. 'Some kind of psychological test?'

'Just trying to relax you.'

But Florence's blue eyelids remained obstinately open.

'It was a rainy night,' she began, blinking quickly. 'A dull, boring sort of a day, a grey evening. I was sitting watching the television when I heard a noise, something in the kitchen. I went out and there were men there, all wearing black masks.'

'Did they say anything?'

'Asked me where I kept my money. I told them I didn't have any, but they didn't believe me. *We'll torture you*, one of them said. I was so frightened, I told them I had money in the tea bag tin. They took it and then they went.'

'What did they look like?'

'I told you,' she said, annoyed. 'They were wearing black masks.'

From the doorway Mike frowned at her and gave the smallest shake of his head.

Joanna drew in a deep breath. 'Can you remember——?'

The interview was interrupted by the ring tone of Joanna's mobile phone. It was Barra calling. 'I think you'd better come over to Spite Hall,' he said. 'As soon as you can.'

They left Florence Price still seated on the terracotta-coloured settee. Barra didn't summon without just cause.

Shadows were lengthening over the two houses as they pulled up on the gravelled drive, but whatever it was that had excited Barraclough, there was no hint of it from the outside. All seemed quiet. Even the incident caravan looked deserted. Joanna drew up right outside the front door.

They found the scene-of-crime officer in Nan Lawrence's bedroom, stood over one of the shoe boxes. The lid was flipped off. The three of them stared into it.

11

Superstitiously Joanna eyed the three objects on the bed, pink tissue paper discarded at one side. They were a pair of brass candlesticks and a pension book, the name clearly printed on the cover: Cecily Marlowe. The pungent scent of mothballs permeated the room.

'We've already fingerprinted the candlesticks,' Barra said.

Joanna already knew what they would have found. 'Nan Lawrence's?'

He nodded.

'Anyone else's?'

Barra shook his head. 'Just hers.'

Mike spoke from behind her. 'She couldn't have done anything to Cecily Marlowe,' he said viciously. 'She was too frail. So that leaves—'

She turned. 'I know. I know exactly who it leaves.'

'Then we'd better speak to him. Now.'

'Not yet.' Joanna checked her watch. 'We've a briefing scheduled for ten minutes' time. And besides, I want to talk to Mrs Marlowe again before confronting Christian with this.'

'We won't get any more out of her, Jo. Let's haul him in.'

Joanna faced her colleague. 'This entire case is much deeper than a series of crimes followed by a murder, Mike. I want the whole story. If we bring Christian Patterson in now, what do we have?'

'We can charge him with malicious wounding.'

'And skate across the surface of the crimes? Why, Mike? That's the point. *Why* did he do it?'

'At her direction?'

'Okay, then why would *she* ask him to assault her friend? And why would he have carried out his great aunt's bidding? Because he was *under her influence*? If you believe that intelligent and personable young man committed a serious assault on his great aunt's old "friend" just because she asked him to . . .' She shook her head slowly. 'See the logic, Mike. There's much more to this case — to these cases — than that. If we watch Christian, knowing what we do, we just might get to the bottom of it. Otherwise . . .'

Korpanski looked disgruntled. 'You're the officer in charge,' he said stiffly. 'But if you want my advice—'

'We should haul him in now,' she finished for him. 'And I say no.'

* * *

Driving back into Leek, Mike made a feeble attempt to lighten the atmosphere between them. He glanced across to Joanna and gave a tentative grin. 'If this was an Agatha Christie', he observed, 'the head-pulping would have been either out of vicious, uncontrollable hatred or to conceal the victim's identity.'

'Rather than to make absolutely sure she really was dead and not just faking?'

'Sure about that, are you?'

'I'm only starting to be sure about a few things in this case,' she said, 'and one of them is that the more I think about Nan Lawrence's murder, the less resemblance it bears to the attack on Cecily Marlowe.'

'Go on,' he prompted.

'Cecily's was planned. They *waited* for her. There was intelligence and direction.'

He waited.

'Nan Lawrence let someone in she thought she could trust. Emily Whittaker was the victim of thoughtlessness; it was an opportunistic burglary where the perpetrators didn't care that she fell downstairs.'

'They pushed her.'

'Yes, but they didn't intend injury to her, they merely didn't care what happened. Florence Price, if you ask me, was not the victim of an attack at all. And Jane Vernon's was carried out by someone she recognised and wanted to protect. She's given us no evidence and is reluctant to help us, if not positively obstructive. So what we have, Mike, is not a series of crimes but a succession of different crimes. What we need to know next is, were they like a pack of cards, each one resting on previous events, or were they mere coincidences?'

They had arrived at the station car park but neither of them moved. 'Joanna—' the scepticism was apparent in Mike's voice — 'I don't know how you can possibly come to that conclusion. It's the most far-fetched, incredible . . .'

'Bear with me, Mike,' Joanna appealed. 'It's just an idea.'

'One of the stupidest you've ever had.'

'Maybe. But if you take the stance that each assault was a result of the previous incident . . .'

Korpanski was unimpressed. 'How?'

'*If* the story about Emily Whittaker was widely reported and gained sympathy, *someone* reads their newspaper and thinks—'

'Who?' Mike demanded.

'Florence Price could have read the account in the paper and been astute enough to realise just how much sympathy — and money — was generated by the assault.'

'Go on,' Mike said scornfully.

'When newspapers report crimes,' Joanna said slowly, 'it has various effects. Some people become frightened of being a victim — we've seen that in action over the last few months. Everyone over the age of sixty who lives within a ten-mile radius of Leek has believed they could be the next intended victim. But to other people it has another result. They realise that if they commit a similar crime they have a ready-made scapegoat. Initially, at least, the gang will be blamed. It's possible that that's how Jane Vernon came to be robbed.'

'And Nan Lawrence?'

'It gave her the idea of taking revenge on Cecily Marlowe using her grandson. Otherwise we would not have found the two stolen items in Spite Hall. No one else really went there; it has to have been him. They were close. He did it under her direction, I'm certain of that. What I can't work out is why she directed it, why he did it and why she kept the candlesticks as trophies to gloat over them.'

'You're jumping to conclusions again.'

'*Her* fingerprints were all over them. *He* would have worn gloves. She kept them wrapped in tissue paper in a box at the bottom of the wardrobe. According to Barra, her prints were not only numerous but un-smudged.'

'So we're not looking for one lot of criminals anymore but a whole bloody bunch of them who all read the newspaper?' Contempt was evident in his tone.

'I think so.'

Korpanski drew in a long, whistling breath. 'Okay, Jo,' he said, the disbelief still making his voice harsh and hostile. 'The million-dollar question. Who killed Nan Lawrence?'

'I don't know—'

'A frail old lady obsessional about security and she lets her *killer* in,' Mike reminded her, 'then sits there sewing.'

'I don't pretend to know everything, Mike.'

'Oh, right. So what's the evidence to support your theory?'

'I thought you understood. I don't have any evidence, except for the candlesticks and pension book turning up in Nan's wardrobe and the detail Barra's gleaned from the scene of the crime. It's more to do with psychology. The assault on Nan was a frenzied attack while Cecily's was coldly done, with a knife and not a bludgeon. And as far as we know, nothing was taken from Nan Lawrence.'

'Unless she did have a cache of money lying around somewhere.'

'There's nothing to suggest that,' she said.

Mike was silent for a moment. 'If you don't know who, then why was she murdered?'

'Try this for size,' she countered. 'What if the reason she was killed was that someone knew she had been connected with the assault on Cecily Marlowe?'

'More revenge?'

'Got anything better?'

Mike sighed again. 'If your theory's even half right', he said, 'you might want to think about this. Two of the crimes are connected by the spoils, and who stumbled across two of the bodies? It just might be worth finding out a bit more about Tylman's milk round.'

Joanna nodded and pushed the door open.

The station was a blaze of light, its warmth welcome after the vicious autumn wind that had almost blown them through the doors. As they passed the desk sergeant he slid the window open. 'I've put the evening paper on your desk, ma'am, and you're not going to like it.'

'He's damned right about that.' Mike spread the copy of Wednesday's *Sentinel* across the desk and scanned the article. 'Whatever you say, Jo, the evening paper is homing in on similarities between the cases — not differences.'

'Let's have a look.' She leaned over his shoulder. The face of Bill Tylman stared out solemnly at her. Joanna winced. They'd got him to pose with a milk bottle in each hand, like the Milky Bar Kid. The headline was equally puerile: 'Hero Milkie Finds Second Victim'.

'And tomorrow they'll still be running the same story', Mike said, 'but the angle will be different.'

'I can't wait for my cornflakes.' She stood up, stretched her arms above her head and yawned. 'Let's get started.'

The room was full. Chief Superintendent Colclough had been generous with resources, pulling all available officers off any job that was not urgent and allocating them to the murder inquiry. A few had been drafted in from neighbouring forces. Joanna sat on the corner of the desk, talking casually, inviting comments and observations from anyone in the room who had a contribution to make. These briefings were less formal occasions than a pooling of information. She began by relating the latest discovery at Spite Hall. There was a ripple of disbelief as they all searched for an explanation. None was forthcoming.

'For now', she continued, 'we should continue to focus on Nan Lawrence's murder rather than on the other crimes. If there is a connection — and I believe there is — our investigations should eventually throw some light on the entire picture. Refresh your memories with all the details of the previous assaults and keep them at the back of your minds. Now, does anyone have any comments to make?'

PC Phil Scott spoke up from the back of the room. Two years earlier he had been a young rookie, eager to please, with sharp blue eyes. In previous investigations he had always been the one furiously writing down all facts as they came out. His methodical approach and structured, logical thinking had frequently borne fruit. 'Just a thought, ma'am.'

'Go on, Scottie.'

'Is it possible . . . I mean, we have plenty of witnesses who saw Nan Lawrence walking home from church on Sunday at lunchtime. Considering the fact that the house had not been broken into, could someone have followed her home from church and then jumped her when she opened her own door?'

Joanna shook her head. 'Matthew put the time of death as sometime on Sunday evening,' she said. 'And Christian Patterson, her great-nephew, claims he saw her sewing in a lit window at about six o'clock — *if* we believe him. When we found her on Tuesday morning the curtains were drawn. She was sewing, so she'd have been unlikely to draw them until the light was gone. The lamp had been switched on; lighting up time is about 5.30. That's enough evidence even without Barra's other details. There were no bloodstains anywhere in the house but near the armchair that faced the window; none in the hall. Fairly obviously, if the first blow had been struck in the hall, she would have had to stagger from the front door into the sitting room, which is where we found the body. It wouldn't have taken much force to have broken her bones or draw blood. All the pathological evidence indicates the primary blow was severe if not instantly fatal. There was not one speck of blood in the hall. No.' She frowned. 'Nan must have left the door unlocked. Certainly she was sat over her embroidery when she was struck — from behind — with her walking stick. And then . . .' She closed her eyes. She didn't want that dreadful vision of the pulped face to haunt her. 'After she had fallen, her assailant continued lashing her face with the stick until—'

WPC Dawn Critchlow spoke up from the back. 'Did she fall face down or was she rolled over?'

Barra answered the question for Joanna. 'She must have fallen face down. It's the only position that fits.'

'So her assailant . . . ?'

Barra nodded. 'Rolled her onto her back so he could aim blows at her face.'

There were a few pale faces around the room.

Joanna continued. 'We might consider the possibility that the assailant hid somewhere around the house only to surprise her later on in the evening, but I think it's unlikely, as she let herself in at least five hours before she died.'

Barra interrupted. 'I didn't find any evidence that someone hid in the place.'

'Right. We have no record of her leaving Spite Hall during Sunday afternoon or early evening, and her home help states she rarely left the place. She wasn't well known for her sociability. Add to that the weather was foul and I think it's likely that she remained at home after her return from church. But it would be a good idea for you to get a list of people at the morning service and visit each one. Maybe they saw someone hanging around the place or following her home; perhaps they spoke to her. Marion Elland was there, for a start, with her husband.'

'I bet her son wasn't there.'

Joanna looked up. 'Sorry?'

'Craig Elland.' It was PC Robert Cumberbatch. 'Nasty piece of work, that one.'

'Should I know this guy?'

'Just come out of prison, ma'am, a couple of months ago.'

'What was he in for?'

'GBH. He was a bouncer at a night club. Someone he didn't like the look of tried to get in to Shaker's one night. Craig went for him. Built like a sumo wrestler, he is. Reckon his mum must have put anabolics in his bottle instead of giving him rusks. A psycho if ever there was one.'

Joanna met Mike's eyes and knew he was recalling Emily Whittaker's description. *A big man, strong, arms like weightlifter's. Head up to the top of the door frame. And he nearly fills it, like a boxer. He moves like an ape.*

Cumberbatch had her full, undivided attention. 'When exactly did he come out of prison?' she asked.

'Couple of months ago, sometime in the summer. Tell you what, ma'am, NACRO will have a problem fitting him back into the community.'

Joanna turned to Mike. 'Does she have a key?'

'Who?'

'His mother, Mike, this psycho's mother, Nan Lawrence's home help.'

'I don't know.'

'Then we'd better find out, as well as getting the date of Elland's release. We don't want to start charging him with a crime carried out when he was still safely tucked away inside Stafford Jail.'

Joanna called across the room: 'Bridget?'

PC Anderton stood up. In her forties, she was the mother of four children, brown-haired, with plain, ordinary features until she smiled, which she did now, and her face lit up. 'Ma'am?'

'Keep an eye on the Pattersons, will you — young Christian and his grandfather — particularly Christian, such a charming young man. I don't want to haul him in just yet, but equally I don't want him escaping us. And while you're at it, I would love to know why his mother threw him out.'

PC Bridget Anderton beamed at her. 'With pleasure,' she said. 'Charming young men are my speciality.'

Joanna glanced up at the clock. It was past nine and she had a press conference in the morning. She spent some more time discussing the case with the remaining officers before dismissing them. They would meet again at seven in the morning. She could feel a great weariness creeping toward her. Murder investigations were always like this. You simply worked; boring, repetitive, exhausting, routine work. You got more and more tired and wondered if you would come to any conclusion. And then dawn would break through and the days gone before would seem nothing but structured work leading inexorably toward the solution. She wanted to go home.

Mike put his hand on her shoulder. 'Personally, I don't know why we're not arresting Christian Patterson and bringing him in. And Elland too. He fits Emily Whittaker's description perfectly.'

Joanna pushed her hair away from her face. 'We have no hard evidence, Mike. It's all circumstantial, no proof at all. We'd have to let both of them go after the usual 36 hours. We have to get more on them than that. As far as Christian is concerned, although we have evidence that his great aunt was connected to the assault on her old friend, we have nothing concrete to link him to the crime. The whole thing would get chucked right back in our faces by the CPS; they'd come down on us like a ton of bricks if we tried to pin Emily Whittaker's assault on an ex-con. So let's get our facts straight. And we wouldn't even have half a conviction; I'm not convinced that it was Christian who battered his great aunt to death. I don't pretend to understand the relationship between them, but nothing points us toward the assumption that hatred played a part in it.' She made a face. 'People have hinted it was an abnormal affection, but no one has stated that Christian disliked Nan. Marion Elland thought that he might have held some amusement at her beliefs, mocked them even. *If*, when Barra looks closer, he finds Christian's fingerprints on the candlesticks or some of Nan's blood on his clothing, we'll go for him, but not now, Mike. It's too soon.'

Korpanski snorted. 'I just hope it's too soon rather than too late.'

12

It was almost eleven by the time she let herself in. Matthew was watching *Sky News*; he looked up as she entered. 'Hi. Everything all right?'

She tried to stifle yet another yawn. 'Not really. No progress, press conference in the morning, some tricky interviewing, and I'm tense.'

'So, I prescribe one glass of wine and a neck massage.' He vanished into the kitchen and she flopped onto the sofa. For a moment she reflected on the contrast between the present and the past, before she and Matthew had finally moved in together. Then she had let herself into an empty house, there had been no one to ask her how the case was progressing, sympathise when things went wrong, pour her a glass of wine. Now she had Matthew, and already she would find it hard to return to the way things were before. He put a wine glass into her hand and she smiled at him. Utter contentment.

'Now sit here on the floor', he ordered, 'and I'll take all the tension out of your neck.' Which he did, his long fingers probing the muscles until they finally relaxed.

She leaned back against him. 'Busy day for you too?'

'Not so nice. The pile-up on the M6 yesterday. Whole family. Multiple injuries.' He paused, then added tentatively, 'Jo.'

She was instantly alert. She knew that tone in his voice.

'Eloise will be here in a day or two,' he said. 'I suppose it's too much to hope you'll eventually become friends . . . ?'

She leaned back into his forearms. 'Don't suppose anything, Matt,' she said. 'Eloise will be here. That's all.' Only to herself would she pose the question, *How would they weather it?* And give the usual answer, *Stormily.*

They went to bed half an hour later. Despite the traumas of his day, Matthew slept well. But she did not. She was often like this during an investigation, her mind restlessly probing the darkest corners of the case. Before she and Matthew had lived together, insomnia had not mattered. She had been able to pad around the house making endless cups of tea, working things through, alone. Now she had Matthew to consider. She did not want to disturb him. She did try to sleep, or if not to sleep then to induce that trance-like state that allowed her brain to consider the case from all angles, but it was hard. She found it had to accept the idea that any of the old women involved in the case might be deliberately lying. *But,* she argued with herself, *why should they be exempt from normal human weaknesses because they are old and, like the very young, we find ourselves blessing them with clichéd, idealised characters?*

In fact their failings could be worse than mere weaknesses. Nan Lawrence had done more than lie; it was almost certainly she who had orchestrated the vicious assault on her one-time friend. Florence Price was almost certainly a liar too; she'd spent the gas money on other things and lied to gain public sympathy. Someone else would pay — had paid — her gas bill. She'd gambled and had won — so far. Jane Vernon had also deceived, but for different reasons. But as she lay motionless in bed, Joanna acknowledged that this was only half of the story; the other part was even more obscure. Why on earth had Cecily Marlowe protected the villain who had assaulted her? What did she have to gain? Or was she simply shielding him through fear of further attacks? Had he threatened her so successfully? But Nan Lawrence was dead now. Surely she had nothing to fear?

Joanna sneaked another look at Matthew; he was curled in the foetal position, his back toward her. He moved his legs slightly, muttered something unintelligible and gave a little snore; he was in deep sleep. Her restlessness would only disturb him.

She rose as gently as she could, threw a towelling dressing gown on, knotting the cord around her waist and throwing her hair out of her eyes. Then she tiptoed downstairs and brewed up a cup of tea. She had an idea, an old idiosyncrasy from when she was a child, disturbed from sleep by her parents' noisy rowing. Taking the tea with her, she sat cross-legged in front of her cabinet of China figures. She never had liked dolls as a child, preferring instead her aunt's collection of Victorian Staffordshire pottery. More real than dolls, the figures had always meant something to her. Knowing this, the aunt had bequeathed Joanna the entire collection, more than forty figures. Joanna still loved them. She had used them before as a focus to aid concentration when a case was more a puzzle than a certainty.

It was hard to say what the attraction of the figures was. Certainly there was something simple, unpretentious, naive almost, that simultaneously inspired and reassured her. Perhaps it was the sense of permanence hanging over from that most powerful and stable of periods — Victorian England. Whatever it was, she could see in the pieces so much more than crude clay figures. She could see the entire spectrum of personality: good, evil, simplicity, complexity, naivety, deceit. She turned the key and opened the glass-fronted cabinet, and as had happened many times before, her fingers selected a piece that seemed to bear some relevance to her current case: an old lady seated in a rocking chair, the lettering beneath describing it. *Old Age*. How very appropriate. She studied it closer. Quite cleverly the potters had portrayed the archetypal old woman: grey-haired, bent-backed, wearing glasses. It could have been any old lady — Nan Lawrence or Cecily Marlowe, Florence Price or Emily Whittaker. Joanna frowned. That had been their mistake from the beginning of the investigation. They had lumped all the old ladies — all the cases — together, when they weren't the same at all. Each crime was as individual as were the women themselves.

Joanna peered closely at the figure. So which one was this really? Nan Lawrence, of course. The old lady was knitting as Nan had incessantly stitched away at her tapestry — a church cloth, according to Christian. Joanna fingered the figure. Pottery, soft as soap, lifeless and cold. It was not the most attractive piece in her collection — *Old Age* — a dull subject, drably painted in grey and brown with none of the splashing blues or reds, none of the daring of Dick Turpin, highwayman, none of the adventure of Will Watch, smuggler, or the romance of Nell Gwynne, king's mistress. It was merely a quiet portrayal of old age, an old woman sat peacefully rocking in her chair, as Nan Lawrence had done until—

'Jo.' Matthew was stood in the doorway, naked to the waist, with black pyjama trousers, bare feet, tousled blond hair catching the light. 'Jo,' he said again, 'can't you sleep?'

She shook her head.

He moved closer and drew her to him. 'Is it Eloise?'

She smiled. How typical that Matthew should believe her inability to sleep was due to the thing he was responsible for, when she was investigating a murder.

She held up the figure to him. 'No,' she said. 'For once it isn't Eloise.'

'Good.' He pushed her hair away from her face and kissed her gently. 'By the way, I almost forgot, she'd have killed me. There was a message on the answerphone. Caro's coming up tomorrow — today.'

'Oh?'

'Doing something on rural crime; a series of articles that's been commissioned by *Country Life*. Comparison stuff, I suppose.'

'*Country Life*? She's doing well, coming up in the world. I only hope the little worm wriggling on the end of the line isn't this particular case. I have a feeling there are about to be some hefty twists before we have any idea who killed Nan Lawrence.'

He was halfway up the stairs before he picked up on her statement. 'I thought it was just a bludgeoning by a couple of overenthusiastic thug burglars.'

'I wish,' she said. 'But I think there's a bit more to it than that.'

'Come back to bed', he said, 'and sleep, Jo. Sleep without dreaming.'

'If only.'

13

Thursday 29 October, 6.45 a.m.

Lydia's hand wandered toward the antimony box again and found another photograph: a plump young woman with her hand trustingly linked to another's, a young man with fair hair, staring, strained and anxious into the camera. She smiled at the picture and brushed it with her fingertips, recalling long ago days when she had touched his face in a similar fashion.

'David,' she said. 'Oh, David.'

* * *

One glance at Mike's set face told her his domestic situation was unchanged. They reached her office before he exploded. 'She is a vicious old—'

'M-i-ike.'

His face was thunderous. It brought it home to her that soon it would be her turn to have an unwelcome guest.

'Hide like a friggin' rhino,' he continued. 'You'd think she'd have the nous to realise she's outstayed her welcome.'

Joanna shrugged.

A little of the mischievous Mike peeped out. 'Kids found a couple of snails in the garden yesterday,' he said. 'Popped them in the old dingo's bed.'

She joined him laughing. 'I think it would take a bit more than that to rid me of Eloise.'

He gave her a hard look. 'You shouldn't cast yourself in the role of wicked stepmother, Jo. It doesn't suit you.'

'It isn't me doing the role selection.'

'When's she coming?'

'Tomorrow or Saturday.' She knew Matthew had been deliberately vague as to her arrival.

Then she remembered Caro. 'Oh, and a friend of mine's coming up from London. You remember Caro, the journalist?'

'I remember her; skinny thing with sharp features.'

'You could call her that. Does she intimidate you?'

'Not her particularly, I'm just wary of all journalists. By the way, Jo,' Mike's eyes were gleaming as he scanned a note lying on top of her desk, 'Craig Elland was let out of prison on July the second.'

She grinned back at him. 'Good.' She stood up. 'So, let's get round there and wake him up.'

* * *

Two cars were stood outside the semi on Blackshaw Moor. One was a Peugeot 205, red, like Joanna's own but a year younger. The other was far more flashy: a gold Vauxhall Tigra, last year's registration. It looked like Craig was home.

Out of habit Joanna checked the tax disc on the Tigra. In date, everything in order. Maybe Craig Elland had learned his lesson, or he was being careful.

Marion Elland opened the door, looking older and more weary than before. 'What have you come back for? It's early. We're hardly up.'

Both Mike and Joanna knew she was perfectly aware of why they had returned. Her eyes were already drifting toward the staircase. Young Craig, it appeared, must still be in bed, snatching some beauty sleep.

'You'd better come in,' she said, moving quickly into the sitting room and closing the door behind her. A man of about fifty was sat on the sofa, reading the paper. He stood up as they entered. 'Hello,' he said guardedly. 'I'm Ralph Elland. What seems to be the problem?'

Joanna introduced herself and Mike and watched Mr Elland Sr's face darken. He and his wife both wore the same tired, world-weary air. Life with their son at home must be hard.

Joanna addressed Marion Elland, who was wiping reddened, soapy hands on her apron. 'As you already know, we're investigating the murder of Nan Lawrence.'

Marion gave a swift, despairing glance at her husband, as though pleading with him to reassure her. Joanna could almost guess her thoughts word for word. *No, not this too. Not murder. Not of someone so old, so defenceless.* Fights outside a nightclub were one thing. This was another.

It was time to winkle out the truth. 'Mrs Elland,' Joanna said quietly, 'did you have a key to Spite Hall?' Marion looked struck, her face crumpled, and suddenly she seemed twenty years older. And Joanna knew she had already faced this fact herself.

'Ralph.' She appealed to her husband.

'Of course she has a key,' Elland said brusquely. 'She has to get in whether the old bat's there or not.'

'And where do you keep it?'

Again Marion looked at her husband to supply the answer.

'In her purse.'

'Which is?'

This time Marion Elland looked around the room, homed in on a shabby black handbag and nodded. 'You want me to . . . ?' She picked it up and fished around the bottom until she found a worn leather purse, opened it and handed a Yale key threaded with blue embroidery silk to Joanna. 'This is it,' she said.

Joanna knew Mike's thoughts would echo her own. The key would be useless for fingerprints; there was not enough of a flat surface. 'You always keep it in your bag?'

Marion Elland nodded warily.

'And you leave the bag lying around the house?'

Again a weary, wary nod. She had been there before. In her worst nightmares.

'Did you take this handbag to church with you on Sunday morning?'

'No,' almost a whisper, 'another one.'

He could have removed the key at any time after it had last been used and returned it at his leisure. She would not have needed to use it: by the time she might have inserted it into the lock of Spite Hall, Nan Lawrence had been long dead and her attentions as home help replaced by scene-of-crime officers. She would probably not have checked if it was still in there, and to acknowledge that, she would focus suspicion on this household.

'We'd like to speak to your son.'

'He's in bed asleep.' Again a swift, worried glance at her husband.

No such delicacy from him. Ralph Elland strode toward the door, flung it open. They heard his heavy tread on the stairs, the sound of voices, angry voices, arguing.

More steps returning and the door was flung open. Mike was big but Craig Elland almost dwarfed him. Mike's muscles were formed by hours at the gym, pumping iron. Craig's bulk was the result of food, plenty of it, almost certainly supplemented, as Cumberbatch had observed, with liberal helpings of anabolic steroids. He stood more than six feet tall, with a shaven head and huge arms decorated with tattooed snakes along their entire length. He was dressed in judo pyjamas, crumpled white with a black belt, and he was glaring at them.

Joanna gave him a wide smile, which he returned with suspicion. 'Craig Elland?'

'Cops,' he said disgustedly, 'smell 'em a mile off.' Mike was treated to a jutting chin and clenched fists. Joanna to a hard, appraising stare.

'That's right, Craig. We are "cops". And I think you've had a bit of experience of our profession.'

'I'm clean now.'

Joanna smiled to herself. They all were. She recalled a visit to a prison years earlier and the officer turning to her, smiling and saying: 'This here is the only place in the world where no one's done anything they shouldn't and everyone's a hundred percent innocent.' Of course Craig was clean now. As clean as a skunk sprayed with perfume.

'What's this about anyway?' he asked.

'We're investigating the murder of Nan Lawrence.' Joanna was slotting pieces together in her mind.

Craig fitted one aspect of the crime perfectly: a brutal, opportunistic, bullying sort of criminal. He would be just the sort of person to stand over an old woman half his size and shove her down the stairs, step over her while she moaned with the pain of a broken hip and then three months later stand over another old woman a third of his weight and batter her with her own walking stick until her head was a pulp.

'I don't see what a murder's got to do with me. I ain't done a murder.'

It was funny, this honour amongst thieves. They robbed, they supplied drugs to juveniles, they committed armed robbery, but charge them with an offence outside their category and they would use their own previous offences as a defence. She could have smiled, except none of it was really funny. With people like Craig Elland there always was, at the end of their acts, a victim.

Mike eyeballed him. 'You nearly did commit murder, Elland. The guy was dead, but they revived him in the ambulance. He was never the same again.'

Elland squared his shoulders, caught something determined in Mike's face and backed off.

'We may need you to come in to the station,' Joanna said quietly. 'We want to interview you and your parents.'

'Why not,' Elland flattened himself against the door. 'I got nothing to hide.'

They never did have. Until they were exposed. Joanna watched him from beneath lowered lids. She didn't have him yet, not by a long chalk, but she was close. Silently she asked herself, *Why look any further?* He had opportunity, he could have got in without breaking a window or splintering a door, he could have reached the old lady without her having left her chair. Surely this was how it had been done? More convincing than that, he even felt right for the charge; he fitted. But they had no motive apart from his psychological profile.

She became aware that Ralph Elland was waiting for her to speak. She forced herself to look Craig Elland full in his podgy face. 'Just for the record,' she said softly, 'where were you on Sunday afternoon and evening?'

At her side, Ralph Elland's shoulders drooped in desperation. It was an attitude of utter defeat. It told Joanna that whatever Marion believed of her son, his father knew he was capable of murder; not only in fisticuffs outside a nightclub but a planned act, brutal and cowardly. But Craig was ready with his answer. They always were. Alibis were practised as assiduously as a part in an amateur dramatic production.

'I was 'ere all afternoon,' he said defensively. 'I were watching the footie with me dad. Man U was playing.' He looked to his father for confirmation.

His father gave it.

Elland leered at Joanna. 'And then we 'ad our dinner.'

'And then what?'

'We went to Evensong,' Marion said faintly.

'I went up the pub with me mates. Watched the rugby on Sky.'

'Which pub?'

'The Cattle Market.'

'And who were the mates?'

'Tony Arrandale, Wayne Chiltern, Scott Trent.'

A well-known set of villains.

'Fine. Okay if we check up with them?'

Joanna knew Mike would be having the same thoughts as she was. What would be the point when alibis from these three could be bought cheaper than a pint of warm beer? Craig shrugged, almost as though he knew the worthlessness of the gesture.

Something struck Joanna. Usually in this type of situation, parents were swift to defend their offspring against police interrogation. They screamed intimidation and victimisation when their beloved sons had recently been released from prison and supposedly wiped the slate clean. Yet neither Ralph nor Marion was offering one word of defence. They knew him best. Even Craig himself wasn't giving out the usual objections.

'We'll want to talk to you again, Craig,' she said, 'after I've chatted to your mates.'

He met her eyes fearlessly. 'They'll enjoy that,' he said. 'Bit of attention from a female dick.'

Joanna gave her widest smile. 'One of the perks of the job, Craig.'

She waited until she and Mike were back in the car before voicing both their thoughts. 'So, there we have it.'

'What if they were all seen at the pub right the way through Sunday?'

'Matthew couldn't be very precise about the time of death. Even if they were seen in the pub, it would only have been until closing time; they could have gone round afterwards, they could have gone round before. What's important is that Craig Elland — a nasty piece of work even by my yardstick — had the opportunity to borrow his mother's key to Spite Hall. It answers some of the questions we've been posing.'

'And motive?'

Joanna chewed her thumbnail for a minute. 'What if Marion hinted that Nan had money stashed away? Easy to get the key; in fact, the entire bunch of mates could be the ones—'

'A bit obvious, don't you think?'

'Well, Craig doesn't exactly strike me as a subtle sort of a guy.'

'No.'

'Try this for size, Mike. We have three mates on a burglary spree. In July they're joined by a fourth, much more violent friend, recently released from prison. As soon as *he's* on the scene, petty theft is no longer the object, the emphasis has shifted so that the objective is the violence and terrorism itself.'

Mike started the engine. 'It fits, Jo. Trouble is, we've no scrap of proof.'

'So, we need to send some officers to interview Craig's three friends. We need to know what they were all wearing and we need to get the clothes to forensics. Agreed? And it might be an idea to speak to Cecily Marlowe again and jog her memory.'

Mike nodded, picked up the phone and rapped out a few instructions.

But as they approached the outskirts of the town he blurted out, 'And what about the candlesticks and the pension book?'

Joanna gave a deep, heartfelt sigh. 'I don't know, Mike,' she said. 'Let's revisit Spite Hall, talk to Patterson and his grandson.'

The day was turning gloomy with thick black clouds bubbling up in the sky. As they turned off the Macclesfield road the clouds finally burst and blasted rain against their windscreen, drowning the wiper blades however fast they swiped at the water. It made the scene ahead even more depressing.

As usual Brushton Grange displayed no lights; it looked derelict, deserted. She and Mike picked their way along the narrow, mossy path, made even more slippery by the incessant rain. Gutters spilled their contents over the brim. 'I'll never forget this place,' Joanna said. 'If Frankenstein himself answered the door I wouldn't be surprised.'

Korpanski resisted the temptation to frighten her with a shout and his King Kong impersonation, instead pulling on the bell handle. The peal of the front-door bell echoed inside the house, and Joanna was again almost tempted to retreat. The house surely *was* empty this time. She glanced up at the attic windows, saw a face jerk back, and picked up the bass thump of techno music. Mike clanged the bell again, and then they heard slow, painful steps tapping across the hall toward them. Arnold Patterson pulled the door open.

'So you have come back.' He twisted his head to stare at the ceiling. '*He* said you would. *He* said you'd want to interview him.'

'Can we talk to you first about your sister, Mr Patterson?'

'I've nothing to say. She's dead. We're well rid. Best she's forgot.'

'Surely you want her killer caught?'

Patterson gave her a long, penetrating stare. In it she read his blunt comment that her killer was morally no worse than the woman herself.

But it did not justify murder. However evil the victim had been, nothing justified the brutality of that assault.

'Mr Patterson,' Joanna tried again, 'the killer might strike again.'

This time Patterson's face gave the ghost of a smile.

'They've struck before.'

He seemed to switch off then. 'What do you want to know?'

'Why don't we go in your living room? You'll be more comfortable there. You can sit down.'

Patterson turned and walked back inside the house.

The hall was as dark as a cave, with a musty smell of damp. Their footsteps echoed unevenly.

Korpanski's huge, flat feet, Joanna's rubber-tipped heels, the metal tip of Arnold Patterson's walking cane, the soft shuffle of his slippers.

The room was as she'd remembered it; scarred quarry-tiled floor, threadbare loose covers on sagging chairs, windows smeared with dust, and that day rain whipping against the glass. It was as cheerless as Bob Cratchit's workplace before the conversion of Scrooge.

Patterson sank into one of the chairs. 'I can tell you nothing about Nan', he said, 'for the past fifty year.'

'Then tell me about Nan the child.'

Korpanski was shifting his weight from foot to foot. She knew what he was thinking, that this was a waste of time. Maybe it was. Maybe it wasn't.

She prompted him. 'You were friends then, Mr Patterson, as children?'

'Aye.'

'All the time you were children?'

'Most of it.' Some of the lines in his face seemed to smooth out. 'All children fall out sometimes,' he said, smiling.

Joanna pushed away the memory of her own sister: hair-pulling, tale-telling, noisy quarrels meant to deflect the attention of rowing parents. But their parents had always been too busy with their own conflicts even to notice.

'But as you grew up?'

'The war came,' Patterson said. 'It changed everything.' He stopped for a moment, his eyes far away from either Brushton Grange or Spite Hall. 'Everything,' he repeated. 'I were called up, plenty others were too — young lads.' He looked straight at Joanna. 'We saw things,' he said, 'things we never should have. It made us different, different from them at home who'd gossiped and sewed their way through those years.'

Joanna leaned forward to see Patterson's face better. 'Was that when you fell out with your sister?'

Patterson seemed not to have heard her. 'Nothing was the same,' he said. 'We wanted to come home, dreamed about being here again, walking through fields that was green and damp and quiet. And when we got back . . .' There was a deep, despairing depression in his face.

Mike cleared his throat. 'It was bound to be different.'

It was his contribution. Joanna turned to look at him. The war had affected him too; his father had been a loyal

Pole, repatriated in Leek, married finally to a local girl. Had it not been for the war, the child of Demetri Korpanski would almost certainly have been one hundred percent Polish, brought up in Warsaw or Gdansk or some other place in the fatherland. German ambitions had changed that too.

'When did you and your sister fall out?'

'The end of the war, as we came home and our father died. Me and David, we'd fought for peace. But when we came home—' Patterson drew in a long sighing breath — 'there was none. It had been blown away by the gunfire.'

It was all the explanation he was going to give them.

Patterson's chin was sunk onto his chest. He was far away. Far away and long ago.

14

Lydia put her pencil down. The time for truth seemed near. Strange how rain, streaming down windows, helped her to see pictures long ago relegated to the back of her mind. Arnold, whipping his hoop along the drive. It wasn't gravelled then; a muddied lane in wet weather, raising fine clouds of dust in hot spells. And the day she recalled had been hot, too hot for her. She had been already too plump to do anything but mope slowly toward the house. Not too hot for her brother and sister. She screwed up her eyes to see the vision all the clearer. Nan, in white pinafore, hair streaming down her back, running behind Arnold, trying to catch him. But Arnold's legs were long and strong — he was five years older than Nan — and he didn't want to give Nan a turn of his hoop. Nan's voice, clear as a church bell, ringing in her ears. 'Wait, Arnie, wait for me. Please wait.' And Arnold had stopped dead.

Lydia dropped her face into her hands. She had forgotten the way Nan had always called him Arnie, the way he had responded to her affection. Arnie, her very own pet name for him. Oh, how cruel life could be.

Lydia leaned back in her chair, gasping with the sadness of it all, tears streaming down her cheeks, mirroring the rain washing down the windows. How cruel. They three had started off with everything — a mother, a father, a home, money — and how empty their lives had become. They had lost it all, ended up with nothing. Their homes were a mockery. Mother and father, naturally, both dead. The money — Lydia's face twisted — little of it left now. They didn't even have each other to share their grief with, or mourn jointly as brother and sister for the lost one of the trio. *'Wait for me. Wait for me, Arnie.'*

Arnie would no sooner come to Quills than she would climb the four steps to the front door of Brushton Grange. Would she even go to her sister's funeral? Would he? Would they forget the past — ever? Or were the scars too deep? Too old? Lydia stood up, pacing the room in a burst of agitated energy foreign to her. She was the lazy one; all her energy had been cerebral, not physical. Nan and Arnold had been the active ones. Always.

* * *

The thump, thump of a bass beat drew them up the two flights of stairs to the top-floor attic rooms. They had thought their footsteps would be drowned out by the noise and their arrival would be a surprise, but Christian was the one to spring the surprise.

As Joanna's foot touched the top step, the door to their right was flung open. Christian gave them a quizzical look.

'Back again, Inspector?'

The dry, sweet smoke of marijuana seeped out from the room beyond. A girl was draped around Christian. Pale-skinned, with long, straggly hair and spaced-out hazel eyes, wearing a long skirt and brown short-sleeved T-shirt. Christian seemed hardly aware she was there.

'Guess what,' he said to Joanna, 'my Aunt Nan's gone and left me everything. Solicitor rang this morning and told me.'

'So you thought you'd celebrate with a joint?'

Christian's eyes regarded her steadily — confidently, overconfidently. 'I don't think you've come about a couple of blades of grass, Inspector.'

'No.'

'So what have you come about?'

'Can we come in?'

'Got a warrant?' It was the girl who spoke, stroppily.

'Shut up, fatso.' There was little sign of affection from Christian in either the direction or the nickname, but the girl was either too thick-skinned or too spaced-out to be offended. And anyway, she was anything but fat. She uncoiled herself from Christian, moved back into the room and dropped into a sofa cheered with a throw. They followed her in. Christian perched on a beanbag, Joanna and Mike stayed standing.

The attic had a different character from the rest of the house. Sloping ceilings instead of the high square rooms found elsewhere. The furniture was cheap second-hand or MFI but bright, and it was clean.

Joanna eyed Christian curiously. He returned her gaze without a flicker, the only visible sign that he was aware of her scrutiny a quick flick of his ponytail.

'Congratulations on your good fortune, Christian,' Joanna began. 'You'll be glad of the money, I expect.'

'What there is. The solicitor did warn me not to go mad. It'll take a time to wind up the estate, and he said it wasn't enough for a life of luxury. But then, as I'm young, my life is likely to last a long time.' Said without embarrassment. 'Anyway,' again the same bold, challenging eye contact, 'isn't everyone *always* glad of money — more money?'

The girl, knees apart, was staring at the floor. It was doubtful if she'd have been aware of more money, except to buy more and more life-escaping drugs.

'Well, you're a student, and I understand your parents—'

'My parents?' It was the first time Christian's guard had dropped. It was like letting a docile tiger out of a cage and watching it turn savage in the space of seconds. 'Aunt Nan told me they would be hostile, jealous of our closeness.

She predicted they would drag out stupid comments, about undue influence and rubbish like that, and she was right. It was surprising how often she was right.'

Both Christian and the girl smiled. The girl offered a comment with a shrewd, sideways glance at Christian. ''Spose the money gives 'im a motive.'

'I told you.' Again the savagery in Christian's voice shocked both Joanna and Mike, but not the girl. She must have witnessed it before. 'I told you, it isn't much. Get that into your thick head.'

'Money is a common motive for murder,' Joanna said, 'if a bit of an obvious one. The first thing we do during investigations is ask ourselves who will benefit from the crime.'

'Me.' It was back to the polite, charming Christian. But now Joanna was aware of what lay behind his charm. And like black wood within a thin coat of white paint over it, she could perceive Christian's dark side even when the side he was presenting — so well — was glossy white.

'Exactly. You're probably the only one who benefited at all from your great aunt's death.'

The statement was enough to rattle the youth. He reacted quickly. 'But I was going to get it anyway. Aunt Nan was old, and not in good health. I only had to wait; I wouldn't have needed to have murdered her.'

'According to her doctor', Mike spoke steadily, as though reading, verbatim, from a notebook, 'all she had was arthritis, and you can live for years with that. Maybe you were in a hurry for the money, Christian? Or maybe she was thinking of changing her will?'

'Who would she leave it to?' the youth said scornfully. 'There was only me.'

It was true.

'A dogs' home, an animal charity.'

Christian broke into peals of laughter. 'Animals,' he said, 'she hated them: cats, dogs, anything.'

It struck Joanna then how very many things Nan Lawrence had hated: her family, all but one of her relations, and now animals. But the question that burned was not how many people Nan Lawrence had hated but which of them had hated *her* enough to kill her. She knew Mike would have liked her to confront the youth with the discovery of the pension book and the candlesticks, but she would keep that hidden for the time being.

'They took my clothes,' he said suddenly, 'searched my room.'

'I asked them to.'

'Get a warrant, did you?' the girl piped up.

This time Joanna answered her. 'They aren't difficult to obtain. Did they find anything, Christian?'

He shook his head very slowly; there was an element of doubt in the action. Joanna could almost hear Mike's palms rubbing together in anticipation.

'Well,' she said sweetly, 'it's been nice seeing you again. We'll see ourselves out.'

She and Mike clattered down the two flights of stairs.

* * *

The assembled members of the press didn't number as many as she'd feared; but, she reminded herself, most of them were freelancers and would submit their copy to more than one newspaper.

Mike had been right about the continued milk diet. Bill Tylman stared out of the front page of the early editions of the evening paper. Joanna studied his blandly smiling face and was pricked with curiosity. She looked up to answer the question of one of the more astute reporters. 'Inspector,' he began, 'the attack on Mrs Marlowe a month ago, is there any *forensic* evidence to link the two crimes?'

By her side Korpanski shifted uncomfortably.

'Not forensic,' she answered smoothly, 'but in both cases there has been very little forensic evidence. If we had a suspect we might be able to gather some.'

A tiny, imp-faced reporter was next. 'We understand you have been interviewing previous victims of crimes, all elderly women.'

'That's correct.'

'Are you able to comment further, Inspector?'

'Only to say that, amongst many theories, we are considering the possibility that the killer of Nan Lawrence has been involved in other crimes in this area.'

Furious scribbling.

'We understand—' an anonymous voice from the back of the room — 'that Mrs Lawrence's brother is elderly and quite frail. Are you prepared to make any comment as to how he's dealing with the murder of his sister so close to home?'

Joanna found herself suddenly staring at the upturned faces. None of them knew it, but this was the hardest question of all. She contented herself with the answer that he was understandably upset.

* * *

The briefing had been set for six o'clock, when the investigations of the day were drawing to a close and hopefully there would be something to report.

WPC Bridget Anderton stood up. 'I've spoken to Christian Patterson's mother,' she said. 'Not much love lost between her and her son. She said she was relieved when he moved in with his grandfather, said he was becoming a handful.'

'Did she mention Nan Lawrence?'

'Only to say that she was a nasty old woman.'

'I think we were coming to that conclusion on our own,' Joanna said. 'No other clue?'

WPC Anderton shook her head. 'Nothing concrete.'

Joanna addressed Sergeant Barraclough then. 'And what did you take from Brushton Grange?'

'Some clothing,' he said. 'I've bundled it all off to the lab, but it'll be a while before we get the results. I also found a Stanley knife. A very, very clean Stanley knife.'

'He's a very, very clean person,' Joanna said softly. 'We can but hope he isn't too clean for our laboratory.'

PC Phil Scott spoke next. He had spent the day, with his team of people, interviewing the entire congregation of Rudyard church, the parish church less than half a mile from Spite Hall. Joanna leaned back in her chair and watched the young blond constable give his account.

'There were thirty-one people at the morning service,' he began, 'mostly locals, regulars. All of them had noticed Nan Lawrence sat right at the front, in a black straw hat. Most said she didn't speak to them. Some people noticed her speak to Marion Elland, but this wasn't unusual. Marion worked for Nan. She was one of the few people, and I quote, "the old dragon did speak to".' He scanned the room, smiling. 'Mrs Lawrence wasn't a popular woman, ma'am. No one had anything nice to say about her.'

Joanna winced at the 'ma'am'; she'd always hated it, would have preferred them all to address her simply as 'Joanna', but police protocol encouraged rigid titles. So long as Mike didn't address her as 'ma'am' she supposed she would have to learn to accept it from junior officers.

'A couple,' Scott glanced down at his notes, 'Mr and Mrs Raynor, actually saw her walking down the road toward her home. They stopped and offered her a lift.' Again he looked up, met Joanna's eyes, knew she would want the statement verbatim. '"We felt sorry for her. She was old. It was quite a step out back to her place, nearly half a mile, and she looked so pathetic, so doddery with her walking stick. It was a struggle for her. We pulled up just past her. Paul—"' that's the husband — '"ran back and offered to take her to her door. She said—"' Again Phil Scott looked around the room. They were all waiting for Nan Lawrence's last known spoken words. Scott bent back over his notebook and read: '""D'you think I can't manage it? That I'm that decrepit I can't get from church back to my own house? I'm not that past it yet, whatever the gossips say.""'

There was a moment of silence. Everyone in the room could picture an old crow of a woman spouting out venom. They could imagine her voice, sharp and cracked. Put that with the image of a woman who had lived for more than fifty years in a house with no name but the one that had built up around its reputation, a name anyone approaching Brushton Grange would have understood. Joanna allowed herself one light thought: how the hell had such an old bag been allowed to live so long?

Then she glanced at the side of the room, at the board where the police photographs had been pinned up, in glorious Technicolour: blood, brains, a face that had been pulped, a body with — how many bones did Matthew say had been broken in the assault? She drew in a deep, depressed breath. Human nature could be cruel in many ways.

'Anything else, Scottie?'

'Yeah.' He hesitated. 'The service was taken by the Reverend Leon Gardiner. He asked if he could speak to the senior investigating officer.' Scottie looked almost apologetic. 'I think he was thinking of taking the funeral service.'

'That's for the funeral director to sort out,' Joanna said sharply. 'Nothing to do with the police.'

'Maybe he just wanted to know when the body would be released.'

'Then he should speak to the coroner.'

'Does he have anything useful to say?' It was Mike who spoke from behind her.

Scottie shrugged. 'Sorry, Mike, I don't know.'

'Anything more?'

Sergeant Barraclough spoke from the back of the room. 'We've had some early reports from forensics,' he said. 'They've done a reconstruction of the room. She definitely was working on the tapestry when she was struck from behind.'

* * *

She could hear Tom and Matthew laughing as she opened the front door, and Caro's clear voice speaking over them: 'So we decided on a June wedding. You know, flowers are cheap, don't need to go abroad for a honeymoon, and the journalists' world is as dead as a dodo then anyway.'

Joanna smiled. Caro, always the cynic, hiding any heart she might have. She pushed the sitting-room door open.

Caro stood to greet her. Tall, pencil thin, with blonde hair and angular features, she gave her friend a hug. Tom was next in turn, still in his solicitor's suit, gold-rimmed glasses almost steamed up in embarrassment.

Joanna looked from one to the other. 'Well,' she said, 'how are you both?'

They exchanged swift glances. Joanna gave a mock groan. 'Don't tell me you want me to be bridesmaid? Can you see me in pink froth?'

Caro gave her a mischievous look. 'You don't fancy a double wedding?'

Joanna felt cold, aware that Matthew was watching for her reaction, as was Tom.

It was Caro who saved the day, by speaking swiftly. 'Funny, isn't it? Tom and I getting married but living apart, and you and Matthew living together in sin. And you a police inspector, my darling,' she finished with mock severity.

'Don't you start.'

Joanna vanished into the kitchen and bustled around searching for a corkscrew and a bottle of wine, anything to escape the hurt look she had just read in Matthew's eyes.

When she had regained her cool she emerged. 'So,' she said brightly to Caro, 'you're up here to do some articles on rural crime?'

'Do you think it's a duff idea?'

'No, but you're going to have to do some digging.' And at the explosion of laughter from both Tom and Matthew she laughed too, and the ice was broken.

She looked from one to the other. 'Are we eating?'

'The takeaway should be here—' Matthew glanced at his watch — 'in 15 minutes.'

'Just long enough for a glass of wine.'

'And for me to pick your brains,' said Caro. 'Tell me, Jo, do you think rural crime is inherently different from city crime?'

'Sometimes,' she said guardedly. 'Certainly last year's murder of a couple of farmers would be very hard to imagine in a city.'

They chatted around the subject, pausing only to answer the knock on the door and serve out the curry, rice, chapattis and poppadoms.

There was only one blot on the evening, when Caro asked when Eloise would be arriving.

'Tomorrow.' Joanne couldn't quite keep the apprehension out of her voice.

15

Friday 30 October, 7.15 a.m.

Lydia hadn't even picked up her pen that morning. Instead she was pacing the room, almost trampling on the two hens as she did so. They squawked out a protest and took refuge in the basket, softly clucking their disapproval. She hardly seemed to notice them. The box of photographs was tipped over, the pictures scattered across the floor. She sank down on the sofa and dropped her head in her hands, swamped by a feeling of utter despair.

* * *

The bike was a luxury Joanna could not afford during a murder investigation, when time was of the essence. And, as always, driving seemed to instil in her a huge impatience to *know* what had happened the Sunday before, in the hours of darkness.

On impulse she drove right through Leek and took the Macclesfield road, past the football club and out toward Spite Hall. She wanted to catch Bill Tylman. Somewhere in the muddled jigsaw puzzle there must be a reason for everything, even his silence on a subject she would have expected him to speak about — the discovery of Cecily Marlowe.

She didn't have long to wait. At 7.40 the milk float trundled up the drive. Tylman didn't notice her at first, sat in her car. She watched him pick up two bottles of milk and disappear round the corner in the direction of Brushton Grange. She met him on the way back, a couple of empties in his hand. He started.

'Good morning, Inspector. Didn't expect to see you here—' a pause — 'so early.'

She gave him a frank smile. 'To be honest, Mr Tylman, I couldn't sleep very well. Something was worrying me.'

He looked wary. 'And what was that, Inspector?'

'Lots of things,' she said vaguely.

Tylman waited.

'One of them was that I just couldn't understand why you didn't mention you'd been the one who found Cecily Marlowe the morning after she was attacked.'

'I can't keep boasting about—'

'But you should be proud of yourself, Mr Tylman. If you hadn't found her, who knows what would have happened?'

'Lucky I was there, that's all. There weren't nothing to it.'

'And Nan Lawrence? Not so lucky, was it? Still, we police would always prefer a body to be found earlier rather than later.'

He met her eyes steadily.

She continued conversationally. 'By all accounts she was a difficult woman. How did *you* get on with her?'

Tylman busied himself noisily putting the bottles in the crates. 'No worse than anyone else. I couldn't call her a friend.' His back was to her.

'She was a bit of a gossip, wasn't she?'

'If you're trying to imply—'

'I'm trying to imply nothing, Mr Tylman.' Joanna laughed. 'I'm just a nosey copper. Satisfy my curiosity a little further. Tell me, did you deliver milk to any of the other people burgled? Emily Whittaker for instance? Or Florence Price? Jane Vemo, maybe?'

'I'd have to look in my book.'

'Surely you'd remember the names? They were *all* victims of crime.'

He was climbing into his cab. 'I've a big milk round, Inspector. I can't recall every single old lady on my—'

'Check your books then, please, Mr Tylman. I'd appreciate it.'

She watched as the float trundled as fast as it could toward the main road.

* * *

She met up with Mike in the car park. His thunderous face discouraged small talk. Instead she suggested the time was ripe for a repeat call on Cecily Marlowe. Even that didn't please him; he scowled. 'We harassed her so much last time she nearly had a nervous breakdown. She was so terrified by the attack, people said she'd lost her marbles, and now Nan Lawrence has copped it we won't get anything more out of her.'

'We must speak to her, Mike.'

'Well, she's not going to able to explain how her candlesticks and pension book turned up in her old mate's wardrobe.'

'You think not?'

* * *

At the time of the burglary Cecily Marlowe had lived in an end terrace on the outskirts of the town — the same house she had inhabited from the day she had arrived as a young bride in 1942 — but from the evening she had been assaulted she had never spent another night in the place. She had flatly refused to return when due to be discharged from hospital. So Social Services had helped her to sell her home and move into a tiny, warden-patrolled flat — red brick, a solid, comforting place. Safe.

It wasn't only Mike who opposed Joanna's visit to the old woman. A stout, sensible-looking middle-aged woman with short brown hair opened the door to her and introduced herself as the warden before letting fly. 'I do wish you'd leave her alone,' she said. 'The poor thing was so traumatised by it. It can't do any good, raking up the past; she told you everything she knew.'

'New evidence has come to light.'

'What new evidence?'

'I'm not at liberty to say.'

'A load of tosh. She can't help you solve this blessed murder.'

'I'm sorry, but I must insist.'

Still grumbling, the warden led the way along a concreted passageway. 'She's only just settling down with us.'

Joanna was stung. 'Well, she's lucky. Nan Lawrence wasn't quite so—'

That made the warden turn around. 'Just don't use the word lucky again. You police are such perverted people. You can't possibly think of Cecily Marlowe as fortunate. Have you seen her face? Please, don't insult her by calling her fortunate.'

'She isn't dead,' Joanna retorted through gritted teeth.

'She might as well be.' It was said very softly.

Without uttering another word, Joanna followed the stout figure up the stairs, standing back while the warden knocked. 'Cecily . . . Cecily, it's Mavis. Can I come in?'

There was an interminable wait before the warden knocked again. 'Cecily, Cecily, my dear.'

The door opened and the scarred face peered out.

Joanna stepped forward then. 'I'm sorry, Mrs Marlowe, but—'

Cecily recognised her, and gave a little squeak. 'Why have you come?'

Mavis swivelled her head to give Joanna a sour stare. 'I'm afraid, Cecily, dear, that the detective wants to ask you some more questions.'

Mrs Marlowe made a feeble attempt to close the door. 'I don't want to answer any more questions. Do I have to?' It was a querulous voice.

Joanna was glad she'd left Korpanski in the car. While his effect on younger women was positive, he couldn't help but intimidate nervous septuagenarians. Ever conscious of time wasted, she moved forward. 'You do remember me, Mrs Marlowe? Detective Inspector Piercy?'

Pale eyes flickered across her face. The door swung open. 'Ye-es, I do remember you.'

Now Joanna had a full view of the disfigured face. Crisscrossed with red lines, flesh and skin similarly puckered, one eye not quite fully open and when she blinked, the other not fully closed. Joanna struggled to keep the revulsion out of her expression. She had thought wounds healed better than this. Quicker. But more than a month later, possibly for the rest of her life, whenever Cecily Marlowe ventured out, people would notice her scars first. When she shopped or went to church or anywhere else, her face would mark her as a victim.

Joanna felt guilty. Mournful eyes were gauging her reaction, assessing it accurately. Joanna smothered all with a quick smile.

It didn't fool Cecily. 'You've asked me all the questions before,' she said. 'Why have you really come?'

'Because someone else has been attacked.'

Cecily fingered her face. 'And does she look as pretty as me?'

Joanna had a swift vision of Nan Lawrence's wrecked features and opened her mouth to answer, but it was Cecily who supplied it. 'She's dead, isn't she? Beaten. Oh, it's all right,' she said quickly, 'I read the newspapers.'

They were stood in a tiny kitchenette; cream Formica, a kettle, a microwave oven, a couple of electric hobs. A claustrophobic little room, lit with fluorescent strips, bright enough to read reactions. Cecily Marlowe felt no grief at the death of her one-time friend. It was hard to read expression accurately on a face so distorted. It looked devious, strange, queer, then — fleetingly — shrewd.

Joanna knew she must be honest. 'I want to know who it was that broke into your house. I want to know exactly what they said to you. I want to know why they picked you out.'

'I've already told you.'

'I know what you've *told* me. Bits. Now I want the whole truth.' Joanna forced her eyes to focus unflinchingly on Cecily Marlowe's eyes. 'Who were they?'

'How many times do I have to tell you? They wore masks.'

'What sort of masks?'

'Stocking masks. I told you all this.'

'Sometimes you say it's stockings over their faces, sometimes balaclavas.'

'All I know is, I couldn't recognise them again.'

'Sure about that?'

Even marred, Cecily Marlowe's face looked cunning. 'I'm sure,' she said, steadily now. 'I am quite sure that I wouldn't be able to stand up in a court of law and identify the people who attacked me.'

It was as learned as a catechism. 'Wouldn't be able to identify them or wouldn't be willing?'

The old lady ignored her.

'And they were waiting for you when you returned from your shopping?'

'It's what I said.'

The warden opened her mouth to intervene, but Cecily Marlowe shot her a swift glance.

Joanna persisted doggedly. 'You did know them, though?'

'No, I didn't. I didn't.'

'How many were there?'

'Two.'

'Sometimes two, sometimes three. Where were they sat?'

'I don't know,' she wailed. 'I was frightened, terrified. Can't you imagine?' Her hands were up to her face. The middle ring finger on the right hand was circled in red. Another suture line.

Joanna steeled herself to ignore it. 'What accents did they have? Irish? Scottish? Local? What's the truth, Mrs Marlowe?'

'I don't know anything. That's the truth.'

'Okay. How tall were they?'

'Taller than you.'

Finally the warden was moved to speak. 'This is sheer intimidation, bullying an old woman. I'm sure, Inspector, that you aren't supposed to interrogate frail old ladies this way.'

'I'm simply trying to get at the facts.'

'Which Mrs Marlowe can't remember. She was shocked, terrified out of her wits. It's probably better that she never does remember.'

'Well, if she had and we had been able to act on the evidence, it's just possible that Nan Lawrence would still be alive.'

'What?'

The colour had drained out of Cecily's face, making the scars stand out, vivid red streaks against parchment white. Her knuckles, blue white, clutched the side of the kitchen unit. 'What did you say? You think it was the same person?'

'It's possible. No, it's likely.'

Cecily Marlowe was shaking. 'No. No,' she said. 'No, not possible. Not possible.' She gathered herself quickly. 'Tell the newspapers,' she said quickly. 'Issue a statement. Whatever you do. Say that I saw nothing of my attackers, because — because this is the truth. From the moment I walked in, I saw nothing. I screwed up my eyes in terror. I saw nothing, I tell you. I heard nothing and I saw nothing. Put it in the newspapers.'

Joanna watched her hysteria with a cold detachment. Something was very wrong here, so she decided to produce her trump card. 'Can I ask you one more question, Mrs Marlowe?'

Cecily looked wary.

'Can you explain how your pension book and a pair of candlesticks, matching the description of the ones stolen at the time of your assault, have turned up in Nan Lawrence's wardrobe?'

Cecily Marlowe fell back against the cabinet. The warden picked her up, fussing noisily over the old woman. Joanna sighed. She knew when she was beaten.

* * *

Back in the car Mike was dozing, his head flat against the neck-rest as she opened the door. He came to with a grunt. 'Learn anything?'

'What do you think? She may be a frail old woman but the inmates of Broadmoor aren't tougher or more stubborn. She's keeping the whole thing back. I used to think it was out of fright, now I'm not so sure. It's more like . . .' She and Mike were back at the station before she finished the sentence. 'More like', she said, 'keeping secrets. That's what it feels like.' She opened her eyes wide. 'It's all to do with keeping old secrets. Nan Lawrence, Cecily Marlowe, old man Patterson, young man Patterson, and the eccentric Lydia, all of them are busy keeping dusty old secrets, protecting other people. But she's frightened. She wants it put in the newspapers that she would be unable to identify her attackers because she had her eyes tight shut.'

Mike stretched his long legs out in the car. 'That's what she says, is it? So who went for Witchie Lawrence, and over which particular dusty secret?'

They walked in through the double doors, straight into her office, picking up some coffee on the way. Joanna sat down behind her desk. 'Correct me if I say anything wrong.'

Mike nodded.

'Cecily Marlowe was attacked on Tuesday September the seventeenth, at four o'clock in the afternoon. Right?'

Mike nodded.

'She'd been out shopping. The details she gave were very vague; they changed from day to day. One thing that changed was the number of men involved in the assault. She said maybe two, maybe three. But Barra found evidence of only one, wearing blue jeans. So we stick at one. Am I still on track?'

'So far.'

'We initially thought her shifting story was probably due to shock, trauma, stress. Call it what you like.' Joanna's eyes were sparkling with something.

Mike waited.

'But in actual fact, shock usually does the reverse. Unless there is brain damage, what you get are uninvited flashbacks. The incident is seared onto your brain, intensified, not dulled, and not removed. It seeps back into your consciousness.'

Mike listened.

'We went back a week later. We questioned her again, and again, and again. And all the time she claimed she could not be sure of anything. Masks? Stockings? Balaclavas? How many men? She *never* said just one man. But Barra said only one cushion on the sofa showed signs of having been sat on by an intruder. Okay, so there were two used cups. One, found in the sink, held traces of tea; the other, found on the table in the sitting room, of coffee. Did the other man stand? Did one drink tea, the other coffee? Was one man tidy enough to put his teacup in the sink while the other left his coffee cup on the table? No. I'll tell you what I think. *One* man was waiting for her when she returned from shopping. The other cup was hers, left over from before she went out. The one man had been sat watching television; it was still on when Tylman found her in the morning. *She* hadn't switched it on, *he* had. So Mrs Marlowe entered her house, with her bags of shopping, and saw someone whose presence didn't worry her at all. It was someone she was used to seeing in her home. She passed the sitting-room door and put her shopping down on the table; it wasn't dropped. The man was not masked or she wouldn't have been initially so calm and unafraid; her coat was even hung up. But then something happened, things changed. He spoke, he threatened her, and then he lunged at her with a knife. And then she really did become traumatised. She cowered, terrified, beneath the kitchen table until Bill Tylman found her many hours later. This is the truth, Mike. She was so terrorised by her assailant that she could not cross the six or seven steps to her front door to help and safety. She was too afraid that he would still be there. Right the way through the night she was still paralysed with fright. That, Mike, is the truth. Christian Patterson worked alone that night.'

'Yes.'

'She knew him and feared him, still does fear him. She thinks he'll come back, even though his great aunt is dead. That, Mike, should tell us something about Christian Patterson.'

They were disturbed by the phone. Joanna picked it up and listened without comment, Mike watching the expression on her face change. Only when she finally replaced the handset did she allow herself a wide grin. 'That was Longton Police,' she said. 'They've picked up a young woman for stealing an old lady's purse after tricking her way into her home. The little thief's name is Carrie Foore and she's asked for thirty other thefts to be taken into consideration. One of them was in Leek. Ms Foore has long, naturally blonde hair and her gran lives next door to Jane Vernon. The net, Korpanski, is beginning to tighten, and I can feel some little fish wriggling inside it.'

'The question is', Mike replied dourly, 'have you got a big fish in there too?'

'I think so.'

* * *

Although the weather was cool it was also blustery. A few hardy yachtsmen were sailing their dinghies around the lake, their sails making bright triangles against a backdrop of dark trees that flung their branches around in the wind. Beyond were the hills of the moorlands, prettily divided up on the lower slopes by a neat patchwork of fields, marked out by the dry-stone walls so typical of the area.

Quills looked a little prettier that day, with a brief burst of autumn sun to brighten it, but the mud hadn't dried from the recent rains; it would still be a mucky approach. This time they left the car outside the gate and advanced on foot. Lydia must have been watching through the window; she met them on the top step.

Her face looked thinner, older and more tired, saggy. New lines had appeared in the days since her sister's body had been discovered. She might not mourn her, but she could not deny she was affected by her death. She greeted Joanna and Mike warmly, as though glad of some company. Quills gave the impression of being a home little visited by humans. There were only the animals to keep its occupant from solitude. Joanna had thought that was how Lydia Patterson had liked it. Not anymore.

'Inspector. Sergeant.' And they both sensed that this time she wanted them to enter.

She shooed the hens down the steps, as they squawked their protests noisily. 'Get out of the way, Sam. Not there, Ella.' Then she gave them a sardonic smile. 'Funny, isn't it?' she said. 'I used to think I was so bloody witty, calling the hens Sam 'n' Ella, the lamb Mint Sauce and the pig Bacon.' She sighed. 'It just doesn't seem so funny anymore. Joke's fallen flat.'

Again Joanna caught the sense that since her sister's death Lydia Patterson's life had altered in some great way.

'Come in. Come in. Sit down.' She paused, suddenly awkward. 'Look, I was about to make some tea.' There was an air of desperation in the invitation, which again puzzled Joanna. She felt that they *should* accept.

While Lydia Patterson was clattering noisily in the kitchen, humming some unrecognisable tune, Joanna prowled, policeman like. Mike, as always, stood in the doorway, arms folded, watching her silently.

It was the surface of the desk that drew Joanna toward the window. It overlooked the miniature farmyard outside. And as though the animals were aware of her interest, the woolly-coated sheep lifted its head and stared at her, so did the hens lately evicted from the house, and the duck. Idly, Joanna wondered what the duck was called. Orange? She smiled, then her eyes dropped to the surface of the desk scattered with sheets and sheets of paper, an exercise book, tightly hand-written, and a couple of skilled line drawings of the animals outside. The hens and sheep were instantly recognisable, so too were the pigs and the goat. But when she lifted the draw-ings, expecting more to be underneath, she found some sepia photographs. Joanna picked one up: heavily posed, children from some vague time between the wars. A tall boy, sausage suited, dark eyes staring at the camera. He held a hoop in his right hand, a stick in the other. Either side of him stood two solemn-faced girls in spotless white pinafores, one about ten, the other maybe five. They too stared at the camera, dark-eyed, solemn-faced. And between the three children there was no hint of the animosity waiting in the wings.

The photograph was more than sixty years old, but there was no need to ask who the children were. They were posing on the front steps of Brushton Grange, the picture taken from quite a few yards away. There was an expanse of flat croquet lawn in front of them.

The photographer must have been stood roughly on the spot where Nan Lawrence would build her home.

Joanna picked up a second photograph. One of the girls was much older now. It was impossible to tell which it was, both were so altered — Nan by the blows of death, Lydia by the wads of fat that now padded her cheeks. But one of the girls then had been very pretty. Jo peered closer. More than pretty, beautiful — with smooth cheeks, large eyes and hair cascading down her back. And on the girl's face there was the vaguest hint of a smile; a pleased, self-satisfied smile.

Lydia bustled back into the tiny room carrying a Formica tea tray and some chipped mugs. Sugar spilled from a glass dish. She handed round a packet of chocolate Hob Nobs with a rueful glance at her bulging stomach. 'Weakness of mine,' she said, stuffing two of the biscuits in her mouth. That day she was wearing a flowered smock that billowed out at the waist. Her eyes picked out the sepia photograph in Joanna's hand. 'Nan,' she explained quietly. 'Just after she was engaged. Lovely picture, isn't it? I've been looking at them.'

Joanna nodded, replaced the picture on the desk, and moved forward to take the mug of tea.

Lydia Patterson aimed a coquettish smirk at Korpanski. 'Surely you're not going to stand in the doorway *all* the time you're here, Sergeant?'

Mike grunted, accepted the tea and refused a chocolate Hob Nob. Lydia offered one to Joanna, who took it.

'Why have you come here today?'

'Just to talk to you, Miss Patterson.'

'And you think just talking to me will help you find my sister's killer?'

'Maybe. Maybe not.'

Lydia Patterson's eyes gleamed intelligently. They followed Joanna's glance across at the table. The picture of Arnold with his two sisters was now on top. She gave a deep, heartfelt sigh. 'Times,' she said.

'Your father—' Joanna began.

Lydia laughed. 'Was a crusty old thing,' she said. 'But he was clever.'

'I've been thinking about his will,' Joanna continued. 'He left your sister land she had no use for. He left your brother the family house he didn't want. What did he leave you, Miss Patterson?'

The eyes appraised her. Lydia stood up, her huge arms quivering with emotion. 'That was the best of it all,' she said, moving toward the desk. 'The very, very best bit. My father—' Her hand rested on the sheets of paper smothered with words and sketches. 'I don't know how much my brother's told you or whether or not you'd understand anyway. His gifts, you see, were not gifts but Trojan horses meant to be indicators of our weaknesses. I was 15 years old when my father died. It was 1945. The end of the war and my father's death are, to me, blurred into one event. I remember Victory parties and somewhere in the middle a wake. I recall flags waving and a day of sombre clothes. Which came when I have no idea. It's all such a long time ago, and I didn't mourn my father anyway. Even as a child I felt little affection for him, I was wary of him. His death was almost certainly much, much less important to a 15-year-old than the fact that the soldiers came home and people felt glad.' She dropped her eyes, wiped her face with the flat of her hand. 'Nan was twenty and Arnold a handsome and wonderful soldier returning from faraway lands. He was my hero.'

Joanna could not reconcile this vision with the bent old man who lived surrounded by such decay. Could time really be such a destroyer, to turn Nan, the dark-eyed beauty filled with such self-satisfaction, into the battered *thing* she had seen on the floor of Spite Hall?

Time and spite, an effective eroder. But age had not withered her so much as her character. She listened to Lydia's account, feeling as though the years were peeling away.

'I do remember the day the solicitor came to the house to read the will.' Lydia swallowed. 'Arnold was given the house — which as you rightly say he didn't want. He always hated Brushton Grange. When he came back from the war, he threatened to pull it down given half the chance. Father used to mutter, "Over my dead body."' Lydia gave a sour smile. 'Just a phrase. Anyway, Nan was given the land — which as you observed was no use to her. She was no farmer.'

'Her husband was though. Why didn't David Lawrence farm the land?'

'He had all but died in the war. He was like a baby when he came home; he couldn't have managed a farm. He had been wounded by a sniper's bullet, but more than that his spirit was broken, his mind destroyed. He couldn't believe he wouldn't be shot at if he ventured out in the fields, so he stayed indoors and allowed Nan to run his life as she found fit. And me? You asked what my father had left me? It was the cruellest gift of all. They laughed when my portion was read out. I was told my legacy was my intelligence.'

'I don't understand.'

'At the time', Lydia said, 'I was considered . . . Oh, these days they would have realised I was dyslexic, possibly through the traumas, the worry of war. Maybe it was lack of good teachers — they all went to the front, you see — or maybe it was simply the way my father tried to destroy what fragile confidence I possessed. I was not subnormal, but nobody knew. They were all too busy with the war effort and afterwards with celebrating. But then no one spent any time with me. There were no nice, tidy labels. I was considered thick.'

She picked up some of the sheets of paper, let them scatter over the desk. 'But the last laugh was on me. David Lawrence, returning from the war, left with little of his physical strength had plenty of time to teach a girl to read. I adored him,' she said simply. 'He unlocked the—' She wiped away a tear that had formed in the corner of her eye. 'Do you know what these sheets of paper are?'

Joanna shook her head.

'I write books,' Lydia said. 'Oh, they're just children's stories. I didn't find a Stephen Hawking level of intellect. They're just life as I know it.' She peered out of the window at the animals grazing contentedly. 'Tales of a smallholding, squabbles between animals, that sort of thing. Shamelessly anthropomorphic, but they sell. Kids like them.' There was more than a hint of defensiveness in her attitude. 'Since the middle 1960s I have made a reasonable living out of my stories.' She gave a lopsided smile. 'My father would have been furious, quite furious. He would hate to know how he had been thwarted, outwitted, and by David Lawrence of all people. He had no time for him. Here.' She tugged a drawer open and pulled out a couple of books, gaudily covered paperbacks, one with a hen on the front, the other a sheep, both with humanoid expressions on their faces.

'Take them home. Give them to your kids. Who knows, I might even gain a couple of new fans.'

Mike caught his. 'Thanks.'

Joanna also caught hers, and realised with a shock that by now she too had a 'kid' at home. It was an unwelcome thought.

16

Joanna and Mike spent Friday afternoon reading through statements, Joanna delaying the moment when she should return home. At the same time, she acknowledged that wherever Eloise Levin was would not feel like home to her. The antagonism between them was far too tangible, because Eloise blamed Joanna for the break-up of her parents' marriage. In her most depressed moments, Joanna wondered if the girl was right. Counsellors might protest that there was only room for a mistress in an imperfect relationship, but Jane and Matthew would have muddled along somehow, like many couples. Besides, what quality of relationship did she and Matthew have now? Not perfect. It was flawed every time Eloise's name cropped up, and her physical presence was a thousand times worse. Eloise was acute enough to sense Matthew's guilt and play it for all she was worth. It was her trump card — constantly overplayed. Joanna's biggest dread was that the girl would one day ask to come and live with them permanently and Matthew would not say no. She gave a big sigh, which Mike quickly picked up on.

'I can guess what you're thinking about,' he said, 'and it's nothing to do with the case.'

She gave him a rueful glance.

'How long's she staying?'

Joanna shrugged.

'Well, don't ask me how to get rid of unwelcome guests,' he said. 'I'd hardly qualify to give you any advice. Can't manage it myself, Jo.'

It brought the faintest of smiles to Joanna's face. 'She's still with you then?'

'We've tried everything', he said 'in turns. Being nice. Being horrible. Talking. Not talking. Listening to her advice. Ignoring it — and her — completely. I tell you what, Jo. Life was good before she came, only we didn't appreciate it, we didn't know how good we had it until it had gone.' He pushed his fingers through the jet black hair and stared gloomily at her. 'I'd give anything to get back to our place and see her cases packed and in the hall. Anything.'

'I know the feeling.'

They felt close, bonded by common enemies. Silently but companionably they worked through the piles of statements, looking up every ten minutes or so to exchange grins and comments. 'Found anything?'

'No.'

'Me neither.'

At 5.30 they were disturbed by the telephone. It was the desk sergeant. Bill Tylman had dropped by asking if they had found out anything new about the case, and did they want to speak to him?

'Hang on a second.' Joanna smothered the mouthpiece and eyed Mike. 'I only spoke to Tylman this morning; what's he "dropped by" for?'

Mike shrugged. 'Only one way to find out.'

'Why not,' she said into the receiver. 'Send him in.'

She put the phone down thoughtfully. 'I don't expect interviewing Tylman will advance the case one jot, but at least it'll delay the evil moment when we have to face our unwelcome guests.' Mike grinned back at her, and the comradeship between them warmed a few more degrees.

Bill Tylman was much as they'd remembered him: ruddy-faced, honest-eyed, filled with a sort of prurient excitement that Joanna found vaguely distasteful.

He began by explaining away his presence. 'I just wondered how you were getting on. I was just passing, thought I'd pop in.' He glanced anxiously from one to the other.

Jo indicated that evening's local newspaper. Tylman interviewed by one of their main reporters, the headline, 'The Trauma of Discovering a Body'.

'Still grabbing the headlines, Mr Tylman?'

He had the grace to blush clumsily. 'Funny, ain't it? Local papers call you a hero for anything.'

'Well, in the case of Cecily Marlowe, you were a hero. If you hadn't found her . . .' Joanna let the sentence hang in the air.

'I know. Don't bear thinking about.' Tylman began to relax.

Always a better situation for worming out the truth. When they were off guard.

'She was in a bad way,' he said. 'Poor old duck, frightened out of her wits. But once the papers got a sniff of it, wouldn't leave me alone.' There was a puff of pride clinging to him.

'And now, Mr Tylman?'

'Leave me alone? Well—' His attempt at modesty was going to fail. They both knew that. 'I just chat to them, almost forget I'm talking to a paper. Get a shock myself, reading my name in so much. Of course, it ain't the same — finding a body.'

'Not so much of a tale to tell?'

He simply wasn't wise enough to know the pair of them were setting him up.

'It's just a different story when someone's dead.'

'And you still made the front page locally.'

And all of a sudden Tylman saw where they were coming from. His honest eyes clouded.

'Now look here. I didn't ask for them to make a story out of it—'

'How did they know?'

'I don't know how they . . .' His eyes seemed to shrink. 'Someone must have told them.'

Mike took a couple of steps toward the milkman. 'I don't suppose you've remembered anything that might help us? Something you *forgot* before.'

Tylman licked dry lips. 'Not a thing, Sergeant. Absolutely nothing, I promise you. I've told you the lot.'

'And we', Joanna put in sweetly, 'can't really discuss the case with you.'

'Fine.' Tylman's eyes darted toward them. He wanted out. 'Well, if I do think of something—'

'Just one more thing.'

Tylman had his hand on the door handle, his back toward them, but even so they could read tension in the set of his shoulders.

'Cecily Marlowe. Did she have her milk left at the back door or on the front doorstep?'

'The front.' Tylman was definitely wary now.

'You heard her call that day?'

'Yeah, that's how I knew she was in distress.'

'From the kitchen, Mr Tylman?'

He half nodded.

'But the kitchen door was shut.'

They had gained few real facts from Cecily Marlowe, but in this she had been certain, because it was *she* who had pulled the door closed behind her. She had heard the front door slam and pulled the kitchen door closed before returning to her frightened hiding place, under the kitchen table.

Tylman seemed to wither. 'Was it?'

Joanna nodded, deliberately holding his gaze with her own until he was quite out of the door.

They laughed as soon as the milkman had left the room. 'That rattled him,' Joanna said. 'Little . . . He was obviously just nosing around to gather more details to feed to the papers.'

'Now, now.' Korpanski held his hand up. 'No bad language, please. Not ladylike.'

She scowled at him. 'Your mother-in-law', she said, 'is beginning to have an effect on you, Korpanski. And I'm not sure—'

'Yeah, well.' Mike gave her a quick grin. 'How about I buy you a quick drink at the Quiet Woman on your way home.'

'It isn't on my way home; in fact it's in the opposite direction.' She narrowed her eyes. 'What are you up to?'

He glanced at his watch. 'It's six o'clock, Jo. Opening time.'

Then she clicked. 'And Grinstead will already be propping up the bar, having queued outside for the last half hour. Well, Mike, whatever you think, I certainly need a drink before facing Miss Eloise.'

* * *

True enough, Grinstead *was* propping up the bar, halfway down at the very least his first evening beer. Opening time meant non-stop drinking time to him. An unsavoury character, he didn't know whether to hail Korpanski as an old friend or a threat — the sergeant could be both. He never had trusted Joanna. He watched the two of them thread their way through the early evening drinkers.

'Hello, sir.' Grinstead had learned it was better to call Korpanski 'sir' until he was sure which hat he was wearing; friend or policeman.

'Buy you a drink, Melvin?'

Grinstead relaxed, while still eyeing Joanna warily. 'Thanks, guv. Don't mind if I do.'

It was hard to decide how old Grinstead was. He could have still been in his thirties. He looked about fifty, but Joanna knew these old lags aged quickly. It was, in a way, a hard life. Not without its stresses.

'Melvin.' Watery grey eyes turned on her. 'We're interested in anything you can tell us about the recent burglaries committed against old ladies.'

He took the pint from Korpanski and drank deeply, his eyes never moving from Joanna's face. He didn't speak until his glass was half-empty and his mouth was free. 'It's Inspector Piercy, isn't it?'

'That's right, Melvin,' she said. And waited while he put the glass to his mouth again.

'I only know somethin' about the early ones,' he said in a rush when he had all but drained his glass, leaving nothing but dregs and froth, which he gazed at with maudlin sadness.

Joanna lifted her eyebrows toward Mike. He took the glass from Grinstead and had it filled. 'Go on,' she said.

'The ones in the spring,' he said, 'they was youngsters. No harm in them. Very young, know what I mean?'

'Habitual offenders?'

'Not for that,' he said.

'Then what?'

Grinstead licked his lips. 'Cars.'

'Locals?'

'They was in an accident early July.'

'Fourteen-year-olds?'

Grinstead nodded. It was enough. It told her everything. Gave them names, addresses, everything.

'What about the other lady? The one that had a broken hip?'

Real fear flickered through Grinstead's eyes. 'Put it like this,' he said. 'Word is he wasn't long out of one of your special institutions.'

Joanna and Mike exchanged glances. Elland.

'And the one in August? The one that had three hundred quid nicked?'

Grinstead's eyes blanked out. 'Don't know nothin' about that. Press bits about the other job put the youngsters off. That and the crash. Two of the lads was hurt, legs broke. Frightened them, so they stopped.'

Joanna was tempted to smile. So nature and the results of their crimes had punished them and taught them a lesson far more severe, more lasting and more effective than any the courts would have meted out. Providence, one could call it. Certainly justice had been done.

She moved closer to Grinstead. 'What about the old lady who had her face cut, Melvin?'

He was paralysed. 'I don't know nothing about that, Inspector. Honest.'

She fixed her eyes on him. 'Sure?'

'I swear . . .'

'Don't use your mother's life, Melvin,' she said softly. 'I have the feeling she might not like it.'

Grinstead put his glass down on the counter and walked out of the pub as straight and as dignified as he could manage.

'So he was worth a little,' Joanna conceded the point to Korpanski. 'You were right. Again.'

'He's a harmless enough old devil.'

'Who'll wander under a bus one of these days, drunk.'

Korpanski gave an uneasy grimace. 'Got second sight, have you?'

'It'll happen,' she said, looking back at the frosted door still swinging. 'It's the way with these old geezers. They drink, they gabble, they stumble on crimes that are far too big for their tiny brains, and they're so easy to dispose of.'

'It's time you went home to your poisonous little step-daughter.'

'And time you went home to your pet dragon.'

Mike made a face. 'And tomorrow?'

'The usual. Briefings, checking statements, reading reports and other such vital work.'

'Sunday the same?'

'No. Sunday I think I shall go to church.'

'Didn't know you were the religious type.'

'I am and I'm not,' Joanna said enigmatically. 'But it was a week ago Sunday that Nan was last seen walking the bare half-mile from the church to her home. I shall retrace her footsteps and see if I can jog anyone's memory. Besides, the Reverend wanted to talk to me, and it'll get me out of the house. I don't think I can face seeing Eloise's face every time I look up from the *Sunday Times*. We're meeting Caro and Tom for lunch so the rest of the day shouldn't be *too* bad, and half-term's only a week long; surely the little blighter has to go back to whatever institution is making an effort to educate her? What about you?'

'I thought I'd hang around Brushton Grange for a couple of hours, see what sort of company Christian Patterson's keeping these days. Never know what might turn up.'

'Fine. Ring if anything crops up.'

They parted company.

The journey home seemed too short, Waterfall Village a mere couple of minutes away, when usually she was impatient to get home and it seemed to take too long. But that day Joanna was not anxious to arrive home at all.

She let herself in and stood in the hall for a second — no longer. The first thing she heard was Eloise laughing. 'Oh, Daddy.'

It set Joanna's teeth on edge. For a couple of pins she would not have entered the sitting room but sneaked straight upstairs and locked herself in the bathroom. But that would have been silly, antisocial and admitting defeat. Instead she walked in and greeted Matthew's daughter casually. 'Hello, Eloise.'

The girl was 14 years old, a clone of her mother. Slim, with sleek blonde hair a few shades lighter than her father's but the exact same colour as her mother's, and sharp, angular features. In the uniform of the teenager — orange crop-top sweater, bootleg trousers, black clompy boots — she was draped across the sofa, opposite Matthew, who was laughing with her. Both stopped when she walked in.

Eloise didn't even try to smile, and her greeting was a sulky, 'Hello, Joanna.'

Matthew made an effort. He stood up and planted a clumsy kiss on her cheek. 'Hi, darling. Busy day?' And not for the first time Joanna realised with an ache how difficult it all was for him. So she smiled back, returned his kiss and flopped into the spare armchair.

'Any chance of a coffee?' she asked.

'I thought we were going out?' piped up Eloise.

Matthew's eyes flicked anxiously from one to the other. 'Hang on a minute, darling. Joanna's just got in.'

'But I'm starving.'

'We could order a takeaway from the Indian, Matt.'

'A curry?' Eloise said, as though she'd suggested they eat rhinoceros droppings.

Of course, Miss Eloise would not like a curry, not if Joanna had suggested it.

She tried again. 'Then what about a Chinese? There's a good one in Leek and they deliver.'

'Okay, then.'

Joanna fished a menu from the drawer and they all made a great show of studying it with absorbed concentration. After they'd ordered, Joanna drank her coffee and escaped to the bathroom. At least in there she would not be disturbed.

By the time the food arrived, she too was hungry, then there was a good film to watch. After that she made the excuse of tiredness and escaped to bed. Six more nights.

17

Saturday 31 October, 8.15 a.m.

Eloise was a child who slept late. Joanna was up, breakfasted and away without hearing a stir from the bedroom. She had taken a coffee up to Matthew just before she left, brushed the hair out of his eyes and read all the guilt, pain and depression at the clash between his daughter and his mistress. She kissed him with pity and he pulled her toward him. 'I believe you do try,' he said, 'but you just don't like her, do you?'

'She doesn't like me, Matthew.'

He stroked her hair and closed his eyes. 'I suppose I'll just have to get used to it; the fact that the two people I love most in life can hardly bear to be in the same room as each other.'

She lay with her cheek pressed against his chest. 'You might try to point out that however nasty, rude or offhand she is to me, it won't make any difference. She won't part us, Matthew, you won't go back to Jane, we'll still be together. That's why she does it, Matt. She thinks if we fall out you'll go back to her mother.'

He kissed her hair. 'My little psychologist.'

'I think . . .' she began. 'I think that if you tried to persuade her just to be civil, it might help. Like and certainly love is asking too much. Here.' She fished Lydia Patterson's book out from under the bed. 'Give her this. Nan Lawrence's sister writes kids' books, she gave me one. Oh, it's all right.' Matthew's sharp eyes had picked up the cartoon hen on the cover. 'I know it's far too young for her.' Joanna flicked through the pages as she had done the night before until she had dropped asleep, and again she was struck by how unlike a children's story it really was. More an adult tale using animals as characters. Like some of the great children's classics, *Watership Down* or *Animal Farm*, it had a message and a moral.

Matthew held the book for a moment, then gave Joanna a sudden kiss on the cheek. 'Thanks,' he said with one of his broad grins. 'We both know it won't work, but thanks for trying, Jo. I appreciate it.'

She felt warm, virtuous and happy.

'And as a reward', he continued, 'you should find my official report of Nan Lawrence's PM on your desk this very morning.'

She kissed him and left.

* * *

For the first time in years, Lydia had put away her exercise book in the top drawer, cleared the top of the desk completely and tipped every single photograph out of the antimony box. She was lining them up, muttering private thoughts, thoughts she would not have spoken aloud if there had been the remotest chance anyone would hear. Sam 'n' Ella clucked softly in the corner.

She laid the pictures out in sequence. One child joined by a sister, and then a second sister; the three children growing up; Nan's engagement; Arnie in uniform; a wedding day. And then the pictures stopped.

Lydia picked up the last of the photographs. 'So,' she said, 'the time has come. It'll soon be too late. We're old now. Nan is dead, and Arnie . . .'

Gazing through the window at the dull day outside, she began, at last, to face up to her sister's murder.

* * *

Matthew was as good as his word. The report, neatly typed, was waiting for Joanna when she arrived. It made ugly reading, every single blow neatly documented, Nan Lawrence's body subjected to the most intense scrutiny, medical facts baldly scripted. Joanna scanned through it, as always impressed by Matthew's thoroughness, if not able to understand every single word. On impulse she picked up the phone. 'I wish you wouldn't use such long medical terms,' she grumbled. 'I only understand half of it.'

'I only resort to medical terminology', he said, 'when layman's terms fail to describe her condition accurately. What particular words are you having a problem with?'

'Well, I can cope with contusion,' she said. 'But haematoma? Fraenulum? Pinna? Gravid? I need a dictionary.'

Matthew chuckled. 'The pinna is a part of the ear,' he said. 'The outer bit. The fraenulum is the flap of skin that ties the tongue to the floor of the mouth. Gravid is a term connected with pregnancy. Haematoma is a collection of clotted blood. How are you doing?'

'Scribbling like mad,' she said. 'I shall have to attend some of these lectures you're always giving.'

'Do,' he said. 'You'll be more interested than half the police surgeons who turn up.'

'So what have you two got planned for the rest of the day?'

'Not sure,' he said vaguely. 'I've got the awful feeling she wants to take me shopping.'

'Oh?'

'I'm sure we'll think of something. What time do you think you'll be back?'

'Late. Eight, nine; maybe even later. You know what it's like during a murder investigation; all fun and families cancelled.'

'Right.' A pause. 'See you when I see you.'

They both hung up.

* * *

Korpanski turned up at lunchtime armed with a bag full of sandwiches, some cake, drinks and fruit. 'Thought you might want feeding,' he said, dropping them onto her desk.

'I do. I do,' she said, leaning back in her chair and opening one of the packs. 'So, what have you got for me?'

'Christian didn't get up to much this morning,' he said. 'Tried to gain access to his great aunt's house.'

'Checking up on his inheritance?'

'That or destroying evidence.'

Joanna picked up a second report on her desk. 'I don't think so. Barra's picked the place clean. Look at this though.'

Mike scanned the note with a dour smile on his face. 'He's a clever sod,' he said. 'Put the bloody Stanley knife through the dishwasher after taking it to pieces. No wonder they didn't find anything.'

'Then get me the make of dishwasher used. Mine leaves loads of debris.'

Mike flipped the papers onto the desk. 'It's an admission of guilt,' he said disgustedly. 'I mean, how many people with nothing to hide would put a knife through a dishwasher after taking it to bits?'

'Patterson's defence will think of a perfectly good excuse. And they'll have months to do it by the time it gets to Crown Court.'

'Do you ever think the law is tipped on the side of the criminal?'

'Never.' Joanna made a face.

'You seem on a high,' Mike commented, 'considering you've—'

'The white witch staying with me? Oh, Matthew and I had a little talk about her this morning. I feel better for airing my grievances.'

167

'Well, I wish I did,' Mike re-joined grumpily. 'Although she is taking the kids to the Halloween firework show tonight. Fran and I are having a meal out.' His dark eyes twinkled. 'Or we may not go out at all.'

'Then take tomorrow morning off; you'll get your over-time in next week. I'm going up to the church anyway, unless you want to come?'

Mike shook his head. 'Strictly a weddings, christenings and funerals man myself.'

They worked steadily through the day and most of the evening too, packing up at nine. Joanna let herself into an empty house and picked up a note from the kitchen table.

Gone to the New Vic to see Cabaret. Trick or treat. Matthew XXX.

Joanna picked up one of his forensic textbooks and began to read.

18

Sunday 1 November, 10 a.m.

Rudyard church was a traditional, stone-walled edifice, built centuries ago and approached by a single-track lane. The rain had started up again, heavy and drenching, pouring from skies so dark with cloud Joanna began to wonder if the sun really was behind it. Like the rest of the congregation she was forced to run from the car park to the porch, where the Reverend Leon Gardiner stood, greeting his flock. He was an extraordinary-looking man. Very tall and powerfully built, with a shock of thick, tawny hair. It was difficult to guess his age; certainly over sixty, possibly even upwards of seventy. He crossed toward her and held out his hand. 'Hello.' She introduced herself and was subjected to a piercing stare from very calm grey eyes. 'You're not at all what I expected, Inspector.'

'No?' She had thought she was used to this reaction but it still stung. 'I believe you wanted to talk to me, Reverend Gardiner?'

He shot a swift look around. The organ was already playing very softly.

'Maybe after the service?' she suggested.

'Yes.' His relief was obvious as he pumped her hand. 'Yes, of course. That would be most convenient. You may be interested in my sermon, Inspector, about neighbourliness.'

'I'm sure I shall.'

She sat near the back of an ageing congregation and was surprised to see how many she recognised. Cecily Marlowe was two rows in front; Florence Price, in a shiny pink straw hat, to the side. As the organ started playing, Emily Whittaker clattered awkwardly up the aisle, her two sticks tapping on the stone floor like the blind beggar of *Treasure Island*, rain dripping from her pacamac. She sat down with an audible groan, which translated to a ripple of sympathy around the pews.

The Reverend Leon Gardiner climbed the step to the pulpit. The slow ritual of an English Sunday service began to the breathy tones of a pedal organ. Handel. Joanna closed her eyes and dreamed of far-off days when her grandmother had insisted she attend church. And she had, glad of the peace and tranquillity, away from the warring factions of her parents, which her grandmother's sharp eyes and ears had picked up. With hindsight Joanna knew the real reason her grandmother had insisted she attend church had had nothing to do with her immortal soul; she had been simply trying to prevent further damage to a sensitive child, caused by insensitive parents. Occasionally, in quieter moments, Joanna allowed herself the luxury of pondering incidents that trickled through her childhood and spilled into the adult woman she was. Understandable that after such turbulence, ending only with the abandonment of her mother for a woman much younger than herself, Joanna was reluctant to tie the conjugal knot. For her mother, her husband's departure had been the ultimate insult. So the years of bitterness and acrimony had ended in yet more poison; poison not even neutralised by her father's death. Still, every time her father's name was mentioned, the muscles in her body would tense up involuntarily. And coming to this service almost made her feel that she would walk away from the church with her hand holding her grandmother's tightly; they would return to the pink-washed cottage, open the door; and the peace of the service would be shattered.

Joanna frowned. Strange that she didn't remember Sarah having been there. But then Sarah had been older, disdainful of her younger sister. They had never discussed their parents; they had never discussed anything. And the only way she had been able to attract her father's attention had been to be the daredevil — the chancer — the son he had never had. So she had ridden her bike the fastest, dived from the highest board in the swimming pool and sailed on the stormiest of seas. Her father had still gone.

She opened her eyes to see light pouring in through the stained-glass window. The sun had been lying in wait behind the clouds. It had taken a giant breath to clear them. The window reminded her of the picture on Nan Lawrence's tapestry. The subjects couldn't have been more different; this was the Virgin with child, not the Slaughter of the Innocent. She closed her eyes again and sat very still, her mind struggling with a new concept she could not quite understand, not fully.

Joanna opened her eyes. The prayers were over and she hadn't listened. They would have been for the dead. Nan. She *should* have listened. She glanced round the rest of the congregation and wondered how many of them had been absorbed in their own thoughts instead of concentrating on the Reverend's words. Or were the soothing words of the matins facilitators for clear and empty minds? She glanced along the row. Marion and Ralph Elland were staring at her curiously; they must be wondering why she was there. She flushed and forced herself to listen.

Stood high in the pulpit in his flowing white surplice, the Reverend looked larger than life. Powerful, strong. Omnipotent. Omniscient. She could almost convince herself he could be omnipresent too. She recalled that the vicar in her grandmother's church had looked much like this when she had been a child; something different from an ordinary mortal. She couldn't believe it the first time she had seen him in normal clothes, strolling down the high street of the small Shropshire town where her grandmother had lived. He had looked so disappointing. So which, she had reasoned later, with a child's confused logic, was the real person? The larger-than-life Reverend or the humble, mousey man who had held his shopping in a brown carrier bag?

But somehow she couldn't imagine the Reverend Leon Gardiner scuttling in and out of shops with brown paper bags, even out of his vestments. He was a man with a presence, a man who emanated power. Leon was a good name for him with his thick mane of tawny hair. She wondered again how old he was. His voice was strong yet soothing. Easy to listen to. And he seemed to be directing his sermon straight at her.

'The last week has been a difficult time for us all. One of our members has died an untimely and violent death, and the police are investigating. Nan was, in many ways, a difficult person to love.' His words were truthful, uttered from the heart. 'And in the words of our Lord, I say: love your enemies. Bless them that curse you. Do good to them that hate you, and pray for them that spitefully use you and persecute you. We will pray today for the repose of our sister's soul.'

A difficult person to love. Not just Nan Lawrence but Eloise Levin, Fran Korpanski's mother — all these people spinning around their lives — were that; difficult to love. But how much more difficult was it to return their spite with prayers and blessings? Back came the answer. Impossible. The Reverend was asking the impossible.

The service ended with a hymn and a prayer, during which the Reverend Gardiner again made reference to Nan Lawrence's death, finishing with a plea that the police would be guided by God's infinite wisdom. Joanna muttered an amen. The organ struck up a valediction.

One by one the congregation filed past the Reverend, each receiving a word, a blessing, a gesture until the church was empty apart from Joanna and him. Outside they heard cars coughing and crunching away over the gravel; a faint acceleration and they were gone. There was no sound but the gargoyles spitting out rain water.

The Reverend Gardiner sat down on an adjacent pew.

Joanna spoke first. 'It was very brave of you to make such an outspoken comment on Nan Lawrence's life. Most reverends would, I think, have said something bland, uncontroversial, possibly even something untrue.'

He looked up and smiled at her. A sweet, sad smile full of pathos and regret but saturated with humanity. 'It would have been—' he was choosing his words with care — 'hypocritical for me to pretend that Nan was other than who and what she was. There was something quite twisted about her. But she was one of Christ's children for all that. She was a lifelong member of this church. We owed her something.'

'You knew her well?'

'She came here every week — one of the faithful. Though what she got out of the services I often wondered. However many times she listened to sermons preaching love, forgiveness, generosity, it didn't make seem to make any difference. But her trip to church was one of the only outings she made. She led a lonely and isolated life.' Again that smile. 'It probably did nothing for her naturally perverse character.'

'I see.'

'Are you making any headway over the case?'

'We've a few suspects but nothing concrete yet. I wonder, Reverend Gardiner, you must have known her better than most. Are you able to shed any light on the case? Have you any idea who might have wanted to kill her?'

He hesitated. 'I suppose you've heard about the Ellands' boy?'

'The villainous Craig?' Joanna smiled. 'We're checking him out. He does seem to qualify for top of the list.'

There was something about this man that invited confidences. Not just his cloth but more — maybe the warmth of the grey eyes.

He smiled again, a different smile, more worldly.

'I'd like to think Nan's great-nephew was in the clear.' A touch of mischief in his face now. 'If only in deference to his name.'

Joanna smiled with him. 'Oh, Christian, you mean. I wouldn't exactly say he's in the clear. We're checking him out too.' She drew in a deep gulp of air. 'Reverend, I wonder about the others of your congregation.'

Instantly he was cautious. 'Yes?'

'Mrs Marlowe, for instance.'

'What about her?'

'Would she lie to the police?' Joanna asked bluntly.

The Reverend pondered the question quite carefully before he answered. He was not a man to be hurried, not easily stirred, but when the kraken wakes . . .

'Cecily is a weak person, fragile, easily frightened. And the assault on her in the summer left her terribly shaken. She was nervous before; now her every waking moment is filled with terrors. Would she lie? What exactly do you mean, Inspector?'

'Her statement kept changing,' Joanna said. 'It made it very difficult for us to investigate the crime, because we didn't have an accurate account of what happened. We still don't know how many men broke in, we don't know what was taken. And . . .' Could she ask him to swear to secrecy? As sacred as the confessional? 'A few of her things have turned up in Nan Lawrence's house.'

Leon Gardiner stood up then, eyes burning with anger. 'What are you saying?'

'I don't know what I'm saying.' Joanna found herself raising her voice too, and listening to the echoes bouncing around the stone walls. 'I don't know. All I know is that we couldn't get an honest story out of Cecily Marlowe. She was cruelly hurt, and then her possessions turn up at the bottom of someone's wardrobe; someone who was supposed to have been her friend and who has been murdered herself a little over a month later.'

'Her friend? What makes you think they were friends? Nan didn't have friends.'

But they had been Christian's words.

'Okay. Okay,' she said quickly. 'So they weren't friends anymore. But there is no suggestion that it was Nan who carved up Cecily Marlowe's face. She couldn't have done it; she was too infirm. Cecily would have been more than a match for her, surely?'

The Reverend Gardiner turned to face the stained-glass window. 'These are murky waters, Inspector.'

And if Joanna hadn't been in a consecrated place she would have replied, *You're bloody well telling me.* As it was, she merely agreed, politely, and asked if he had anything further to add that might help them.

Leon Gardiner didn't even turn round. 'I have not.'

It was all she was going to get out of him.

All the way to the pub she pondered the Reverend Gardiner's statement. More important than what he had stated had been the hidden statements, the veiled sermon, the judgement on Nan Lawrence's character. And if she wasn't very much mistaken, he wanted to believe that Craig Elland had been Nan's killer.

19

She arrived late at the pub, at one o'clock instead of 12.30. Matthew, Eloise, Caro and Tom were already sat at a table, and their laughter wafted toward her as she pushed the door open. Obviously Eloise's resentment did not extend to Joanna's friends. Or was she trying to prove to her father that she was a nice girl really? A nice girl who could relate to *anyone* — anyone except her.

Joanna had reached the table before anyone noticed her.

The child was wearing make-up, quite skilfully applied; a touch of dark mascara to fringe her father's green eyes, plum-coloured lipstick. Eloise looked a 14-year-old, but the woman she soon would be was easy to spot: intelligent, forceful, direct.

She stared defiantly at Joanna. The others all greeted her, Caro pushing a schooner of white wine toward her. 'If it's warm', she said, 'don't blame me. We've already ordered the roast beef. So,' she grinned at her, 'how did the morning go?'

'I went to church, the one Nan Lawrence attended.'

'Lovely, darling.' Caro was almost writing notes. Too late, Joanna recalled the article; the backdrop of an English village church would be too tempting to pass by.

Caro moved conspiratorially close. 'Do tell. Thunderous guttering, resplendent gargoyles, lead roof? That sort of thing?'

'Pretty much.'

'And the vicar?'

'Resplendent too.'

'What did he want to see you about, Jo?' At last Matthew was managing to insert a word into the conversation.

'I don't know, Matt, nothing really.' She realised she didn't have a clue what the Revered Leon Gardiner had wanted to see her about, and he hadn't even mentioned the funeral service. Maybe he had spoken to one of the other officers and had the situation explained, so that by the time she had visited he had no longer had any need to speak to her. Certainly there had been no offloading on his part after the service. The others were all watching her. 'His sermon was—' She turned her attentions back to Caro. 'For goodness sake, I wouldn't want this appearing in your article.'

'Off the record,' Caro said blithely. 'Meanie.'

'Well, it was about loving your neighbour, doing good to those that spitefully use you,' she quoted. 'It wasn't quite what I'd expected, but apt.'

Tom's eyebrows moved upwards. 'Appropriate, but an unusual line to take.'

'Nan Lawrence was an unusual woman,' Joanna said.

'So was that the reason she was murdered?' It was Eloise's attempt to join the adult conversation.

Joanna nodded. 'In a way.'

Caro interposed. 'But I thought it was a gang of serial burglars, inner-city stuff?' She looked accusingly at her friend. 'That's still the official line.'

'I know. I can't go into it, Caro.' To her right Tom was nodding approvingly. 'All I can say is the case isn't what it initially seemed. It isn't straightforward. There's something devious, strange about it. You'll have to wait. I'm sorry.'

Tom steepled his fingertips together. 'I must say I thought from the beginning there was more to this case than met the eye. I read an article in one of the papers.' He grinned apologetically, pushed his gold-rimmed glasses back up his nose. 'You know, long sit-out sessions at court, tend to read the paper.'

She had always valued Tom's opinions, as a friend, as a lawyer. She never had known anyone quite so deliberately impartial. 'Go on.'

'Struck me — I mean, burglars are a predictable lot, stick to the same MO and all that.'

'So?'

'I'm sure I don't need to go into it. But it's all wrong, Jo.' Joanna nodded her head.

And what was most wrong was having found the booty from Cecily Marlowe's place stashed at the bottom of Nan Lawrence's wardrobe.

'Thanks for the kids' book,' Eloise said suddenly. 'It's weird.'

Joanna looked full at her, saw less of her mother, more of her father. And behind the made-up facade she read emotion too: unhappiness, insecurity, anger. 'You think the *book's* weird,' she said, 'you want to meet the old biddy who wrote it.'

'Oh?'

'Lives in an old shack full of animals. A couple of hens called Sam 'n' Ella.' Joanna laughed. Suddenly the situation seemed so funny, so bizarre. Nan had lived in Spite Hall. Her brother in a rambling old mansion, decayed as Miss Havisham's wedding cake. Lydia, huge and fat, lived in a place called Quills — in deference to her profession. But it was part pigsty, part chicken coop, part lambing shed. They made the Addams family seem like Hyacinth Bucket: staid, middle-class, ordinary. Joanna was still laughing as she finished telling Eloise about Lydia's tenants. 'There's a lamb called Mint Sauce.'

'You're joking.' It was the first time they had laughed together, at the same thing. It was a sobering realisation. 'And there's more.' Tears trickled down her nose.

Caro was alert. 'Does this elderly eccentric fancy doing an interview?'

'She might, then again she might not. You'd better ask her yourself.'

The meal arrived then, and plenty of it. Traditional roast, steaming hot with potatoes browned in the oven, thick slices of meat tender enough to carve with a fork, lashings of onion-flavoured gravy and fresh Brussels sprouts and carrots. Could you cook better than the food provided by a good moorlands pub? They did justice to it by suspending conversation.

Apple pie made with *real* Bramleys. Crusty pastry sprinkled with sugar the way Joanna's grandmother used to do, dripping with thick yellow custard. Joanna glanced at Eloise. The child was tucking in greedily.

During coffee they were all mellow and chatty. Matthew regaled them with a couple of tales from work, Caro with the gossip of the London journalists' scene, Tom with some typically wry observations from the courts. Joanna and Eloise were the silent ones, each eyeing the other up like boxers before a really big fight.

Every time Joanna's eyes left her plate she was aware the child was watching her, but as soon as she knew she was observed, the green eyes flickered away. Joanna turned her attentions to Matthew. He seemed happy. She watched him tease Caro about the forthcoming wedding, pull her leg about the service at a hotel, about her loving, honouring and obeying.

'For the first time in your life? Caro the rebel? Go on,' he said, still laughing. 'I bet you're even planning on wearing a white meringue.'

'And why not?'

Joanna watched her friend. Caro always looked so sophisticated, city-dressed even at a Sunday lunch in a rural Staffordshire pub, scarlet pencil skirt, black tailored jacket, the vivid colours setting off her blonde hair to perfection, make-up applied skilfully. Perfect enough for a model's photoshoot. Scarlet lips even at the *end* of a meal. How did she do it?

'It's about time I did something conventional, Matthew.' Caro was at her most arch, her fingers stroking Matthew's bare forearm. Joanna watched the pale hairs standing. Caro then linked arms with Tom. 'Besides, who but darling Tom could possibly put up with me? You know I'm sharp and unpredictable, but I do have my more conventional side. Who knows, in a year or two we might even go for the baby scene, those pink and blue things, provided I can get a decent nanny.'

The casual reference to babies shook Matthew. It was an accidental dart that shot straight into his Achilles heel. And Eloise? Joanna glanced curiously at her. How had she reacted? Her green eyes darted toward her father. Joanna leaned back in her seat. So — in this — mistress and daughter were united against the father. Neither of them wanted a child. Joanna studied Matthew's face. He had turned slightly pink, and there was a soft shape to his lips. But he did want one.

They ordered second cups of coffee, and Joanna searched for some neutral subject to introduce to remove all the undercurrents. But her main preoccupation would soon be *sub judice* and she didn't quite trust Caro. Given the choice between loyalty to a friend and a good story, a good story won hands down, every time, and Joanna had learned this to her cost.

The men lined up at the bar to pay the bill, and the three females were left together.

'And how is life in . . . ?' Already Caro was floundering.

'It's okay.' Eloise's eyes looked accusingly at Joanna. 'I miss my old friends, I miss our old house, and I miss my pony. Most of all . . .' Even at fourteen she couldn't quite finish the sentence, and tears threatened.

Caro headed for the safest part of the speech. 'You didn't take your pony with you?'

'It wasn't possible; we live in a flat. A friend has him.' Spoken as Jane would have done, emotion squeezed out by sharp diction.

And for the first time Joanna badly wanted to apologise for the disruption to a young life, to say she had not meant it to end like that; but it would have been inappropriate, sounded insincere. Besides, did she mean it? Had she really cared what happened to Eloise?

The men came back, chuckling over something they'd heard at the bar. They looked light-hearted, relaxed. It was the three women who looked tense, each of them sat up straight, carefully not looking at the others. Joanna stood up. 'Look, you lot go on. I really have to—'

Matthew put a restraining hand on her arm. 'No, Jo.' He was frowning. 'Please. Don't—'

'I do. I really do have to go back. I've got a main briefing in the morning. There are things I want to get clear in my—'

Matthew was shaking his head. 'Jo.'

'I won't be long, half an hour at the most. Why don't you get the Scrabble things out?'

Eloise was watching her scornfully. She escaped.

* * *

It was already dusk by the time she arrived at the station. The duty sergeant looked surprised to see her but made no comment. She only understood his guarded glance when she climbed the stairs and rounded the corner. A light was on in her office. She was tempted to knock. But this was *her* office. What was anyone doing there? She pushed the door open. Korpanski was slumped over her desk, a can of beer in his hand, looking as startled to see her as she was to see him.

'What the hell are you doing here, Mike?'

He gave a long sigh. 'The whole thing finally got too much. I've come down for some peace. And you?'

She nodded and sank into one of the chairs. 'Much the same,' she said gloomily.

'Mike,' she said a moment later, 'I've had a thought.'

'Glad one of us has, my mind's a blank.'

'Has Barra gone through the bedroom looking for prints?'

'He's dusted a few surfaces.'

'And come up with nothing?'

'Except Mrs Lawrence's.'

'And I take it the shoebox and the candlesticks?'

'Nothing.'

'I thought so. Look, I want us to haul young Patterson in for fingerprinting.'

'Why?'

'It's a bluff,' Joanna said. 'I simply want to rattle him. I know the whole thing's a bit half-baked.'

'Well, leave it in the oven a bit longer.'

'Thanks, Korpanski. You got any better suggestions?'

'Yeah. Let's haul Elland in for questioning.'

'Fine by me. But what tack are you going to take? And you know how protective NACRO are of their innocent little lambs out in the cruel big world.'

'He had access to a key; that'll do for me. He could have got in. We can set up an ID parade too.'

'If Mrs Whittaker will play ball.'

Mike finished his beer and stood up. 'I'd rather put my money on her making a positive ID than Marlowe. Perhaps we should invite both Elland and Patterson in for questioning. Put the heat on a bit.'

'And while we're at it, I wouldn't mind talking to Lydia Patterson again. There's plenty she isn't telling.'

Both were silent until Mike started speaking, moodily. 'Know what, Jo? Sunday evenings, when I'm at home, used to be my favourite time with the kids. Watch a bit of telly, have a nice tea, chat a bit.' He shook his head. 'Tell you what, last night was Halloween, I was really tempted to send the old witch trick or treating.'

Joanna laughed. 'Come on, Mike,' she said. 'We should both go home.'

He gave a lopsided grin.

It was dark as she drove through the moorlands, passing the small isolated farms, each with its own homely light — far more welcoming than the thought of a Sunday evening at home with Matthew and his daughter.

She found them nestling together on the sofa watching a wildlife film — *Bears in North America*. She perched on the chair opposite them. Apart from a brief smile from Matthew her arrival was barely acknowledged; their eyes didn't leave the TV.

'Anyone hungry?' she asked.

Neither looked up.

'No.' Eloise spoke shortly. The temporary truce must be over now they had moved from neutral territory.

Matthew stood up. 'I'll make a couple of sandwiches.'

Joanna gave a deep sigh. She couldn't go to bed early *every* night. Five more to go before normality returned. Next Saturday Matthew would return Eloise to York and the bosom of her mother.

'Tom and Caro . . . ?' She called into the kitchen.

Eloise laughed at some antic the bears were up to. It sounded forced and strained. Unnatural.

Matthew appeared in the doorway. 'They went home, wanted to be on their own. Lots to talk about, I guess.'

A few minutes later and he was back with a heap of clumsily cut doorsteps piled high on a plate. He balanced it on the chair arm. Joanna took one, not even hungry. It seemed to stick in her throat.

Eloise grabbed one, almost upsetting the plate.

It was Matthew who admonished her. 'Hey, careful. Manners.'

Eloise ignored him and chewed noisily.

Joanna had never been so thankful for the telly; its noise, brightness, colour, diluted the tension in the room. The wildlife film finished, changed to a fly-on-the-wall documentary about a car dealer. No one switched it off so it remained on. A little after ten, Joanna gave a theatrical yawn and announced she was turning in. Matthew looked disappointed.

20

Monday 2 November, 7 a.m.

The morning of Monday dawned bright and clear; cold maybe, but Joanna threw off the covers, leaving Matthew muttering in his sleep. She would cycle in; they could use Korpanski's car all day, and if it got dark before she was through, either Matthew could pick her up or Mike could run her home.

She showered, never so glad for a Monday morning. Matthew was taking the week off to spend time with Eloise, with something special planned for every day.

There was a nip in the air that warned of winter, but as she pedalled across the ridge, Joanna felt a strange exhilaration, a gratitude for life in these parts. Mist clung to the valley but the moorland rose above it, mysterious, high, chilling. Lost in thought, she seemed to arrive in the town quite suddenly, meeting the rush of morning traffic without warning. It was something that had always struck her about the town: even on a bike there was little transition. One minute moorland, the next the bustling town. Even at eight o'clock there was an air of busyness around the streets that contrasted vividly with the peaceful moorland. Joanna turned right into the police compound, locked her bike to the railings and walked into the station.

She and Mike had planned an early briefing before interviewing their suspects. She met Korpanski coming out of her office. He took in her cycling leggings and top. 'You haven't cycled in?'

'I have.' She wiped her cold nose, laughed and vanished into the locker room, emerging a few minutes later in a white roll-necked sweater and black trousers. She pushed her sleeves up as far as the elbows and proceeded along the corridor at a rate of knots, feeling an impatience to begin, a sudden surge of energy that had so far been missing from the entire case. A solution was beginning to feel near her grasp.

And the officers sensed that, speaking clearly, precisely and quickly, concisely sticking to facts.

She took Phil Scott's observations first.

'I've looked at all the statements from the churchgoers,' he said. 'There's nothing there. Nan Lawrence left at lunchtime, a little after 12.30. Plenty of people saw her walk home, and that's the last they saw of her.'

Joanna turned to Mike. 'What's the earliest time of death Matthew gave us?'

'Four pm,' he said. 'Dinner almost digested, and she can't have eaten it much before one.'

'And the latest? The very latest if she'd eaten late rather than straightaway?'

'About 12 hours later.'

'She was alone all afternoon?'

'But alive at six o'clock in the evening — if we can believe her loving great-nephew.'

'*If*,' she repeated. 'Bridget?'

PC Bridget Anderton piped up from the back of the room. 'I've interviewed Craig Elland's mates,' she said. 'As we expected, he's got an alibi right up until midnight. And according to the landlord of the Cattle Market, which is our merry friends' haunt, he has a corroborated alibi for the entire 12 hours — until closing time, in other words.'

'Go on.'

'His mates called for him right after his Sunday dinner — which was about one, according to his mother. He was drinking at the pub solidly until 11 o'clock, when he and his mates were so drunk the landlord called a taxi to take them home. He says they fell into the car.'

'Great,' Joanna said through gritted teeth. 'Just great. The one villain who could have done it and had access to a key has a bloody alibi.'

'Corroborated,' Bridget Anderton added.

Joanna turned aside to Mike. 'I still want to interview him. If he is innocent it'll be the first time in his nasty little life, and I don't quite believe he's altered his habits somehow. Too neat.'

'The person who bashed Nan over the head would have been covered in blood,' Mike reminded her. 'Even if he and his mates "nipped out for some fags" or something similar, they would have come back to the pub looking like something from *Nightmare on Elm Street*. And devoted Mum though she is, I can't see Marion Elland laundering her son's bloodstained clothes without some questions.'

'I know, I know,' Joanna said irritably, turning aside to him. 'So what better idea have you got?'

'Patterson,' Mike hissed. 'We've left him alone too long. He's had time to think about alibis, get rid of evidence. We should go through his room again. Something will be there — unless he's already disposed of it.'

She turned to meet his dark eyes. 'What?'

'Something.'

She gave him an incredulous look. 'He's had *a week* to get rid of any evidence; and besides, Barra's been through his rooms with a toothcomb. He knows his job. If there was anything there, he wasn't going to miss it.'

Mike gave a lopsided grin. 'I want to see young Patterson's face when we tell him what we found in his great aunt's wardrobe.'

'So do I, Mike, but patience. The last thing I want is to haul suspects in, believing they're guilty, and to have to let them go through lack of evidence. When we arrest them I want it to stick. I want them refused bail and put in remand, nice and tidy. Understand?'

Mike nodded.

She threw the next question out to the room. 'Anything else turned up?'

The blank faces gave out a negative. 'Okay then, you can go. Apart from you, Barra. Can I have a quick word?' She waited as the officers filed out.

'What is it, Jo?'

'How meticulous were you around the bedroom at Spite Hall?'

As always Barra thought carefully before answering. 'Not as thorough as the living room. Why?'

'I want you to go back there,' she said. 'Dust every surface, bottoms as well as tops. I want evidence that Christian Patterson has been in there.'

Mike quickly objected. 'But he might have had a perfectly legitimate reason for going in. He spent enough time there — by all accounts. Even if his dabs were all over the place, it's hardly going to make him the murderer. It wasn't even the murder room.'

'I'm not after hard evidence at the moment. I simply want to rattle him, destroy as many of his statements as I can. We can wait for our killer, Mike. It's the usual game of links; one thing leads to another. I'm looking for the answer as to why a particular old woman was terrorised. If we can connect Patterson to Cecily Marlowe's sad little items we will have a liar, and more importantly we may just have, hopefully, a reason for him to have lied. Let's start with that and hope it takes us somewhere else we want to go — that is, to the killer of Nan Lawrence.'

'You have a funny way of going about things,' Mike said. 'Why not just bash his door down and charge him?'

Joanna laughed and touched his arm. 'Because', she said, 'that isn't the way I work. Now let's go and talk to Elland.'

* * *

The gold Tigra was still stood outside the Ellands' house, alone this time. The upstairs curtains were still drawn. At a guess they would be waking Elland from his beauty sleep, long after both parents had set off for gainful employment.

Joanna hammered on the door until he appeared, bleary eyed, a towel loosely draped around his bulging middle. He glowered at them. 'What do you want?'

'To talk to you.'

'Look, I never touched the old goat. Didn't my mates tell you? We was at the Cattle Market all afternoon. We was seen there by plenty of people. You can't pin this on me.'

'Why don't you put some clothes on and make us a nice cup of tea?' Joanna suggested. 'Then we can have a friendly chat.'

'And why don't you go fuck yourself.'

Joanna pushed her foot in the door. Mike's elbow found its way to Elland's chest.

'I'd rather have a cup of tea, please,' Joanna said. 'Now be a good boy and put the kettle on. And cover up that big body of yours, it's turning me on.'

Still muttering, Elland ambled up the stairs, returning a minute later in jogging pants and a vest. It was an improvement though not exactly a transformation.

Elland occupied Mike's favourite place — blocking the doorway — and stood, arms akimbo, glaring at them. 'So, to what do I owe this pleasure?' he sneered. 'Apart from the fact I strayed from the straight and narrow once.'

Joanna fixed her eyes on his pasty face. 'Well, put it like this, Craig,' she said pleasantly, 'Nan Lawrence was found murdered in her own home. She was a nervous old lady, always kept doors locked, didn't open them to strangers, but somebody got in. Understand?'

Elland's pale eyes didn't leave her face. Neither did he nod. He simply waited for her to continue. This was the behaviour of a hardened felon; only first-time criminals babbled.

'You do understand, don't you, Craig? We're wondering how somebody *did* get in.'

The barb hit home. For a split second something wild and animal flashed across his face, then he settled down. As quickly as it had brewed, the storm had abated. But it was a warning. Elland had done time for attempted murder.

Joanna continued in the same calm, even tone. 'What's been puzzling us is the fact that this vulnerable and frightened old lady who never answered the door to strangers was bashed over the head as she calmly stitched away at a bit of sewing.'

Nothing intelligent seemed to register in his doughy features.

'How did he get in, we asked ourselves, didn't we, Mike?'

Mike regarded her steadily.

'And then we found out, Craig, that you had access to a key.' Joanna smiled.

Still nothing seemed to be registering. Craig seemed to be taking some while to sort out the facts. Then he gave a slow grin. 'But I got an alibi for when she was done, hasn't I?'

'We don't know exactly *when* she died.'

'I ain't daft, you know. I can work it out. Mum saw her at church that mornin'. Hypocritical old cow, sittin' there, singin' psalms and prayin'. And she never collected her milk in on the Monday mornin'. I read the papers you know. I weren't on me own at all then except—'

'After closing time.'

'I couldn't 'ave bashed a chicken over the head the state I was in. Let alone crept up on a old lady and done 'er in. Don't remember nothin' about Sunday night. Pissed I was. Me mum put me to bed.'

But if it was true that Marion had actually undressed her son, his clothes couldn't have been bloodstained. She wouldn't have covered that up for him.

'Lots of people commit murder under the influence,' Joanna said innocently. 'Unfortunately, it doesn't always work as a defence plea, balance of mind and all that.'

Again that ugly, mad look flashed through Elland's pale eyes. 'You got nothin' on me,' he grunted. 'Nothin'. You couldn't pin a soddin' parkin' ticket on me. You're just goin' for me cos you got no one else and I done time. Well, I ain't done nothin' this time. You got the wrong man, Inspector. You better try again.'

21

A little over an hour later they were again driving through rain. Wind battered the car. Mike leaned forward and switched the headlights on. It was almost as dark as night, yet it was still only a little past eleven in the morning.

They turned up the now-familiar grassed track that led to the two houses, the contrast as great now as when Joanna had first been introduced to Brushton Grange and its ugly neighbour. Mike parked as near as he could to the front doors of both houses and they dashed along the path toward Brushton Grange.

They clanged the doorbell and prepared to wait; they had grown used to the time it took Arnold Patterson to rise stiffly from his chair, cross the large hall and tug the door open.

Patterson obviously felt he knew them well enough to drop any niceties. 'You keep comin' back,' he grumbled. 'I don't know what for.'

'To see Christian,' Joanna said. 'But I want to talk to you first.'

'I don't know what about,' the old man said, his face still angled toward the floor. 'I can't enlighten you. She's dead. How can I say I'm sorry with *that* there?' He lifted his head briefly, only enough to sweep a gaze across the gully before, exhausted with the effort, he dropped his head again toward the floor. 'If you must know, I do regret her death, Inspector. Mainly because it were violent and because she *were* my sister. But I can't say I'm mournin' her. She is just dead. It's up to you to find out who killed her and let the courts take their justice. There is no point you keepin' comin' back. I got nothin' to tell yer.'

'You were friendly once,' Joanna said.

'Aye, as children.' He jerked his head in the direction of the concrete edifice. 'As you can see, the friendship failed to last.'

'Why? That's what I want to know.'

The question took the old man aback. He straightened his back again to stare Joanna full in the face. 'Are you mad?'

Joanna met him full in the face. 'Why did she build it?'

Something softened in the lined cheeks, and Arnold Patterson's eyes moistened. He licked his lips. 'So,' he said quietly, 'that's what you want to know, is it?'

'Yes.'

In deference to his age, Joanna had dealt gently with Nan Lawrence's brother so far, but she needed facts now. Even if she had to bully them out of him she would get them. Nan Lawrence's death must be dealt with by the law, whatever events had taken place in her life. It made no difference. The crime was still murder, and she wanted no more murders, robberies, attacks. She wanted Leek to revert to the pleasant, safe town it had been. And Patterson was being deliberately evasive. Obstructive even.

'We just grew up,' he said. 'Nothin' more. Brother and sister as children doesn't always mean bosom pals for life.'

But his eyes had told her this was not the truth. He didn't even *expect* her to believe him.

'You quarrelled, didn't you?'

'I can't remember.' Another lie. Eyes that flickered from side to side.

And she was running out of patience. 'Then I suggest you try to remember, Mr Patterson, because I have a suspicion it will have some bearing on the case.'

Again he tried to bluster. 'What nonsense. What utter . . .'

But she and Korpanski had already whisked past him and were halfway up the stairs. It was a measure of how little she valued his statement.

This time there was no loud, thumping music coming from Christian's room. Instead they heard something dreamy and watery; music that seemed to trickle down the stairs, music that conjured up dolphins swimming, music one might smoke hash to.

Which was exactly what he was doing, with a vague, abstracted look on his face as he tugged the door open, a roll-up dangling from his fingers. 'Hey,' he said, 'it's the Inspector.'

Joanna could have rubbed her hands with delight. Pot, better than a truth drug, a suspect right under the influence. She and Mike exchanged looks of sheer triumph. Of course, there was always the risk that Christian would pour out a stream of absolute rubbish. But—

She sank down onto the cheap, foam sofa, ignoring the girl sat wedged into the corner, staring into space. 'Tell me about your great aunt, Christian.'

'She was a lady and a half,' Christian said, waving his hands around. 'A real lady.'

'Some say she was more of a witch.'

Christian smiled, his arm around the pale girl, who was swaying with the dolphin music.

'She could cast spells,' he said enigmatically.

'What sort of spells?'

'Get people, man, do her bidding.'

'And is that what you did — her bidding?'

Christian was rubbing his fingers together. His head was inscribing a circular movement.

'Of course. Powerful persona like that.'

'What bidding did you do?'

'Closed dangerous mouths. People ought not to talk, Inspector.'

How much of the stuff had he had?

'It depends, Christian.'

'I don't think it depends at all. Talking is just . . . Cool arithmetic.'

Typical of the sort of roundabout interview one had with a suspect who was high; just when you thought you were getting somewhere sensible they tailed off into dolphin land.

'Did Nan have her dinner as soon as she came back from church?'

His eyes flipped open. 'Hey . . . You called her Nan. You knew her?'

Joanna was getting bored with this, bored and frustrated. 'Her dinner, Christian?'

'Any old time, Inspector. Hunger—'

'One other thing, Christian. Did you *ever* go into her bedroom?'

'Inspector,' there was a lazy smile, 'what *are* you suggesting?'

'Did you?'

Christian closed his eyes and carried on rasping his fingers. 'Like the music?'

* * *

Mike was steaming all the way down the stairs. 'Well, that was a bloody waste of time. We didn't even get the point across to him that we found some booty round at the "cool witch's" lair. You should have charged them both with possession and hauled them in.'

'Did you see anything lying around, Mike?'

'No, but it was obvious the pair of them were—'

'Did you smell pot?'

Korpanski stared at her. 'They must have been high.'

'Or playacting.'

'Ne-v-er,' he said.

They crunched back over the gravel. Barra's squad car had joined theirs and was neatly parked in front of Spite Hall. The door was wide open. It was a good opportunity to check on the results of his fingerprint search.

The hall looked even dingier than Joanna remembered, dark and airless, with all the doors closed and taped across except the first one on the left, leading to Nan's small bedroom. Barra was in there, so absorbed in his work he didn't even look up until Joanna spoke. 'A bit more interesting than I'd thought. There are three distinct sets of prints. The dead woman's, of course, all over the place. Some others that I guess are probably the home help's. And another set,' Barra scratched his square chin, 'on the drawer of the dressing table as well as a few on the wardrobe door. Nowhere else, interestingly.'

'We'll have them marked out on a diagram and get the home help and the nephew in to check.' To Mike she added, 'At last. I think we might be beginning to get somewhere. I feel that familiar tingling in my toes.'

'It's that bloody bike of yours,' he said.

22

And suddenly it was eight o'clock. The day had flown past, but Joanna was reluctant to go home. Home? It didn't seem it anymore; at least not the comfortable, peaceful haven the cottage used to be, but an uneasy place where she dreaded the evenings.

She glanced across at Korpanski. 'How's your mother-in-law?'

Mike grinned with sudden optimism. 'Gone awful quiet over the last day. She's brewing something up, another spell, maybe. How's—?'

She held her hand up as though to ward off evil. 'Don't even mention her name without brandishing the holy book, a clove of garlic and a cross.'

Mike's face softened. 'That bad?'

She nodded.

'You have my sympathy, and for once—' he gave another jaunty grin — 'my complete understanding.'

The compulsion to avoid returning home was over-whelming. She stopped even trying to resist it. 'Look, um, Mike . . . Drop me off, will you?'

'Where?'

'At Quills.'

'You want me to come?'

'No.' She didn't want to explain anything. 'Thanks, but no.'

* * *

The thought of an evening spent with Lydia Patterson and her animals heartened Joanna. As they drew up in the car, she could see that inside the wooden shack lamps were switched on. The animals grouped curiously around the gate as Mike's headlights picked them out, eyes staring, reflecting red: the sheep; a mangy-looking black-and-white border collie, which slunk away as Joanna pushed the gate open; and two ducks waddling as fast as they could behind her toward the doorsteps.

Mike accelerated away, leaving silence as she waded through the mud toward the door. Suddenly the bulky figure of Lydia Patterson loomed up, blocking out the light behind her. In silhouette she looked even more enormous than usual, enormous and threatening. It was with a shock that Joanna realised Nan Lawrence's sister was levelling a double-barrelled shotgun at her with the steady hand and intense concentration of someone who would use it. She was about to call out when Lydia Patterson lowered the gun. 'How nice,' she said calmly. 'I thought I heard a car, Inspector. Come on in, have a slab of cake. I tried my hand at baking this afternoon. Must have been expecting a guest.' Her eyes searched through the gloom. 'Your bulky friend gone home?' She answered her own question. 'Back to the station, I'd imagine.'

'We don't work nine to five — particularly during a murder investigation.'

'Families must dislike that intensely,' Lydia observed. 'Tricky things, aren't they, Inspector, families?'

Silently Joanna agreed and followed her into the sitting room while Lydia continued talking.

'Went for animals myself, although they can be tricky too, temperamental beasts; loyal though. Not allergic to feathers are you?' And without waiting for Joanna to reply, she closed the door behind them. In the corner, in a basket, Sam 'n' Ella clucked softly.

'Little buggers,' Lydia said affectionately, throwing a glance toward the two hens and locking the gun back in its cabinet. 'But they did present me with a couple of brown eggs this morning, so I really shouldn't complain about them. It was that that gave me the idea to bake. Fortuitous really. Didn't *know* you were coming. Must have had a premonition though that someone would come, and I always felt you'd come back.' Her eyes penetrated Joanna's with piercing understanding. 'Had to, didn't you? No chance of discovering the truth without learning about the past. Hang on a mo, I'll get the tea tray.' Halfway to the kitchen she turned around. 'You *have* come to talk, haven't you? About Nan.'

'Not just about Nan,' Joanna said. 'This isn't just about Nan, is it? It's about all of you.'

Without answering, Lydia walked into the kitchen. Joanna had gained the impression she was pleased at her statement, although it was hard to judge. Lydia's thought processes were jerky and disconnected; she made statements then leaped to other topics without leaving a clue as to what the intermediate thoughts were. One could only guess. Joanna settled back on the sofa and half closed her eyes, breathing in the scent of animals, which seemed to fade the longer you were in the room. She felt relaxed.

But the illusion of a safe haven was sharply blasted away by the irate tone of her mobile phone. And as she answered, she couldn't quite keep the resentment out of her voice, even though it was Matthew. 'I wondered if you fancied a lift home,' he said tentatively. 'We've just got back.'

'I'm with, um . . .' Lydia would hear from the kitchen. 'I'm interviewing a relative of Nan Lawrence's. Why don't you pick me up from here in an hour? Bring Eloise with you. It's the lady who wrote the entertaining book. Maybe she'd like to meet her.'

'Little madam's in a sulk,' Matthew said softly. He didn't want to be overheard either. 'To be honest—'

She didn't want him to have to admit it — that his daughter was difficult — even with him, her adored father. She wanted to spare him the self-abasement, so she didn't let him finish.

'It's okay, Matt. We women can all be difficult.'

'Yeah.'

She gave him swift directions to Quills and finished the call, switching the phone off. Its presence could be intrusive, her awareness of it an obstacle to concentration. She was just putting the phone back in her bag when Lydia returned carrying a tray heavy with a teapot, milk jug, sugar basin, two mugs and a plate of home-made cake. A farmhouse fruit cake. It opened a keyhole of memory, transporting Joanna straight back to six years old, the house of her aunt and the wonderful taste of home-made cake mixed with tea, very milky in deference both to her youth and to the trend then when milk had been thought to be universally, nutritionally good.

Lydia hacked off a crumbly slab and dropped it onto a tea plate. 'Here,' she said, 'you look as though you could do with this.' Then she poured the tea.

'Now then.' A fringe of crumbs had already planted themselves round her mouth; she'd been snacking in the kitchen. She dusted the crumbs off and settled back in the shabby armchair, ignoring the two hens, which were clawing at the straw in their box. 'I think I know what you want to learn,' she said wisely, fixing Joanna with her strange amber eyes. 'You're interested in our family, aren't you? You're curious as to how it all came about.'

Joanna nodded.

'And knowing a little of our history — and our various inheritances — you don't think Nan's death was by chance, do you? This burglary thing was a red herring, a wild-goose chase, a distraction. Call it what you will, Inspector, it isn't the answer, is it?'

Joanna shook her head, almost mesmerised by the voice, which had softened and was lullingly gentle. 'I want you to help me,' she said evenly. 'Just point me in the right direction. You have a duty not to obstruct the police. Others might be in danger.'

'You think I haven't thought of that?' Lydia regarded her steadily for a few moments. 'Look at these photographs, Inspector, before you ask me anything more or even try to make judgements. If you're unable to read evidence, I don't see why I should enlighten you.'

'You must,' Joanna said.

'Well . . . I believe you are an intelligent young woman, Miss Joanna Piercy. Not a hack and slash sort of police-woman at all. I think in the end you will understand. You see, understanding is more important than simply knowing. It is the key, after all. The why. Without that, you might have a physical arrest but not a full comprehension of the case. It is complex. Even I can't tell you everything, and I have been close to its centre for fifty years.'

She reached behind her for the ornate antimony box and set it on the sofa beside Joanna. 'Go on,' she prompted, 'open it. Take your time. It's all there if you've the wisdom to read it. And if I've judged you correctly, you will only be content with the whole story.' She smiled, scratched at a reddened area on her elbow and smiled again.

Joanna glanced downwards. This, then, was the symbol of Pandora's box. What evils would be exposed when she lifted the lid? She was at once afraid yet unable to contain her curiosity. She raised the lid. It was full of photographs, black and white, or rather sepia and cream, and all were old.

'Tip them out,' Lydia directed. 'Study them. The years are written on the back, start from the beginning, Inspector, like a good story.' She was leaning forward, eagerly, hands on huge knees, mouth very slightly open, her breathing heavy.

Joanna did as she was told, tipped the photographs out onto the sofa, and began to sort them through. It was easy to find the earliest; they had been at the bottom. Photographs of children, one, then two. And using the dates on the backs, by 1930 there had been three. Pictures of Arnold came first, born 1920, a baby lying on a lace shawl who grew into a sturdy toddler then a small boy.

And by the time he was five years old, Arnold had a sister, Nan. No hint yet of what was to come.

First pictures of Nan showed a contented, happy little baby, jealously guarded by an older brother. If the camera was not lying, Arnold had doted on his baby sister. His expression was clearly the fierce mixture of pride and protectiveness frequently seen in the attitude of an older brother to his tiny sister. As Nan grew, the bond between brother and sister appeared to remain close, the photographs still portraying them frequently hand in hand, sharing toys, a hoop and whip, a wooden horse, a toy train. And then in 1930 along had come Lydia, always a fat child, plump-legged, bursting out of her dainty dresses.

Joanna looked up through seventy years to see her reading her mind, chins wobbling as she laughed. 'I was a right little fatty, wasn't I?' And Joanna joined in her laughter before she bent back over the photographs, curious to learn more from them.

The children grew with the years, games changed, school uniforms appeared; solemn, studied shots with hockey sticks, a cricket bat, a rugby ball. The vision swam before Joanna's eyes of Arnold Patterson as an old man, bent almost double over his stick. He had not always been a cripple; at the age of fifteen he had been active at school. By the time Arnold was a leggy 19-year-old in 1939 he had swapped his Oxford bags and polo shirts for an army uniform. His sisters now clung to him as though every moment spent with their brother was precious. It must have felt like that. 'Arnie', the back of the photo called him now. Fourteen-year-old Nan and nine-year-old Lydia had still, quite obviously, adored this handsome, jaunty young soldier. Joanna peered closer and began to read emotion behind the sepia.

Arnie's eyes peered out of the photograph with desperation. Joanna could read the terror that lay behind the bold, plucky grin. Frightened? He must have hated it but been just as afraid to let his sisters know that the boldness was all a front, that behind every hero is a coward. Joanna put the photograph back in the box, on top of the others, wondering just how much Arnie's two younger sisters had really understood.

She picked up more prints of the two girls, clinging together, missing their brother, a bemused puzzlement now lying behind their stares into the lens. There were only a few pictures left.

Joanna stretched out her hand and picked up a couple of prints dated 1944, when Arnie must have been home on leave, fear now etching deep lines across his face. But the three had still been inseparable. Arnie had an arm around each sister, and there was no mistaking the adoration mirrored in the girls' faces as they gazed up at their older brother. Behind them, probably imagining the shot would miss him, glowered an older man. Joanna peered at a thin, hard face. Even though it was fuzzy and slightly out of focus, she could still read resentment, meanness, spite. He must be the father who had died and left such a legacy. There was the vaguest resemblance to Arnie, Arnie without the brave grin. But Joanna could see no resemblance to either of his daughters.

There was only one photograph left. 1944: Nan Patterson marrying David Lawrence, neatly ascribed on the back. Joanna stared at Nan Lawrence, looking determinedly in control, staring into the camera lens, dressed in a surprisingly lavish wedding dress, her hand linked with that of her husband, in uniform but still looking like a farmhand, doltish, clumsy and uncomfortable. It was the last photograph. There were no more. Not one that dated beyond the end of the war. Yet they had, all three, survived. Joanna felt cheated. Something should have been there; Lydia had promised her. But whatever clue there was, it had eluded her.

She looked up to see Lydia Patterson watching her with a veiled expression in her eyes; some disappointment that Joanna had not been as perceptive as she should, but there was triumph too.

'*Now* what do you want to know, Inspector?' Her voice was soft — kind — but clearly she would answer only the questions she was asked, and Joanna didn't know what to ask.

'Why did you fall out?'

Lydia seemed to stop breathing. 'I thought you'd ask that,' she said, 'but it isn't my tale to tell.'

'Then whose is it?'

'It *was* Nan's,' she said, even more softly.

'Nan can't tell it,' Joanna said brutally. 'She's dead. You must tell it for her.'

Lydia opened her mouth to speak, then shook her head gravely. 'I can't,' she said. 'I can't.'

'It wasn't only the will, was it?'

Lydia shook her head.

'Was your sister happily married?'

'That was something between her and David.'

'Tell me.'

'I only know a part,' Lydia said. 'Some was never told me. I was too young — only fourteen when the war ended. And girls of fourteen were considered young then. Now, well . . .'

'Do the events of so long ago have any bearing on your sister's death?'

'They had a huge bearing on her life,' Lydia said quietly. 'As to her death—' she stared straight at Joanna, then shrugged her huge shoulders — 'I don't know. I don't *know*.'

'Then you must tell me all', Joanna said, 'and let me be the judge.'

Lydia's face seemed to crumple. 'Nan's story is not unique,' she began. 'It happened to lots of women in those times — war times. Their menfolk were away, they strayed. Nan strayed, and Arnie never could forgive, neither could I. Arnie because he knew what men went through over there. He knew that for all their bravado they were terrified. The "girls they left behind them" sustained them through terrible times. And I — I couldn't forgive Nan because I loved David Lawrence, I worshipped the very ground he walked on. With my 14-year-old's clear-cut passions, I couldn't see how she could have betrayed him.'

'Who with?'

'She didn't tell me, her kid sister, who adored . . .' Lydia frowned. 'No, idolised her. She didn't tell me.' Even fifty years later, Lydia Patterson still managed to look hurt; something of the adolescent resentment was visible. Her sister might have been murdered, but Lydia was still cross with her over a secret never shared. Suddenly Joanna was gaining insight, seeing how lives, as one grew older, condensed so that the emotions of fifty years earlier were *yesterday's* hurts. And revenge? Hatred? Was that as hot now as then? As hot eight days ago as fifty years? Surely no one would wait for revenge for so long?

'Does anyone know who your sister's clandestine lover was?'

A car drew up outside. The gate clicked open. She had not thought it possible that Lydia Patterson's plump face could shrink in fright. Like a pricked balloon, the fat seemed to deflate, and her eyes flicked across to the gun cupboard. She was on her feet in a millisecond, her eyes wide and frightened, tea upset down her flowery dress.

Footsteps outside, Matthew calling to Eloise: 'Mind where you step, darling. It's muddy.' They must have made up their quarrel; his voice was warm. A soft screech from Eloise. Transparent relief on Lydia's face. Matthew's hard knock on the door. The look of alarm on Lydia's face for a fleeting moment.

Joanna was swift to reassure her. 'It's all right, Miss Patterson. It'll be my boyfriend. Don't worry.'

Lydia Patterson crossed to the door in three short strides and tugged it open.

Matthew stood there, Eloise clinging to his arm.

Lydia stared at them both before turning effusive. 'Come in. Come in, the pair of you. You must be cold.'

23

Joanna had never seen Eloise act shy before. She sat still, clinging to her father on the big, shabby sofa, and stared at the floor; she looked smaller. Lydia had come alive with the two visitors. She bustled into the kitchen, produced more cake, another cup of tea, lemonade for Eloise. She must have assumed it was what *children* drank. Matthew she virtually ignored; all her questions were addressed to the shrinking child.

'And how old are you, my dear?'

'Fourteen.'

'And where do you go to school?'

The formulaic questions continued, and Joanna met Matthew's eyes with a trace of amusement. She hadn't thought his daughter could possibly be so demure. Neither had he, judging by the lift of his eyebrows.

Suddenly Eloise looked straight at Lydia Patterson, and the reason for her behaviour was explained. 'I've read one of your books,' she said, flushing slightly.

Instantly Lydia looked wary. Maybe this was a penalty of writing books; meeting the readers, having to take their criticisms on the chin and still smile.

Eloise continued. 'They aren't about animals at all, are they? You just use fur and feathers as a ploy. They're about people, aren't they? Really nasty people doing horrible things to each other. You just pretend, don't you, that they're animal stories, just to get away with being horrible about humans. But it doesn't fool people, you know, especially children. They know. What I'd like to know is, where do you find such shitty people?'

'Eloise!' Matthew's face had also turned pink. They shared this tendency, father and daughter, to colour in response to embarrassment.

'Real life,' replied Lydia.

Eloise was unabashed. 'Why do you feel you have to pretend they're animals?'

'Because I think it makes it more interesting — more fun.' Lydia's eyes seemed to have shrunk to tiny, sharp pinpoints.

'But it doesn't.' Eloise was persistent. 'It would be more interesting if the stories were about real people and you stopped hiding and pretending and laughing.'

'Then what sort of stories would they be, young lady?'

Eloise stared. The silence in the small room thickened so that even Sam 'n' Ella seemed affected by the atmosphere. They stopped clawing at their straw and their clucking stilled, their beady eyes jerked around the room.

Joanna cast her mind back to the gaudy picture of a brown hen cartooned on the book's cover. It had been a story about a treasured possession, about pride, about destruction, jealousy and deceit.

A satisfied smile softened Lydia's face. Her strange eyes were staring at a point far beyond Joanna's head.

'I still think you should write about people,' Eloise persisted.

'Eloise,' Matthew admonished for the second time.

Joanna stood up quickly. 'Thank you very much, Miss Patterson. You've been a help.'

Lydia ushered them to the door, stopping to speak again to Eloise. 'Thank you for your advice, young lady.

Maybe one day I will—' her eyes locked into Joanna's — 'do as you suggest and write a story about real people.' Her huge body seemed to shake with amusement. 'Though what my publishers will have to say about my transfer of affections, I don't know, and the stories won't suit my young readers at all.'

'They might.' Eloise's bluntness was unabated. 'It strikes me you don't really understand children at all.'

'Many children's writers don't,' Lydia countered swiftly. 'Maybe it's that that makes them write such good stories.'

Even Eloise could find no reply. She clattered down the steps and stood at the passenger side of the car, waiting for Matthew to unlock the doors. To insist on a front seat would have made Joanna look petty; she climbed in the back of the car and said nothing. She had plenty to chew over.

* * *

Matthew waited until Eloise was running a bath before he made his comment, in typical understated, quiet tones. 'Perceptive little blighter, isn't she?' His pride was obvious.

* * *

Joanna dreamed that night of hens and eggs and foxes, of rabbits with cheeky furry faces, all paddling in thick, sludgy mud that somehow turned into a battlefield where three children, hand in hand, crossed toward enemy lines. Two girls in white pinafores stepping elegantly as ghosts toward huge guns spewing out bullets. Death, carnage, suffering all around — a blood-splattered field — yet their pinafores remained purest white. No mud. No blood. No soot or dirt. A youth in battledress helped them over the tussocks. The Arnie of the photographs. Dapper, strong and confident as he helped his sisters. But even with his support, one of them slid into a deep, mud-lined puddle and held her arms out. 'Help me, Arnie.' It was Nan, her pinafore altered into the brocade wedding dress of the photograph. Joanna watched her slither down into the mud, the white still startlingly bright right up to the point where she vanished altogether. And through the sludge rose a stone. *Massacre of the Innocent*, it read. *Massacre of the Innocent*.

Joanna woke in a cold sweat, her arms still reaching out to pull Nan Lawrence from the mud. She picked up the alarm clock.

It was five o'clock in the morning.

She padded downstairs, her mind working overtime, clear and sound in the early morning, the world around her silent in the cottage full of sleepers. She boiled the kettle, made some coffee and went through into the small sitting room. She took the figure of *Old Age* from the cabinet, studied the lined face, the bent posture, such a contrast from the figure of youth. She wanted to wake Matthew, but he slept above. She waited until seven before disturbing him with a mug of coffee, perching on the end of the bed.

One good thing about him being a medic was that he seemed to have the capacity to be alert seconds out of a deep sleep — necessary in a doctor, useful in a lover too. She bent forward and kissed him. 'Morning, my darling.'

He sat up, took the coffee and grinned. 'What are you looking so happy about?'

Eloise goes in a couple of days.

'I think we might be about to crack the case, Matt. At least, I'm getting a bit of insight into it. It was nothing to do with the attacks on old ladies, except for one of them.'

'That old biddy helped you last night then?'

She nodded, rumpled his hair and kissed him again.

He spotted the figure in her hand and quickly made the connection. 'And more answers in the night?'

'I've just realised how obvious some of it was, Matt,' she said. 'Some of it has stared me in the face right the way through. Everything was sat there, waiting for me to rediscover it, but I was too distracted by the burglaries. And you, Matthew, gave me the very biggest of clues.'

He pulled her head across his chest. 'You know what, Jo?' he said softly. 'You are at your best when you're just about to bring a case to its conclusion.'

She lay for a while, breathing in the faint tang of after-shave. 'And you, my darling,' she replied, 'are at your very best first thing in the morning.'

24

Tuesday 3 November, 8.30 a.m.

By 8.30 she was in the station, impatiently waiting for Korpanski to turn up. Never at *his* best in the morning, he arrived at 8.45 and listened to her ramblings without comment.

'So,' he said, 'where first?'

'Christian Patterson, don't you think?'

Mike still looked confused. 'But I thought . . . ?'

She tried to suppress the bubbling excitement in her voice. 'He thinks he's got away with it, Mike. One thing I can't stand is cocksure villains.'

She dangled her car keys in front of him. 'And for once we'll use my car and I'll do all the driving.'

He winced. Joanna's battered Peugeot 205 was not the smoothest of rides, nor was it speedy. He opened his mouth to object but she had already whisked through the door. As he scampered down the steps he heard the unmistakable purr of a diesel engine.

They covered the distance to Spite Hall in ten minutes. The clouds hung low over the ugly building, shrouding the house behind. As they turned up the drive, Joanna reflected that however many times she turned off the Macclesfield road, she would never fail to be revolted by the ruination of such an elegant building. 'I wonder—' she raised her thoughts — 'when they'll pull it down?'

Mike shrugged. 'Wills and things,' he said. 'Probate. I bet it'll take years.'

She looked at him. 'I bet it won't.'

She clicked open her seatbelt and opened the door, met mist so heavy it saturated her skin. 'Let's go.'

'Are you going to arrest him?'

'Oh yes, we'll haul him in now. He's had his freedom. We've got our evidence.'

She was used to waiting for Arnold Patterson to answer the door, but that day he surprised her. He must have been in the hall already. 'Inspector,' he said.

She looked at him through new eyes, seeing not only the bent, arthritic old man but the young soldier, the doting older brother, adored hero to Nan and Lydia.

He regarded her very steadily before dropping his eyes to the floor. 'You'll have come to see Christian.'

He knew. He'd known all along what his grandson was capable of, and yet he had shielded him, said nothing. Through a misguided sense of family loyalty? Joanna didn't think so. Through fear? But even peering hard into the old man's eyes she could pick up no trace of fear. The realisation came to her with a shock. He hadn't wanted to interfere.

Arnie dropped his eyelids and shuffled along the corridor.

Joanna wanted to speak to him, to tell him she had seen the photographs, that she understood that they had been extraordinary times, that nothing then had been normal, that events had taken place that could not have been justified in times of peace. The words stuck in her throat; nothing seemed appropriate.

She made a gesture — half friendly, half professional — and she and Korpanski walked past the old man, along the hall, up the staircase.

They made no effort to soften their steps as they crossed the landing and followed the curving stairs to the attic floor.

Joanna glanced at Mike, reading his instinct like an open book. She knew he wanted to crash through the door, grab Patterson by the collar, click the cuffs on and frogmarch him downstairs, without caring if he missed a step or two — or six.

She threw him a warning glance and rapped on the door. 'Christian. It's the police.' She waited a moment, then pushed open the door.

He was stood in the middle of the room wearing bulky headphones, his head jerking in time to the beat. He must have seen them out of the corner of his eye; he crossed the room and switched the decks off.

'What a nice surprise,' he said politely.

Joanna gazed at him. Why, she wondered, had he allowed himself to fall so deeply under her influence? Long ago events could have had no interest to him or bearing on his life. And yet . . . She met Christian's frank stare. Was there any point in questioning such an accomplished liar? Should they just charge him and sweat it out in the station?

'Let's caution him, Mike,' she said.

Christian looked astonished. 'You can't think . . .' He looked from one to the other, perspiration dampening his brow. 'You don't think *I* . . . ? You *can't!*'

And to Joanna's intense satisfaction she realised he was finally rattled.

25

Korpanski liked the new caution; plenty of words for him to spin out, intimidate his victim with. He drew himself up to his full height of six feet three inches. 'Christian Patterson,' he said, 'you are charged with inflicting grievous bodily harm on Cecily Marlowe on the second of September of this year. You do not have to say anything. But it may harm your defence if you do not mention, when questioned, something which you later rely on in court. Anything you *do* say may be given in evidence.' He finished with a hard, hostile stare.

Give Christian his due, he had recovered himself. Still pale, slightly frightened, but in control, he very quietly gave his name and address and fixed his eyes — and, it seemed, his hopes — on Joanna.

'Is there anything you want to say, Christian?'

He shook his head. 'I'm saying nothing,' he said, 'except that I want the family solicitor summoned.'

Joanna sighed. She had not expected a full confession, but all her questions remained unanswered. Christian returned her gaze with a clear, defensive stare. Unabashed. Unashamed.

And believing him guilty, Joanna felt a surge of frustration and anger. She wanted to challenge him, accuse him. *You carve up an old lady, terrorise her so she never returns to the house she's inhabited for more than fifty years, and you won't even tell us the reason?*

Christian Patterson leaned forwards, his eyes glittering. 'Prove it,' he said. Joanna said nothing, merely studied him. Christian's face slowly changed. 'Hang on a minute,' he said. 'I didn't kill *her*. I didn't kill my great aunt,' he repeated. 'I couldn't have done that. You couldn't believe I would. I couldn't have hurt *her*!'

And yet, at her bidding, you could commit an act of cruelty against a woman you must hardly have known, for a reason you probably never knew, let alone understood? She was beginning to understand what a dangerous old woman Nan Lawrence had been.

There must have been other old enemies, plenty of them; not only her brother and sister but another, more sinister one. Something must have pushed him beyond tolerance, so that he had been the one to strike first. No wonder so many bones had been splintered and with such force. The blows had been struck with the accumulated anger of years. More than fifty years.

Arnold Patterson was waiting for them downstairs, his face upturned to meet his grandson's glance. 'Always knew you were a chip off the block,' he said. 'Got 'er in you, and my father too; all that was rotten.' He stumped back toward the sitting room, Christian watching him without saying a word.

* * *

They began the interview an hour later, when the family solicitor had been summoned from his offices.

Korpanski flicked a couple of pictures of Cecily Marlowe across the desk. They had been taken two days post attack. Christian glanced down, lifted his eyes again, and dropped them. Behind the bravado Joanna could read something almost approaching shame. Remorse? That favourite solicitor's plea for the guilty.

Christian looked up boldly. 'Nasty injuries,' he commented. Joanna nodded coldly.

214

'What evidence have you against my client?' demanded the solicitor.

And as the law required, she laid the evidence before him: primarily the booty from the robbery at Cecily Marlowe's that had turned up at Nan's house — where Christian was almost the only frequent visitor.

By four o'clock that afternoon they'd gleaned all they were going to from Christian Patterson. Nothing. He was playing for time, using silence as his weapon. None of Joanna's questions had been answered. All the time she was speaking to him, her mind was battling furiously with the problems. Christian didn't strike her as a compliant sort of chap, who would blindly do what he was asked, and she didn't really swallow the theory that Nan Lawrence had held some sort of a Svengali influence over him. She was relying on the assumption that Cecily Marlowe would finally admit it had been Christian Patterson who had assaulted her. But the motive continued to baffle her, until she saw Christian's gaze drop to the photographs and his eyes brighten. That was when she knew why. He had done it because he had wanted to; he had enjoyed terrorising Cecily Marlowe. Cleverly hidden behind a convincing facade of urbanity was the familial streak of cruelty. He had used Nan Lawrence's desire for revenge for his own purposes; not because *she* had asked him, but because it had suited him.

But now her mind grappled with the next questions. Why had Nan Lawrence wanted revenge on her old friend, and what connection did it have with her own murder?

* * *

The weather was as crisp as a winter's day as Joanna and Mike again took the Macclesfield road toward Brushton Grange and turned up the now-familiar track. Behind the great house the sky was a cold Wedgwood blue, promising imminent frost.

'Just leave me alone for a moment, Mike,' Joanna said as he switched the engine off. 'I want to think.'

She walked slowly all the way round Spite Hall and tried to imagine the days when it had been built. As she rounded the back, she noticed a movement in the dust-shrouded window of Brushton Grange. Arnold Patterson must have anticipated her return. He was watching her, as he must have watched the construction of this ugly edifice, from that very window, powerless to stop it.

Joanna stopped in her tracks, suddenly sensing some other, darker purpose. Why had Spite Hall *really* been built? Because of the terms of the will? Or had there been another, more powerful reason? Now Joanna believed so.

She watched him through the window. As still as a statue, staring through the glass as though oblivious to her. Maybe like many ancient folk he had one foot too firmly in the past ever to be entirely in the present. And as Joanna stared at him she realised he hardly knew — or cared — that she was there. He was seeing something else — the green fields and croquet lawns of pre-war days?

She rounded the corner and returned to the car. Mike was leaning against it, arms folded, occasionally kicking the tyres with impatience. He looked relieved to see her.

'Solved it?'

'Not quite', she said. 'But we're getting there, Mike. We are getting there.'

'I'm really glad you included me in that,' he drawled sarcastically.

She didn't answer him but led the way toward the steps and the front door of Brushton Grange. And this time Arnold was waiting there to meet them. He straightened up to stare deep into Joanna's eyes, saying nothing. But there was a line of communication far more effective than any that had yet been established between them. She read pain, shame, deep, deep regret. After a brief pause, he nodded as though satisfied.

They followed him into the high-ceilinged living room, both sensing that this would be a long, sad, slowly-told story.

'So,' he said at last, 'she had her way. She said I would pay.' He peered from one to the other. 'It's what you're here for, isn't it?'

Joanna nodded.

He picked up his walking stick. 'Do I have to come with you?'

'Not now, not yet. But you will eventually.'

Patterson leaned heavily forward on his stick, his rheumy eyes focused on his hands, knobbled with arthritis. After a while he stopped looking even at them. 'I nearly got away with it, didn't I? Old age almost had you beat. I can't have long to go now.'

Joanna nodded.

'Happen I was . . .' He seemed to be having difficulty saying the next word.

'Sorry?' She tried to supply the word.

He shook his head very slightly. 'Wrong. All I know is, it didn't feel so at the time. I couldn't bear . . .' He stared beyond Joanna's shoulder. 'It's right that she lived there,' he said softly. 'Camped on my doorstep, never letting me forget.'

'You killed . . . ?' Korpanski was staring at the old man in amazement.

Both Joanna and Patterson swivelled round to look at him.

'Not, Nan.' Joanna answered Korpanski's mute question. 'He didn't kill Nan.'

'No, not my own sister. Times I wished I had, but I didn't, young sir. It weren't me. Though I hated her for what she'd done to—'

Joanna supplied the words. 'To David, to her husband. And what she did to you.'

'How much do you know?'

'I *think* I know it all. I could be wrong.'

Patterson tossed his head in an age-old gesture of defiance. 'They've clever words for it now,' he said. 'They would

217

excuse me, saying how the things I'd seen at war was reason enough to kill.' He tossed his head. 'Post-traumatic something or other.'

Mike turned to Joanna for explanation. 'Nan?' he said again.

Again she shook her head. 'Nan's child,' Joanna said. 'It was in the post-mortem report but I didn't understand the phrase. *Gravid*. She'd borne a child. But whose was it? Where was it? Where *is* it?' The second query was addressed to Nan's brother.

For answer he continued to stare beyond her shoulder.

'Christian?' Mike ventured.

'Far too young. We're talking about fifty years ago, aren't we, Mr Patterson? The end of the war, a soldier about to return home to find his adored wife was already pregnant.'

Arnold nodded. 'It would have finished him off; he didn't deserve that.'

And Joanna knew now. It *had* to be there, buried in the foundations of the house. 'You killed it, didn't you?'

'I didn't want David Lawrence returning from war to that. He'd suffered enough.'

Joanna waited until Patterson continued.

'It were such a little thing . . .' There was something evasive in his old eyes, some secret he still believed he could conceal. 'It were nothing, really.'

'We must exhume,' Joanna said. 'Let the courts decide.'

Patterson bowed his head.

'Can you tell me any more?'

'You know enough.'

Joanna stood up. 'We'll let ourselves out, thank you, Mr Patterson. And you do understand, we *will* be back.'

This time the old man didn't respond.

She closed the door behind the old man, leaving him with his memories, staring, unfocused, straight ahead, in shock.

* * *

They found Cecily Marlowe in her tiny kitchen, watching a cling-film-smothered dish revolving in the microwave. She didn't move as Joanna and Mike walked in. When the bell pinged she removed the dish, uncovered some cauliflower cheese and walked back into the sitting room. 'You weren't going to give up, were you? I thought you would. That was my mistake, thinking anybody would give up.'

They watched her munching the cauliflower cheese, the scarred face puckering grotesquely as she ate. 'They don't like me eating with the others,' she said quietly. 'They say it puts them off their food.' She gave a cynical laugh. 'To think I was the Rose Queen of Leek once, long ago.'

She carried on eating, seemingly uncurious about the reason for their visit. But Joanna realised much of the hysteria had vanished from her manner. As soon as she had formed that thought, she knew the reason why. Because Nan Lawrence was dead and word might have reached her that Christian Patterson was in custody.

'I think', Joanna said slowly, 'that it's about time you started telling us the truth, right from the beginning.'

Cecily's hand flew up to her face.

'He won't be back,' Joanna assured her. 'We've finally charged him with your assault.'

Cecily nodded. 'It took time.'

'Yes.'

Mike was sat in the chair opposite, his face serious. For once he was showing not aggression but frank pity for the old woman. Joanna smiled inwardly; Korpanski was learning her methods. Over the last few years he had been changing — slowly. He always would be Korpanski. But he was a different Korpanski from the one she had encountered when she had first come to Leek. He was acquiring a heart.

As if to manifest her thoughts, he spoke. 'We won't let that villain come within a mile of you again, Mrs Marlowe.'

The old woman gave a watery smile of thin confidence. She turned to Joanna. 'So where do I start?'

'At the very beginning.'

She was still cautious. 'And what is the beginning?'

'The war.'

'The war.' She gave a cynical laugh. 'Perhaps we can blame it all on the war.'

'Perhaps.'

'We was friends through it, me and Nan. Flighty young things I suppose you'd call us. Teenagers for nearly all the war years. Life was hard. No men to speak of except farmers, imbeciles, soldiers home on leave — and that was short and uncertain. Pushed us into things too quick. Made us reckless, made us not want to wait. 'Cos wait and you might be dead, that was what me and Nan used to say, might not get another chance. She and David Lawrence, we-ell, he'd always had a soft spot for her, and she liked having the ring. Vicars was always ready to tie the knot double quick; cheered everyone up, a wedding. Good for morale. Forty-four, Nan did tie the knot. But it wasn't five minutes before he was off back to the front. Germany.' She paused for a moment, seemingly reluctant to continue. Yet neither Joanna nor Mike prompted her. 'We felt life was slipping us by. No fun. Husbands away fighting, while for those of us here life was mundane, boring. We just wanted something — anything. Anyway, young bride or not, Nan took up with a man. He was kind to her. I don't suppose either of them *wanted* it to go so far, but it did, and Nan got pregnant. Then Arnie came home. He went mad. He'd seen action, real action — friends of his blown up, dying horribly. It'd made him hard, inhuman, different from the Arnie who'd gone away.'

'Go on,' Joanna prompted softly.

'Summer was coming. Nan had the baby early. We could see the war was nearly over. David would be home. The . . .' She looked desperately at the two police officers. 'He . . .' She swallowed. And suddenly the horror of the situation touched Joanna.

'What happened to the baby?'

'He was a tiny thing,' Cecily said, her eyes dark with horror. 'A tiny thing. He hardly cried. But he was born alive.'

Joanna waited.

Cecily bowed her head, her evening meal hardly tasted, left on the plate. 'Arnie killed him with a shovel,' she whispered. 'I saw him do it,' she looked up, 'so did Nan.'

And now Joanna understood.

'Nan never forgave him or me. The baby was buried and Nan built her house. That's the real reason it's called Spite Hall. People always thought it was because of where it was. She put it there as a reminder to Arnie, so he'd never forget. Nothing to do with her father's will at all.'

'She hid the baby in the house for a while, and when they put in the concrete for the foundations, she put him there. When David came home there was no baby. He never knew about the child.'

'There's only one thing to add,' Joanna said. 'Who was the man?'

26

The little church was shrouded in heavy, damp mist as she and Mike approached. They opened the wicket gate and walked along the wet path, running the gauntlet of dripping trees. Yews, a holly bright with berries. She had known she would find him there, kneeling in front of the stained-glass window, praying to the Madonna and Child. What were his prayers? For forgiveness? Or for the truth never to be discovered? From somewhere in her own past an ancient hymn swam through her mind. 'The day Thou gavest, Lord, is ended.' It was ended.

By a stiffening of his shoulders, a tautness in the set of his head, a jerk of his large hands, she sensed he was aware of their arrival at the top of the nave.

Mike gave her a swift glance. It was impossible not to be affected by the cold silence.

Joanna's shoes were low-heeled, rubber-soled. Even so, her footsteps echoed loudly on the stone flags. Korpanski was close to tip-toeing. Neither of them spoke a word.

They had almost reached him when he stood up, quite suddenly, and turned to face them.

And now, at last, Joanna caught a glimpse of the killer beneath. She should have read his face before.

She had witnessed this wildness without seeing where it could lead. But him being a man of the cloth, she had discounted him, trusted him without question, believed him innocent, beyond suspicion. She should have peered behind his eyes and perceived other characteristics. His relationship with Nan Lawrence had developed not from pastoral kindness or consideration for a young woman in difficult circumstances, but from simple lust.

'Inspector,' he said quietly.

She motioned him to sit on the front pew, then she and Mike sat either side of him. Leon Gardiner appeared unable to meet her eyes. His searched the walls of the old church, reading, it seemed, the rolls of honourable dead, victims of the two wars. Finally he focused only on her, ignoring Korpanski. He was making the mistake other suspects made, that someone of her gender would be kinder on a felon.

'I've led a long life,' he said, 'a very long life. I am a man of the church, Inspector, someone who should have spent the last fifty years close to God. After all, I claim, by reason of my profession, to be His mouthpiece.' He looked away, a tired, defeated old man, his energy finally depleted. 'Him, I could not deceive. But everyone else . . .' He dropped his face into his hands. 'My parishioners, my flock. I. . .' Joanna had the feeling he would have liked to have cried. But any emotion must have been drained out of him over the years, the final drop squeezed out as he had killed her. All that came now were dry, cracked sobs.

'She was a malicious woman,' he said. 'I don't believe any other person could have made me pay as she did. Every Sunday for years she would sit here and watch me fumble through my sermon. She always spoke to me at the end, asked me questions anyone who heard might have believed to be innocent. But she read all my deepest fears and played on them, never telling me the complete truth. For years she told me the child was alive, looked after by another family. She asked me for money for its clothes, its food. I lived in fear that one day someone would arrive on my doorstep. Oh yes. Nan Lawrence played with me like a spiteful child pulling the legs off a spider. Even after I retired from working full time for the church, she still plagued me that so I dreaded the Sundays I would have to take the sermons. She loved to see me squirm.'

'Why didn't you give up the church?' Korpanski's voice was rough. Maybe Gardiner's judgement had been astute. There was no trace of sympathy from DS Korpanski.

Gardiner took the comment on the chin but still kept his gaze on Joanna. 'Because that would have meant she had won, beaten me. Because I—' He stared ahead, back to the stained-glass window. 'You're right. I should have resigned, or at the very least confessed and let the authorities judge me. But—' He stopped, glanced shrewdly at Korpanski. 'Other people were involved.'

Joanna nodded.

'In the early years, I told myself it would have been cruel to David Lawrence to tell him what had happened while he had been suffering for his country. She held that over me, that it would have destroyed him, he was left so weakened by his war experiences. After he died, I told myself I had left it too long, that there was no point in confessing. It's a lame excuse. The truth is I simply couldn't face up to it. The years passed. She had her hold.'

'Until . . .' Joanna prompted.

'Something snapped,' Gardiner said simply. 'It started earlier this year. I was suspicious that the assault on old Mrs Marlowe was in some way connected with Nan. I was aware that Cecily had known about us. Nan had told me the child had been born early and dead and that she had buried the body in the grounds of Brushton Grange. For all I knew it was another lie, but it was what I *wanted* to believe. And then one day Cecily finally came to me and told me the real truth.' Gardiner's eyes were full of anguished pain. 'I confronted Nan and she flew into a rage. She was absolutely furious with Cecily for telling me, and Cecily paid the price for her honesty.'

Gardiner's gaze appeared transfixed by the stained-glass image of a gentle woman with a plump, healthy child that seemed to dominate the church. 'Last Sunday Nan spoke to me, as usual, after the service. She began by asking me about the judgement of Solomon, a favourite topic of hers; the wisdom connected with the decision of the mother to let her child live, even though he would be brought up by another woman — better than to watch him slaughtered. Her eyes never left that window. Then she told me she was embroidering a cover for a prayer stool for the church, depicting "the Massacre of the Innocent". I corrected her, told her she should use the plural. "Oh no," she said, "I'm talking about the one, just the one. And when it is finished I shall donate it to the church so it will sit here, on a prayer stool, in perpetuity."'

He dropped his head into his hands. 'She asked me to call on her that evening, and when I arrived, she told me the entire story in all its ugliest detail. Things she had not said before but must have kept, waiting for her moment, savouring her final revenge. I had this terrible picture of Arnie.' He shuddered. 'She told me he used a shovel to murder my child, my very own flesh and blood. She blamed *me*, my lust and my weakness, for that hideously cowardly attack on Cecily Marlowe. She told me how Christian had taken a knife to her face; again, in the ugliest detail. It was horrible; you have no idea. And all the time I was there, she wouldn't stop stitching, and I knew she had been planning this moment for years. She looked up and smiled at me, then told me it was time for the whole story to be finally laid open. Can you imagine?'

Leon Gardiner wrapped his arms around himself. 'She invited me to admire her handiwork. And then, as she was calmly threading her needle with silks, she quite casually mentioned I was probably standing on the bones of our dead child. She was smiling. The hatred inside me was like a rush of air. I picked up her stick. I just wanted to obliterate that smile.' He was silent, his hands clasped together.

'She didn't love me, ever. I was simply a plaything to a bored, flighty young woman. Something to pass the time. I am an old man now, Inspector, but once . . .'

Joanna could imagine. Once he would have been a powerfully attractive man. A tempting conquest.

'She was so much more than simply beautiful,' he said. 'She was the siren of ancient myths who lured sailors onto the rocks — powerfully sexy. If she exerted it over you, you lost your morals, your free will.' And now he looked Joanna square in the eye. 'I'm not trying to excuse what I did, Inspector. But when I am judged by my fellow man, I want them to see why. Over the years I have watched Nan Lawrence twist in both character and body.' He stood up. 'Did you ever see a bonsai tree?' Joanna nodded. 'Twisted, bent, misshapen?' Again she nodded. Gardiner walked slowly along the nave. 'It springs from the roots, you know. You trim them, prevent them from growing normally, then wire the stems. Nan's roots were rotten, and the environment of Spite Hall ensured she could not lead a normal life.'

Leon Gardiner had reached the top of the nave and was level with the font. He moved the cover aside and peered inside the granite bowl. 'She *asked* me to visit her that Sunday. She wanted to provoke me. She knew ultimately I was capable—'

'Of murder?' Joanna asked curiously. 'Are you telling me Nan Lawrence deliberately provoked you to murder her?'

Gardiner nodded. 'I hadn't touched her for more than fifty years,' he said. 'Not even to shake hands. Her flesh made me sick. I didn't want to go.' The font was not quite empty of water. He dipped his fingers in and pressed them to his face. 'But she still had the power to manipulate me. It was the final humiliation.'

'So you beat her to a pulp,' Mike said brutally.

Gardiner nodded. He looked relieved when Joanna cautioned him.

In the car he still wanted to unburden himself. 'The child', he said, 'is unshriven, unbaptised. I must do it for my final peace of mind.'

To old bones?

They spent the next few minutes in silence. As they neared the police station, he seemed to rally and realise his position. 'I didn't set out to kill her that night,' he said. 'Will it be murder or—?'

Joanna looked him straight in the eye. 'That's for the courts to decide.' She had finally lost the last vestiges of respect for him.

She sat very still, her mind moving through the succession of crimes. He had defiled his position of trust. While the soldiers had defended the country, they had left their wives at home, believing them safe, and that if they needed pastoral care it would be given.

They pulled up outside the police station and she helped him out of the car. As she did so, she picked up on the terrible sadness in his eyes.

'I have had', he said, 'a wasted life.'

27

Wednesday 4 November, 10 a.m.

Solving a murder should bring satisfaction, Joanna lectured herself angrily. But so often all it gave her was a tired feeling of unnecessary destruction — of lives, people, time, money, effort, emotion. She felt drained. How often murder was the result of weakness, not strength, of ducking the truth, responsibility. Gardiner would pay for a short indiscretion and a very long lie, and she had the feeling the courts would not be lenient. He would die in prison as he had lived in one.

She and Mike sat opposite each other in her office. He kicked the desk and she stared at the floor.

'Poor man,' she said.

Korpanski stared at her. 'I don't know how you can say that, Jo. You were at the post-mortem.' His dark eyes held accusation, puzzlement. 'He broke how many bones?'

'She goaded him for all those years, robbed him of his principles, his life, his vocation. Everything he valued.'

'He could have owned up at any time.'

'But he didn't. And the longer he left it — it became impossible, Mike.'

'They deserved each other.'

She gave a tight grimace. 'Maybe.' She gave a long sigh. 'And then we've got the other little matter.'

'Christian?'

'No. Arnold Patterson. He murdered—'

'Surely we aren't going to pursue that?'

'We've no option, Mike, but to let the law grind its course. And have they hauled in Elland yet for his little visit to Emily Whittaker?'

'Can't you hear the noise out there?'

Both were silent until Joanna looked up. 'So, Korpanski,' she fixed her eyes on him, 'what about Eloise and your mother-in-law? Our unwelcome guests?'

His mind must still have been lagging behind. He looked startled. 'We'll get rid of them.'

'How?' she challenged.

'She's an old bag, but not that . . .' Then he caught the humour in her face. 'You didn't mean that.'

She laughed, and after a short pause Korpanski joined her.

Outside in the corridor two PCs listened. 'They must have cracked it,' one said.

'And feel sure of a conviction,' the other, Cumberbatch, answered.

* * *

After Mike had left, Joanna sat for a while in her office toying with a pencil, and ideas. There was a similarity between Nan Lawrence and Eloise Levin. Nan had set out to ruin a life for no reason other than malice. She could have hoped to gain nothing. She could not have believed Leon Gardiner had any intention of marrying her, ever. Nan Lawrence had been young, twenty years old when her child had been brutally murdered by the brother she had once adored. And Eloise? She would love to ruin Joanna's relationship with Matt. But she would not part them. She must not part them.

Joanna picked up her handbag. It was time to go home.

28

Monday 1 February, 9 a.m.

Three months later, in the thickest snowstorm of winter, Joanna drove again along the Macclesfield road. She had heard rumours.

Spite Hall had gone. Vanished as though it had never been. The shape of Brushton Grange loomed through snowflakes like Bronte's Wuthering Heights. The scene had been returned to the vista of fifty years earlier. They must have come in the previous weeks to demolish it.

Now Matthew would be summoned, because somewhere beneath the rubble lay the skeleton of a child that had lived long enough to draw breath once. Or twice? No more.

She turned her car around and went back to the station, welcoming the warmth that greeted her as she entered. The desk sergeant saluted her with a grin.

From somewhere in her office was coming a strange noise — cracked tones. Joanna winced. Korpanski was singing. For him happiness had returned; Fran's mother had gone. But she didn't feel much like joining him in the tune. Eloise would be back.

THE END

ACKNOWLEDGEMENTS

With apologies to the real inhabitants of Spite Hall. I've borrowed the name only, I couldn't resist it, but the entire story comes, as usual, straight from my head!

Thank you for reading this book.

If you enjoyed it please leave feedback on Amazon or Goodreads, and if there is anything we missed or you have a question about, then please get in touch. We appreciate you choosing our book.

Founded in 2014 in Shoreditch, London, we at Joffe Books pride ourselves on our history of innovative publishing. We were thrilled to be shortlisted for Independent Publisher of the Year at the British Book Awards.

www.joffebooks.com

We're very grateful to eagle-eyed readers who take the time to contact us. Please send any errors you find to corrections@joffebooks.com. We'll get them fixed ASAP.